Books by Gloria Herrmann

Single in Seattle

Reeling in Love
Puppy Love

I0542740

Puppy Love

ISBN # 978-1-78686-149-8

©Copyright Gloria Herrmann 2017

Cover Art by Posh Gosh ©Copyright 2017

Interior text design by Claire Siemaszkiewicz

Totally Bound Publishing

Single in Seattle

PUPPY LOVE

GLORIA HERRMANN

Dedication

For Herbie aka Mr. Meaty, my snoring muse,
who is such an adorable character all on his own.

Chapter One

"It's just us now, old girl," Tiffany said as she clinked a champagne flute against Mackenzie's.

"I'm not so sure about that. Jason's been calling me a lot more," Mackenzie teased.

"Oh, please. That won't ever work. He's in Vegas and you're here. It's me and you, woman—single in Seattle."

Mackenzie laughed and they both sipped the glittery drink. Tiffany watched as the bubbles climbed the walls of the glass and released a heavy sigh.

She was thrilled for Molly and happy to be getting drunk as they celebrated her friend's engagement to Owen. But being on this large boat with so many people that she didn't even know? Not so much. She couldn't deny that the setting captured the purest element of romance quite beautifully. White lights were strung above them and the soft flickers from the candles in crystal vases were casting magical shadows everywhere. A canopy of stars seemed to be twinkling to the beat of the music and the brightest full moon was hovering just above the dark water. If this wasn't the most Hollywood version of a happily ever after, she didn't know what was.

Am I a tad jealous? Absolutely. Where in the hell is my Prince Charming? Should I hang out at Pike Place and wait to get clobbered by a fish, too? Tiffany knew her perfect guy was out there somewhere, but she wanted her fairy tale now. Being surrounded by all this lovey-dovey nonsense made her itch for it that much more.

She was a little dizzy and the constant rocking of the ship had made all the bubbly she'd chugged down slosh in her stomach. Maybe it was the rich crab cakes. Tiffany really shouldn't have eaten so many. Molly had warned her not to. Food and drinking didn't not go hand in hand when it came to Tiffany. It had to be one or the other. She held her stomach and prayed the queasiness would go away.

Mackenzie stared at her with concern. "You gonna be sick?"

Tiffany nodded, unable to speak. She put her hand over her mouth.

Molly rushed over after having sensed trouble with her friend. She looked every bit like the bride she would soon be and was gorgeous tonight. Molly wore a long white dress that hugged her body perfectly. Her hair was pinned up with baby's breath tucked in the nest of curls but there the smile she'd worn all night left her face now.

"Tiff, are you are okay?"

Mackenzie shook her head. "I think she's going to be sick."

"Crab cakes? You ate them, didn't you?" Molly frowned. They all knew where this was headed.

Mackenzie laughed. "Of course she did. This is Tiffany we're talking about."

Molly scolded her. "Knowing that you were going to be drinking, you should have known better than to eat so much, Tiffany. Like Vegas all over again is all I have to say." Molly rolled her eyes as she started to lift Tiffany out of her seat.

They walked her to the port side of the boat and Tiffany's her stomach squeezed. *Not good.* The crab cakes made their appearance.

When she was done, Molly handed her a napkin for her to wipe her mouth.

"Thanks," she said. Tiffany felt better now and accepted the bottle of water Mackenzie offered. "Did I ruin your party?"

Molly shook her head. "You didn't puke on me, so we're good. If you'd done that, I would have had to kill you.

This dress cost a fortune." Molly ran her fingers through Tiffany's wind-swept hair. "You look stunning tonight, Tiff." Molly looked at Mackenzie. "You both do."

Tiffany blushed and Mackenzie looked equally flattered.

Molly smiled and wetness filled her eyes as she pulled them in for a hug. "Thank you for being here, guys."

After they broke their embrace, Mackenzie turned her attention to Molly. "Okay, let's cut to the chase, shall we? Who gets to be the maid of honor?" Mackenzie asked with a hand on her hip. She wore a pale blue dress, almost aquamarine, that complimented her tan. It was short, flirty and sexy, even by Tiffany's standards. Her blonde hair was gathered in a small, low ponytail at her neck and long, silver earrings shimmered as she moved.

Molly looked away. Even as dark as it was, Tiffany could still see the smile on her lips.

"She's going to pick me. I can just tell," Tiffany squealed.

"Why would she do that? You just puked at her party." Mackenzie pushed Tiffany to the side and moved in front of her. "You do realize that she just threw up, right, Moll?"

"But I always get sick when I drink too much," Tiffany defended herself and tried to creep in closer to Molly. She swished some of the water in her mouth and spit it over the side.

"Real lady-like, Tiff," Mackenzie commented in disgust.

"Mack, we all know that she gets sick anytime she drinks too much and eats things we tell her not to." Molly shook her finger at Tiffany. "But that doesn't change the fact that I want you *both* to be my maid of honor." Molly grabbed each of their hands.

"Wait, what? Both of us?" Mackenzie looked a little upset.

Tiffany shouted, "I call dibs on doing the bachelorette party!"

Mackenzie let out a huff as she threw her hands up in the air. "What the hell? You can't just call dibs on something like that."

"You can have the bridal shower," Tiffany offered. "Those

are more uptight anyway. I'm just kidding, Mackenzie."

"You are impossible, you know that?" Mackenzie stomped away, leaving Tiffany and Molly behind.

"Sorry. I wasn't trying to piss her off. I can't help it that I'm more fun," Tiffany apologized.

"You both are fun, and I love you, so work it out, girl," Molly said as a laugh escaped her. "I suggest you go tell her you're sorry."

"But we're good, right?" Tiffany didn't want to mess up what was supposed to be a perfect night for Molly.

"We're good. Trust me." Molly hugged her again. She then headed in the direction of Owen, who smiled at his future wife and linked his arm through hers as they walked together to visit with more of their guests.

Tiffany sighed. She wanted someone to look at her the way Owen looked at Molly. She exhaled again. *Time to go grovel to Mackenzie.* Tiffany clutched the bottled water and set off in hopes of finding her friend.

Tiffany hadn't paid attention to where she was going. She was still a little tipsy and didn't quite have her sea legs when she felt arms suddenly holding her.

Tiffany noticed the tailored suit first. It was her weakness. A man in a good suit was an enormous turn-on for her. Then she heard his voice. Words of concern slipped off his tongue in a sexy Irish brogue. *Oh my.* The words were like honey. The sweetness dripped from his mouth. She could listen to him recite the alphabet and probably have an orgasm. Maybe it was the champagne that clouded her reasoning or just being submerged in this romantic atmosphere for way too long. Either way, Tiffany was losing all self-control. It was too late to pull back now. Tiffany didn't hesitate as she put her mouth on his. He pulled her tightly against him then released her. It struck her that that she'd just kissed a complete stranger. Tiffany should have been mortified, scurrying away and running off to go hide. Hell, even jumping overboard would be an acceptable option at that very moment.

Why aren't my feet moving?
Because she was too busy leaning in for another kiss.

Chapter Two

"Ugh...my head," Tiffany whined from the warmth of her bed. The softness of the blankets, the luxurious feel of the sheets against her skin and the firm pillows were more incredible that she'd ever recalled.

Wait, this isn't my bed.

"Oh, you poor thing."

Tiffany's ears perked up at the sound of the voice. *I know it from somewhere, don't I?* Her brain was foggy and her stomach moved in uneasy waves. Fear prickled her skin. Tiffany wasn't at home. *Oh God, where in the hell am I?*

Tiffany tried to sit up in the bed and she took in an immaculate room. It looked like a hotel suite of some kind. *Oh shit, what did I do? Don't panic, Tiffany.*

"Would you care for some tea, lovely?" There stood a tall man with a lean but athletic build. He had dark, smoky eyes, a day's growth of a beard on his strong jawline and his hair was wet from just having showered. She could smell the fresh scent of soap wafting from him and it delighted her senses. He was dressed in a crisp white dress shirt with charcoal-gray slacks that hugged his toned thighs perfectly.

Tiffany's mind raced as she tried to remember what sort of trouble she may have gotten herself into. Mackenzie and Molly, her two best friends in the world, must be sick with worry. Then her brain offered her a sneak peek at the evening before—lots of champagne, Molly's engagement party, Mackenzie being royally pissed off at her then... *damn.* Her brain seized up, withholding any other precious information.

"I'll have you know last night was quite unexpected,

love."

Could he quit talking until I figure some crap out? But that voice was so sexy and very Irish. It had Tiffany even more confused. *Am I in Ireland? Oh dear, I've really done it this time.*

He pulled up a chair and seemed to be surveying her. "You have no recollection of last night, do you?"

Tiffany shook her head and admitted, "No, I'm sorry. Where am I?"

"Certainly not in your home or mine, as you can very well tell." He winked and threw her off with by giving her a sly and sexy grin.

"Yeah, I kinda gathered that much. Thanks. So, where then?" Tiffany was growing agitated, the queasy leftovers from drinking far too much were beginning to surface.

"You look a little ill, dear. You should probably rest." He frowned sympathetically. "Sadly, I have some business that I need to attend to, but you're welcome to order something to eat and make yourself comfortable." He rose from the chair and began to fuss with his cufflinks. He kissed her on her forehead and started to walk away. He paused briefly to grab a blazer that had been draped over the chair then he left without another word. The automatic lock echoed in the room. *Time to think, Tiff.*

Tiffany officially had no clue what the hell had just happened, but she needed to get her butt out of there and *quickly*. Like a frantic tornado, Tiffany searched for all her belongings. Her shoes were proving to be a little difficult to find. She looked high and low and finally caught sight of them, tucked neatly next to the large armoire. This room was nice, way too nice. The pain in her head and icky feeling in her tummy reminded her how champagne was *not* her friend. After finally locating everything she looked back at the room once more—the tangled mess of sheets, the empty bottle of even more champagne and no memory of even being in this room the night before.

Oh Tiff, what have you done?

* * * *

"Where in God's name are you right now?"

Tiffany sighed. She'd known this was coming. "Mac, I'm almost home."

"You weren't at your apartment, so where in the heck were you?"

"When did you drive by?" Tiffany asked. Maybe she could sort of fib her way out this, otherwise Tiffany would never hear the end of it from her overprotective and mother-hen bestie.

"That is not the point. I expected you to be home, especially after how much you drank last night. Do you realize how worried I was?"

"I'm sorry." Tiffany looked out of the window of the cab that was turning onto her street. The sun was bright and her large sunglasses were doing very little to shield the magnificent rays from burning holes into her hungover eyes.

"Today is about Molly," Mackenzie stated firmly.

Guilt crept inside Tiffany. Of course she knew that going shopping for the perfect dress was important to Molly, even more so because the girl she'd known since high school hated shopping with a passion. It took a lot of convincing just to get Molly to agree to go looking for a dress.

"I'm quite aware that it is. Sorry I wasn't here waiting for you," Tiffany spat, as the mustard yellow cab dropped Tiffany off in front of her apartment in a trendy area of Seattle. Well, it hadn't been so trendy a while back, but it was now becoming filled with hipsters and chic little businesses. Plus, it was home to the Fremont Troll, a giant concrete-sculpted creature under one of the bridges in her neighborhood. It had become a huge tourist attraction, a novelty that had people wondering what kind of weirdos lived in Seattle. And everyone thought Portland was weird.

"Are you okay?" Mackenzie asked, her voice was now full of concern.

Am I? She'd just woken up and left a strange hotel suite. That wouldn't exactly classify as a normal, run-of-the-mill morning in anyone's book. To add to the mess she was already in, Tiffany was late meeting Mackenzie and Molly for breakfast and wedding dress shopping. *Why do they even want to go today? They know I'm going to be hungover. Torture. Because that is what best friends do to one another.*

"I just drank too much. I don't even know why we planned to go on this dress shopping expedition today," Tiffany complained.

She handed the cab driver several bills and hopped out. He winked at her when she turned back. Her walk of shame was not going unnoticed by him or the several neighbors that were outside. Tiffany tried to cover her face. *Can this day get any worse?* She could almost hear life snicker, *"It's still early."*

"Not today, Tiffany. I just can't fight with you today, okay? I want to focus on Moll," Mackenzie said with a huff.

Mackenzie and Tiffany were close but had only been friends for the last ten or so years. Molly was their shared buddy, but what Mackenzie needed to remember was that Tiffany had been there first. She had been besties with Molly since their junior year in high school, Mackenzie had come along quite a bit later. The problem with Mackenzie was that she felt the need to scold and parent both Molly and Tiffany. *Why?* They were in their mid-thirties, just like her. They were grown-ass women and didn't need the extra mothering.

Molly was a world-famous photographer who created book covers for tons of best-selling authors and was doing quite well for herself. *Well* was an understatement. She had a gorgeous studio that had the most magnificent view of the waterfront in downtown Seattle. Within the last several months, their girl had found herself engaged to one helluva guy.

Mackenzie taught kids to not eat glue and how to color in the lines — or at least that's how Tiffany viewed her friend's job as a kindergarten teacher.

Then there was her. She was an assistant to a CEO of a small corporation—but a corporation, no less, that owned several other small coffee shops. They weren't anywhere near the size of the famed Starbucks, but they were well-known. Their coffee was also *amazing* and Tiffany loved her job. It didn't hurt that she also loved coffee, too.

Mackenzie really had no cause to worry. They were all doing just fine in their little lives. A gnawing thought bit her. *Didn't I just wake up in some devilishly handsome man's hotel room?* Okay, perhaps Mackenzie had good reason to be a little concerned about her, considering the fact that Tiffany still had no clue how she had wound up there.

"You're so cranky, Mac," Tiffany stated. She kicked her heels off and started to peel off her clothes as soon as she crossed her threshold. A hot shower to scrub away the memory of whatever may have happened the night before was now a top priority.

"I wouldn't be if you'd been home and ready like you said you would be."

"Just tell me where to meet you guys, okay?" Tiffany said as she stood in her bra and underwear, waiting to get into the shower. She decided to brush her teeth. The minty paste started to foam in her mouth as she listened to Mackenzie continue her lecture.

"Are you brushing your teeth?"

"Yeah, why?" Tiffany asked then spit into the glass-bowl sink.

"Because it's gross. I just heard you spit."

"So? Don't you spit when you brush or do you just swallow?" Tiffany asked playfully. Her real intent was to push a few more buttons. She swished water in her mouth and spit again.

"Good grief. Of course, I spit—just not when I'm on the phone with someone. You shouldn't even be brushing your teeth when we're talking. It's kind of rude."

Tiffany rolled her eyes and caught a glimpse of herself in

her mirror. She looked like hell, so that gorgeous guy had gotten quite an eye full this morning. *Great. This is exactly why I'm single.*

"Mackenzie, if we are done with the lecture, can I go? I need to hop in the shower and then I will catch up with you guys. Go ahead and have breakfast without me."

"You are impossible, Tiffany. We'll see you at the diner. Just hurry, please," Mackenzie said and the hung up.

Today was a whole mess of craptastic. Tiffany hadn't even had coffee yet. Maybe that's why the world didn't seem right and nothing made any sense. Molly had a severe coffee addiction that was worse than Tiffany's but not by much. Mackenzie loved coffee, as well, but always made it too sweet and added too much creamer. Different strokes for different folks. But after doctoring it up like that, what was really the point?

Showered and properly caffeinated, Tiffany was dressed and ready to conquer the quest of finding just the right dress for her bestie. If there was anything that Tiffany was great at, it was shopping.

* * * *

"There she is," Molly cooed from behind the rack of tons of wedding gowns wrapped in crinkly plastic.

"It is I." Tiffany hugged Molly and ignored the scowl that was etched on Mackenzie's face. They still hadn't resolved their tiny fight from the engagement party the evening before. Leave it to Mackenzie to stew about it and make it a far bigger deal than necessary.

But Tiffany didn't hold grudges. That wasn't her style. She hugged Mackenzie and ignored how rigid she was. "We can discuss our issue later, but please don't make this today miserable," she whispered to Mackenzie.

Mackenzie rolled her eyes and turned her attention back to the rack of dresses she stood by.

"Save me," Molly begged.

"Oh, stop. You see anything you like or want to try on yet?"

Molly shook her head. "No, this sucks. I hate shopping and this is like pure hell. No one told me what a nightmare it would be."

"Oh, girl, we haven't even started on the accessories or shoes. This is the easy part," Tiffany teased. "We need to figure out shoes, the veil, lingerie and don't get me started on the jewelry."

Molly let out a loud groan.

Mackenzie added, "You could easily eliminate all that and get married in Hawaii. Think about it—barefoot and a simple dress."

"God, yes!" Molly's cocoa-colored eyes grew wide. "That's brilliant. I could totally do that. A beautiful beach wedding. Why in the heck didn't I think of that?"

"Because you barely got engaged and this is all moving a mile a minute." Tiffany held out a dress. "What about this one?" It was silky with incredible bead work.

"Nah, that doesn't scream 'beach wedding'." Molly scrunched up her nose. "What about a swimsuit?"

"Do you think Owen would actually go for a beach wedding in Hawaii?" Mackenzie asked. "You know I was just kidding, right?"

"Yes. But it would be kind of amazing, don't you think?" Molly slid dresses across the metal rack, not stopping to really look at any of them. "I love Hawaii, I did a couple shoots there. Anywhere tropical is good with me."

"Well, you should probably talk this over with Owen first. He might be a church wedding type of guy. Maybe he wants the whole traditional thing. You never know," Tiffany pointed out.

"If he wanted traditional, then he wouldn't have proposed to me. I am the furthest thing from traditional," Molly explained with a giant grin.

Tiffany and Mackenzie nodded in agreement.

Mackenzie held up a beautiful option. "You do have a

point there," Mackenzie said, placing another dress covered in plastic back onto the rack.

"What about this one?" Tiffany held out another dress. It was a soft cream color and had a sweetheart cut, perfect for Molly's big boobs.

Molly shrugged. "I'll try it on for shits and giggles, but I'm kind of diggin' this whole beach idea."

"I'm going to run to the restroom," Mackenzie excused herself.

Molly waited until their friend was out of earshot. "Okay, what the hell is going on?"

"What?" Tiffany tried to act surprised.

"A couple of things actually. One, why didn't you come to breakfast? I know you were a little hungover, but still. Then you and Mackenzie. Um, I guess you guys haven't made up yet." Molly gave her a tight-lipped smile.

"Well, I'm sorry about breakfast." Tiffany wasn't sure if this was the time to go into detail about her whereabouts and all that mess. Maybe Molly would be able to help solve the puzzle, but then again, Tiffany wasn't in the mood to be scolded. The guy was obviously someone that either Owen or Molly knew, otherwise he wouldn't have been on the boat. She just needed a little more time to figure things out.

"Forgiven. But what about you and Mackenzie?" Molly twisted her neck to check to see if Mackenzie was headed back. "Hurry. She'll be back soon."

Tiffany released an exaggerated sigh. "What's there to say? She's pissed off at me, end of story."

"Uh, you were supposed to apologize to her last night and straighten everything out, Tiff." Molly looked past Tiffany in search of Mackenzie. "I don't see why you can't both host the bachelorette and wedding shower? But I do think you hurt her feelings a little."

"Mackenzie always gets bent out of shape. She'll get over it." Tiffany reached for another dress, peeked at the price then gasped.

Molly peered over her shoulder. "Holy mother of God.

See? This is insane." She motioned toward the entire rack. "Why am I even doing this?"

"Because you're madly in love with Owen," Tiffany said with a large smile.

"I suppose, but to go to all this trouble? What about just getting hitched at the courthouse?"

"God, no. There's always Vegas?" Tiffany suggested.

"Yeah, true." Molly almost appeared to be considering it for a moment.

"But I do think Mackenzie is right. A beach wedding would be incredible."

Molly nodded. "It's just that this is so overwhelming already and we haven't even started. I know that women spend hours poring over bridal magazines. I haven't even bought one yet."

"Or some spend their entire childhood planning for this event." Tiffany smiled.

"No! Seriously? Did you?" Molly's dark eyes went wide.

"Well, kinda. I thought all little girls did—the dress, the flowers, that first dance and, of course, the groom." Tiffany had dreamed of getting married since she could remember. If this had been her getting married instead of Molly, she would have had nearly everything picked out, even the caterer, by the time the engagement ring had been slid onto her finger.

"Yeah, he sort of plays an important role, huh?"

"So how are you and Owen?" Tiffany asked.

Mackenzie appeared and immediately set to work sorting through the gowns that Tiffany had draped over another rack to be tried on.

Molly smiled. "Things are good. Last night was amazing. Just being there with everyone… It was so special." Molly's eyes filled with happy tears.

Tiffany and Mackenzie circled her. Now that one of them was marriage-bound, it set in how much it sucked to be single. Tiffany was thrilled for Molly and wished her all the happiness in the world, but she'd love to find her Mr.

Right, too. She wanted the beautiful engagement ring, the excitement of planning a fantastic wedding, and of course, someone to spend the rest of her life with. Tiffany was getting pretty tired of being unattached and lonely. Then her brain kindly reminded her that she hadn't been so lonely this morning.

Chapter Three

When her alarm on the bedside table let out a horrible shrill, Tiffany slapped at it, causing a terrible crash. Her glass of water from the night before was now on the ground soaking her carpet. *Crap.* A couple of books she'd attempted to read but served more as decoration were now scattered about. She fumbled for the lamp in the darkness. *Where in the heck is it?* Her bedroom had no sunshine coming in yet because it was early. *Too early.* Tiffany was always a little disoriented in the mornings. *Coffee.* Her brain and body begged her to caffeinate as soon as possible.

After finally getting her alarm to shut off, she yawned and rubbed her eyes. It took a great deal of willpower to get herself up and showered for work. She was exhausted even after having gone to bed earlier than normal. They had shopped like crazy the day before and, unfortunately, had not found the perfect dress, mainly because Molly was now sold on the idea that everyone could just come in their bathing suits. Her friend was really running with this whole beach wedding idea.

Tiffany whimpered and managed to leave the warmth and comfort of her bed. She started her morning ritual — coffee, shower and more coffee. Then she was off to work, braving the thick river of morning commuters. If she made it into work without her pulling out her hair, then the day stood a chance of being halfway decent. Everyone pegged her for being this little ray of sunshine and happiness, and for the most part, Tiffany was, but what they didn't see were the dark bits. The ones that Tiffany had kept hidden as best she could, the ones that were covered in a dirty layer of insecurities. *But what human, especially female, doesn't have those floating around?* Too much time in traffic meant too much thinking.

She zipped her tiny compact car into the parking garage, gathered her stuff then raced for the elevator. Tiffany felt the spill before she looked down. She was late but knew what had just happened and what was going to make this Monday even more craptastic. The doors opened, several people that were clutching their briefcases and coffees were tucked inside. Tiffany excused herself and squeezed in with them. She tried to rummage through her large designer purse. *Okay, it's a knock-off, but no one can tell.* Tiffany tried to find a napkin or something to wipe up the coffee that was quickly staining her gorgeous and slightly expensive turquoise blouse. A maxi pad, that's all she had. Desperate times called for desperate measures. Tiffany was a resourceful girl, always had been, and she could make this work. Tiffany unwrapped the pad and tried to ignore the stares of people eyeing her curiously. As Tiffany blotted her blouse carefully, she smiled.

"How 'bout them Mariners? What a game last night," Tiffany said loudly, hoping to ease the uncomfortable silence. She got a few polite nods in response.

Has no one ever spilled anything on themselves before? Are these corporate schmucks so perfect? Granted, Tiffany probably should wear a bib. This wasn't her first time at the rodeo. She knew that her chest was often the splash zone for food and drinks. She was a little clumsy. *So what?* The annoyed glares that several people shot her made Tiffany feel uncomfortable. *Note to self, pack more napkins in purse. Hell, a whole roll of paper towels to be on the safe side.*

Only Tiffany would have a Monday that involved spilling coffee on herself and having to clean it up with a jumbo overnight pad. This sucker was not some dainty nondescript thing. No, this was one size away from being a diaper. Last month she'd had a heavy period and she'd packed it just in case. Tiffany didn't think its purpose would have been to absorb coffee, but that was life — or at least how hers was.

The elevator finally took Tiffany to her floor. Her office was right next door to her long-time boss, Patty. Tiffany had climbed the ranks from mail clerk to the marketing president's assistant in a matter of a few years. Patty was charmed by Tiffany. Their shared love for knock-off designer bags and coffee had made them instant friends and the rest was history. Fast forward nearly six years and Tiffany had one of the best offices in their building at Blue Moose Coffee Corporation. She had a terrific view of downtown Seattle and could see the legendary Space Needle. Well, her view was more of the other skyscrapers next to it, but Tiffany would swear that on a clear day she could make out a tiny bit of the Space Needle. *That counts, right?*

Her hands were sticky with coffee as she juggled her purse and travel mug. Her heels clicked against the gleaming, spotless wood floor. She was almost to her office, where Tiffany hoped she had an extra shirt of some kind. Tiffany prayed that she hadn't used the last emergency blouse then hadn't replaced it. She couldn't recall and tried to hurry without being seen. But in order to get to her office, she had to pass by Patty's first.

Tiffany peeked at her watch. Hopefully Patty was in a meeting and she could take care of her little laundry mishap before being noticed. Not that it really mattered. Tiffany adored Patty. Her boss was an intelligent and powerful woman. Tiffany kind of envied how successful she was. She teased Patty all the time, telling her that she wanted to be just like her when she grew up. Patty wasn't exactly the maternal type even though she had kids and even a few grandbabies. Her boss didn't try and project that onto Tiffany. She treated her like an equal and didn't offer motherly advice. Their relationship was rock solid. Tiffany kicked ass at her position, taking care of so many details and important aspects of the company that no one could possibly believe everything she did on a daily basis. Patty entrusted Tiffany with a great deal, giving her tons of tasks and responsibilities that had made other assistants' heads spin. Not Tiffany… She delivered every time. She loved her job and was damn good at it—simple as that. It was the waking up and driving there that sucked. Once she was properly caffeinated and in her element, it was all rock 'n' roll.

Tiffany zipped past some cubicles and several desks. She waved and smiled, but avoided any chit-chat. When Tiffany finally reached Patty's opened door, she tried to scurry past, but her eyes became glued to the man sitting across from her boss. Then Tiffany heard him laugh. *That voice.* She knew it from somewhere. She was confused and started to slip into a bit of shock. It was *him.* Then he turned around in his seat. He smiled at first then it fell off his handsome face. It was *definitely* him.

"Good morning, Tiffany," Patty greeted her and smiled. "Please come in and join us."

There was something in her eyes that caused Tiffany to be alarmed. *Sadness? Bad news?* Something wasn't adding up. Patty's smile was forced and why was *he* here? Too many questions and not enough coffee to process them all.

He stared at her then smiled politely as Patty introduced him, "Tiffany, please meet Colin Murphy. He's going to be the new CEO of Blue Moose Coffee."

What the hell? New CEO? It hit Tiffany hard, like someone had punched her in the gut. *Am I losing my job? Yeah, today is going to be just super.*

* * * *

"Wow, so it sounds like you're having an awful day. Sorry, Tiff," Molly said as they sat in their favorite coffee shop.

Tiffany stirred the long straw that was partially submerged into a dark iced coffee. "Ugh, don't even get me started. It can't get any worse. Right, Moll?"

Molly raised her eyebrows. "Don't tempt fate."

It was Tiffany's lunch break and she'd called Molly to meet her. She needed to vent and to get another shirt, which Molly had brought. Thank goodness for having besties that were willing to help at a moment's notice.

"This new boss-guy... Where's he from and how come you didn't know about him? Patty didn't know?" Molly twirled her own straw.

Tiffany had left out one important detail about Colin Murphy, the one about waking up in his hotel room. Tiffany was still trying to figure out what all had happened. She hadn't talked to him after Patty had introduced her. He was quiet, reserved and probably just as surprised to see her again.

"I'm not sure anyone knew. It was totally weird, Moll." Tiffany took a long sip of her iced caffeine. "I think she may have been forced out. Maybe this whole Murphy Enterprises is going to clean house. I'm a little scared, to be honest," Tiffany admitted.

"So, do you still have a job? Otherwise, I could hire you, you know?" Molly's eyes grew bright.

"Moll, you would make me your slave and only pay me in coffee. At least Patty pays me real money. Besides, you couldn't afford me."

"True. So what now?"

Tiffany exhaled a loud breath. "I go back and learn my fate."

She was terrified. Bills...enough said. Seattle was not a cheap place to live. It wasn't New York or anything, but it was still pretty darned expensive. Tiffany dreaded having to hunt for a new job. She'd worked so hard to get where she was.

"Tiff, it'll be okay. I promise." Molly covered her hand with hers and smiled. "You'll find another job, probably an even better one. But no matter what, just remember. You got this."

Tiffany appreciated Molly's words of encouragement, but

that still wouldn't pay her bills or feed her shoe, handbag and coffee addiction.

"Well, I better get back. Wish me luck." She got up from her seat and hugged Molly before leaving. "Thanks again for bringing me the shirt." Tiffany plucked at the royal purple blouse.

"It's totally your color. Remember, purple is a power color." Molly winked at her. "You got this, bitch."

Tiffany laughed and walked out of the coffee shop feeling a little more confident and with more pep.

It was a gorgeous day in Seattle—the sun was high, the sky was a perfect shade of blue and not a single cloud dotted it. It wasn't too hot, but Tiffany was glad that she had worn her dark gray pencil skirt. The sun felt great on her bare legs and they could use a little a color.

She wished she didn't have to go back to her office. Fear was knitting a sick web inside her. Today would have been a wonderful day to go on a picnic or to do anything that didn't involve her dealing with what waited for her back at work. *Ugh, being a grown-up sucks.*

* * * *

Tiffany managed to sneak back to her office unnoticed as Patty and the new ruler of Blue Moose Coffee were away at lunch. She shut her door and tried to focus on work, but her brain had been miles away. Tiffany had stared at spreadsheets and promotional materials with none of her usual interest. *What if this isn't my job anymore? How large will my severance pay be? How soon can I find a new job?* All these questions kept her from working. She didn't know what to expect and was praying that maybe no one would bother her for the rest of day.

Tucked away in her office, surrounded by silence and her thoughts, Tiffany jumped when the phone on her desk rang.

"Tiffany, can you please join us?"

Her prayers had gone unanswered.

"I'll be right there, Patty," Tiffany tried to reply confidently as she swallowed back the growing lump that formed in her throat. She was sick with worry. *This could be it. Hello, unemployment.*

Taking a deep breath, Tiffany entered Patty's office. *He* was there. Tiffany tried to avoid his gaze but could feel him assessing her. *Didn't he already have enough of a gander this weekend?*

"Take a seat, Tiffany," Patty ordered and pointed to the empty chair next to Colin, aka the new enemy, destroyer of jobs and all things wonderful in her world.

She sat and scooted her chair a little farther away. She heard him let out a laugh.

"I'm not going to bite." The accent was strong and utterly sexy.

Tiffany didn't dare look at him. She'd already noticed the pink dress shirt and charcoal-colored slacks earlier and she couldn't help but find him incredibly hot. However, this man was about to fire her, so she wasn't going to allow her stupid carnal desires to get in the way of her hate right now. He was going to be the reason she'd have to consider moving under a bridge and taking up residence with the Fremont Troll. *Homelessness is anything but cute.* She was accustomed to hot showers, a warm bed and food. Shit was about to get real and she didn't need her dumb hormones making her all crazy and flustered over this jerk. *God, he is so hot. Be strong, Tiff. He's the enemy.*

"I know this is all very unsettling and must be quite confusing for you." Patty offered her a tight-lipped smile. This didn't reassure Tiffany one ounce.

"Yes, I'd say so. Patty. Why didn't you tell me?" Tiffany was hurt that Patty had kept such an enormous game changer from her.

"We weren't certain that the deal was even going to go through, to be honest. I didn't want to cause panic or alarm. Besides, the CEO only told me yesterday."

Colin, aka the devil, sat there listening to them, quietly invading their space. Tiffany was tempted to ask him to leave. *Why does he need to sit in on this conversation? Can't he give us some privacy?*

"Patty, I understand. I suppose my concern is my place here." There, she'd said it, regardless of how hard as it had been to spit out.

"Oh, Tiffany, you aren't going anywhere." Patty laughed softly. There was a nervous undertone that Tiffany still found unsettling.

Now she was confused. *So why were the two of them acting so strange, like they were smuggling some kind of secret?*

"Well, that's not quite true, is it now, Patty?" That damn Irish brogue asked.

"I guess not." There it was again, the sad eyes and the frown on Patty's face. "Tiffany, you will be moving, actually. It wasn't decided until a little bit ago."

"Moving?" Tiffany asked cautiously. *So I'm not losing my job. Yay!* But why was Patty acting so odd? Maybe she was the one being let go. "Patty, are you moving?" Tiffany tried to ask politely.

Patty shook her head. "Nope, I will still be the president of marketing. You will be changing positions."

Tiffany sat and waited. She watched Patty throw a Colin a look. *Shit, are they going to put me back in the mail room?*

"It would seem that Mr. Murphy —" Patty started.

"Colin, please," Colin interrupted. Of course, anything said in that hot-as-hell accent came off as proper and polite. Even if it were some smug remark, he'd still sound charming. She was starting to hate and fall in lust with Colin Murphy, all at the same time.

Patty huffed then finished, "That Colin wants you to become his assistant."

"Wait…what?" Suddenly Tiffany felt like merchandise and that didn't sit too well with her. *I can't be traded and exchanged, can I?*

* * * *

"Ooh, that burns." Tiffany cringed as she swallowed it down.

"It's vodka. It's made to help you forget your problems. That's part of the burn. Here, have another," Mackenzie ordered. They were seated around the large glass table inside Molly's studio.

The Seattle city lights twinkled in the background of the enormous floor-to-ceiling windows that covered one wall. The ample view was incredible, to say the least.

"So you didn't get fired? This is good." Molly drained her shot glass and asked, "Why are we drinking these straight?"

"Because Tiff needs it. Hell, we all need it." Mackenzie laughed and poured another round of shots.

"Didn't realize that you were having a rough week, Mac. Hell, it just started." Tiffany frowned.

"I'm bored. School's out and you guys are at work."

"I would think you'd be happy for some quiet time, Mac," Molly said as she patted Mackenzie's hand.

Tiffany realized why Mackenzie probably hated the quiet. It meant she had to deal with her grief. It had only been a few months since her sister had died. Mackenzie didn't talk about it much and that worried both Molly and Tiffany. They were concerned that it was festering inside their friend, but they also knew that she was one of the strongest people they knew and there was a comfort in that. Mackenzie could handle just about anything.

"So what about work and this new boss of yours? Is he hot?" Mackenzie's words slurred a bit as she poured them each another shot.

"Single?" Molly wiggled her eyebrows.

Tiffany wanted to tell them everything, to completely let it all out. But she didn't want a lecture from Mackenzie or for Molly to worry. It was best to keep it quiet for as long as she could. *Is it the right call to keep this from them? Probably not.* These were her friends and it killed Tiffany not to blurt it all out. She would love to tell them that she had no clue what to do, that she'd been an emotional wreck and had to hide it when they were out shopping. *Will they understand?* Molly might offer sympathy, but Mackenzie would have plenty to say on the subject. Maybe Tiffany deserved that, but it wasn't like her to wind up at a hotel suite with some strange guy. This was a whole new low for her. The thought made Tiffany cringe. The fact that he was now her boss only made matters worse. She eyed the clear drink in front of her. *Maybe that li'l sucker will help me forget just how terribly embarrassing and awful my life has become?*

* * * *

Drinking on a work night was never a good idea, *ever*. Vodka hadn't usually hit her like this. Then again, she had been throwing back shots until Molly and Mackenzie had finally cut her off. How else was she going to forget the nightmare that her life was quickly becoming?

Tiffany wore her large, white Kurt Cobain-like sunglasses that she'd purchased during the nineties and her brief fling with the whole grunge fashion scene. Tiffany couldn't help but think of the days when she'd rocked flannel and ripped jeans—*strategically* ripped jeans. Tiffany, after all, had always been a girl that explored all the latest trends. Now she oozed office casual—khaki capris and a rose-pink blouse. The giant white bug-like sunglasses added an element of cool—or at least she thought so. Plus, they matched her white flats. Either way, for being hungover, at least Tiffany looked pretty darn good.

Carbs were usually not her friend, but today they were. Tiffany dipped another golden fried piece of potato perfection in the ketchup.

"These are friggin' amazing," Tiffany commented happily.

"The perfect cure for any hangover." Mackenzie snatched a fry from the pile in front of Tiffany.

"Hey, these are mine." Tiffany playfully shooed Mackenzie's hand away as she reached for another.

"So? You didn't seem to mind sharing my cheeseburger." Molly looked down at her food, it was untouched.

"What's wrong? Not hungry?" Tiffany asked with concern.

Molly pushed the plate away. "Not really. I feel just blah today."

"PMS?" Mackenzie asked as she managed to swipe another fry.

"Probably." Molly yawned and then turned her attention to Tiffany. "So how was work today?"

"Why do you have to ruin a perfectly good time? Jeesh."

Tiffany looked around at the diner. This place oozed charm and nostalgia in the best remembered way. The red vinyl booths to the jukebox against one wall were all iconic images of a time so long ago. The 50s theme was well cherished here, but so was the food. The fries, milk shakes and burgers were amazing. This place stayed open twenty-four hours like a diner from a Hollywood movie. You could grab coffee and a slice of pie when you weren't quite ready to say goodnight to your date. Or coffee after a night of dancing and drinking. Tiffany had been coming here for years and nothing had changed. She bit off a bite of fry and gazed out of the window at the busy street.

Change was everywhere, even right in front of her. Molly was getting married and she was no longer Patty's assistant. But this diner stayed the same after decades upon decades. It was incredible that this diner on the corner could remain untouched and unchanged. *Why couldn't life be like that?*

Chapter Four

"It will be fine, Tiffany."

Tiffany rolled her eyes and doubted the words Patty had said. "I like how I had no say in the whole matter, Patty," Tiffany said as she grabbed another empty cardboard box and started to fill it with knick-knacks and awards from her bookshelf. Her office was nearly empty now. "It's as though you didn't even fight for me."

"I wasn't given much choice, Tiffany. He simply said he would need an assistant, then we visited a couple of other departments and when we came back... Well, he chose you."

"And there was no way for you to tell him no?"

"Tiffany, is that really an option? Saying no to the CEO is like a death sentence." Patty grabbed another box and started to carefully set items from Tiffany's desk into it.

"We had a good run though, didn't we?" Tiffany asked. She could feel tears threatening to spill.

"We sure did. Tiffany, you are talented and need to think of this as a promotion. If anyone deserves this, it's you. You'll have a nicer office and a bigger salary. Try to see the positives here," Patty explained.

"I just wish that I had been given the opportunity to decide if I wanted that position."

"Tiffany, what's the real problem? I know you like working for me. We're a great team, but this is something that most assistants would give their right arm for. You, on the other hand, are trying to run as far away from Mr. Murphy as possible. Why?"

"Patty, I can't explain it, but I'm not interested in leaving this department. I love my job."

"So are you going to quit?"

Tiffany sighed. "In a perfect world, yes. A perfect world that didn't have bills or the need for money."

"Hell, then neither of us would be here." Patty laughed as she finished clearing off the desk.

"True."

"Let's go check out that new office and get you settled in," Patty suggested.

Tiffany didn't really have much choice, did she? There was no getting out of this.

Patty put a box in Tiffany's arms and ordered her to start walking. They each carried a box to the elevator and up they went. *Top floor.*

Patty had tears in her eyes as the doors opened. "Bet your office is bigger than mine."

They walked up to the receptionist and asked to see Mr. Murphy. They were directed down a hall and came to two large doors. *This is it.*

Working with Patty the last several years had been wonderful. They had a comfortable rhythm, knew each other so well and were completely in sync. She wasn't sure that was going to be the case with Colin.

Tiffany could hear Patty exhale louder than necessary. They faced each other and it took everything for them to both not burst into tears.

"Just don't forget to visit me, okay?" Patty said, her voice was rough as she was obviously trying to contain all her emotions.

Tiffany could only nod. *God, this is so hard.*

They knocked and waited.

Colin, aka the one who was ruining her life, opened the door with a large smile on his face. He was oblivious to the pain that she and Patty were feeling. It didn't matter to him. He'd gotten his way. The amusement and light in his dark eyes made her feel like some shiny, brand-new toy. Tiffany groaned, apparently *not* to herself.

"What is that about?"

Shit, that was out loud. Tiffany inhaled again and lied, "I'm sorry. I was trying to clear my throat."

Colin nodded, but the smirk on his face told her that he knew that hadn't been the case.

"Thank you, Patty. I've got it from here," he excused Patty, who stood there holding a large box. Colin lifted it from her hands and dismissed her with a slight nod.

Patty smiled politely then looked to Tiffany. *This is it.*

"Well now, let's get you settled in properly," he said. The sound of his voice caused her core to warm.

Tiffany hated herself right now. She didn't want to feel any attraction to this man that had completely disrupted her life, both professionally and personally. Tiffany wanted to stay as far away from him and make him a distant memory, but that wasn't likely now that she would have an office right next to his.

"Don't look so glum."

"Mr. Murphy—"

He stopped her. "Colin. Come on, Tiffany. We've been through this already." Colin led the way to a door that was inside his office, which was huge. Even with the giant desk, floor-to-ceiling bookcases that lined one of the walls and a small sitting area, the room still managed to look spacious.

Wow. Her view was killer. She could actually spot the Space Needle from her desk. Tiffany's new office was miniature version of Colin's, except there was an enormous bouquet of flowers on her desk. Tiffany placed the box she was carrying down and let her finger touch the velvety soft petal of a massive sunflower.

"Glad to see you smiling," Colin said from behind her. Instantly Tiffany frowned.

"These are from you?"

"Yes, a little welcome gift."

"That wasn't necessary," Tiffany whispered.

Colin looked at her and closed his eyes, as if he were summoning the strength to deal with her. "Tiffany, we really should discuss a few things."

"There's nothing to discuss. You made the decision for me to be here and there's not a whole lot I can do about that, right?" Tiffany squared her stance.

"Yes, I did make the decision, because I can." His rich tone was arrogant and smug.

Seriously? If she didn't have a stack of bills on her counter and near to zero dollars in her bank account, Tiffany would love to give him a piece of her mind, or at least see how that severance package looked.

* * * *

Mackenzie stared at her with concern. "Tiffany, what's going on with you? You aren't acting like you."

Mackenzie had made a valid observation, Tiffany wasn't being her usual perky self and it had everything to do with Colin Murphy. Tiffany grabbed her strawberry margarita and took a healthy chug. *Ouch, brain freeze!*

She sat across from her friend and stared at the bowl of salsa. Chunks of tomatoes and green leaves of cilantro swam in the spicy mixture. She plunged a perfect tortilla chip in and scooped up an ample amount. Her throat burned and her tongue begged for water. Her margarita took care of that. Another icy sip and Tiffany saved her from the spicy invasion.

"Mac, it's just work." Simple enough of an answer.

Mackenzie nodded. "I know it has to be hard, but try to look at the positives. You got a pay raise, a promotion that most of the other assistants would die for and Colin sounds kind of hot."

That was a huge part of the problem. He was very hot. She'd only been his assistant for one day and thankfully he'd been occupied in a ton of meetings. Tiffany dreaded the time coming when she had to actually work with him, like possibly tomorrow. Maybe she would luck out and he'd be called away to more meetings or whatever else evildoers who steal assistants do.

"So, what new with you? Have you been talking to Jason?" Tiffany decided to turn the tables and steer the conversation away from her.

She watched Mackenzie blink and swallow some of her drink. *Jason*, now that was a fine-ass man, tattooed and muscular and completely not Mackenzie's type. He was a bouncer they'd met when they had been in Vegas during the spring on an impromptu girls' trip.

"Well, it's funny. We talk just about every night," she answered. Mackenzie paused and took another sip of her margarita. "I'm actually flying out to see him soon."

"Really?" Tiffany almost choked on her chip. That was an unexpected response from Mackenzie. Tiffany had no idea that Mackenzie was entertaining the idea of trying to carry on a long-distance relationship with this guy. Sure, he was hot, but with that said, it was doubtful he was being faithful in the city of sin. "Are you sure that's such a great idea?"

"I don't see any other eligible men knocking down my door." Mackenzie laughed and dove a chip into the salsa.

"Well, that makes two of us."

"So what do you think about Molly and Owen? Can you believe they are actually going to get married?"

"It's friggin' nuts. We have so much to do. Dress shopping was a bust this weekend."

Mackenzie rolled her eyes. "You can say that again. It's like pulling teeth trying to get her to try on anything."

Tiffany was thankful that Mackenzie didn't go into their squabble.

"If it were my wedding, I would be trying on so many dresses and shoes. I can't wait until I get married," Tiffany gushed.

"Yeah, I didn't quite get to the whole dress-shopping portion of the engagement with Gideon." Mackenzie looked sad and it broke Tiffany's heart.

Tiffany reached for her hand and said, "Someday we won't be old maids. The right guys are out there for us—

somewhere."

"Yeah, true." Mackenzie looked hopeful.

"But just not in Vegas." Tiffany shook her finger at Mackenzie and they both laughed.

* * * *

"Tiffany, please come here," Colin asked.

Tiffany's door was cracked open and she sighed. She had been working hard to avoid him all morning but knew she couldn't hide in her office forever.

"Yes, Mr. Murphy?" she asked politely.

"Tiffany." He tossed her an annoyed look. "Colin, remember?"

Calling him Mr. Murphy was her own way of getting her digs in. She enjoyed how much it irritated him and it also kept an invisible professional line drawn between them. *Can't he see that?* They hadn't discussed Saturday night and the horror of Sunday morning yet and it was almost as if it hadn't happened. *Maybe it didn't? Is it possible that it was all just a drunken delusion? God, that would be wonderful.*

"Please sit," he commanded.

Tiffany sat down in the chair across from him. She stayed rigid, keeping her posture straight. He clasped his hands together and looked at her, studying her, which only caused Tiffany to grow more nervous. She could almost see the gears in his handsome head turning. He was silent, thinking. Tiffany waited for him to speak. *Might as well take in the view.* The man was gorgeous. It was as simple and as complicated as that. There were fine creases near the corners of his eyes that she imagined would bend as he laughed. His lips were more on the full side, definitely kissable. She *had* kissed them and right now wouldn't mind another go at it. Then she saw him move his tongue across his lips, leaving a slight sheen as it passed. *God help me.*

"Tiffany, we need to discuss a few things. I want you to fully understand what I expect." His voice was firm but he seemed to choose his words carefully.

A curt nod was her response and she became even more uneasy. *Shit is about to get real.*

"I know you aren't thrilled that you were selected to become my assistant. You've made that crystal clear. My first question is why? What is your aversion to me?" He looked like a wounded little boy. The pouty stare he gave her seemed as though Tiffany had just kicked his puppy or something. She'd had no idea he was sensitive. One minute he was this powerful man then next a complete softie. He was an enigma.

"Mr. Murph—" she started.

"Colin."

Fine, he can have this one.

"Colin," Tiffany continued, gathering her thoughts so she didn't sound like an idiot. She could hardly think straight with him in the same room, much less with him only a few feet away. "I'm less than thrilled, I'll admit. I have worked for Patty for years and feel that we make a great team."

"I know. I could sense that right away," he agreed and motioned for her continue.

"I wasn't even given a choice in the matter," she complained.

"Tiffany, this wasn't up for negotiation. I will decide where everyone is placed and I chose for you to be here. I only want the best."

Her train of thought had derailed. Stumbling over her words, she began, "Then there's that other thing. You know?" Tiffany winced as the words left her mouth.

He frowned and replied coolly, "Let me be clear on something. I don't mix business with pleasure."

Wow. She wanted nothing more than to retreat to her office. A sudden wave of disappointed crashed over her. *Why?* What had she expected him to say? Did she think he would profess his undying love and sweep her off her feet? No, he was the one in charge here. Any dreams of fairy-tale bullshit, a knight with an Irish brogue carting her off to his castle, were all dashed. It wasn't until those words had been spoken—slaying the sleeping dragon that had been there since she'd seen him only days earlier—that Tiffany realized she might be in quite a pickle. The ridiculous attraction she felt for Colin drove her nuts. What if she wanted to mix business with pleasure? Again, Tiffany didn't have much say in the matter and that was starting to piss her off.

Chapter Five

A soft tap on her door caused Tiffany to look up from the monitor in front of her. Her papers were all in neat rows and her concentration had been trained on the project.

Colin was in a black suit—some faint pattern could be seen on the jacket—and a crisp white shirt made his skin tone appear more olive. *Why do I have such a thing for suits?*

"Tiffany, I need you to drop everything and get my boy."

Boy? He has a son? This was news to her.

"Okay, where?" Tiffany saw the relief in his eyes as he instructed her to go to his condo. He explained that she was to bring the boy back to their office.

"Something happen with his babysitter?"

"No, she just wasn't able to watch him today."

"He's all alone? How old is he?" Tiffany asked. As she grabbed her purse, worry started to build up inside her for this youngster.

"He's two, and I have car taking you to go get him now," Colin answered as he spun around and left the room without another word.

Tiffany's mouth hung open, she was shocked. Two years old? He'd left a toddler by himself? *What kind of man does that?* So he could run a company, but he obviously failed as a father. Great, this was the guy she was attracted to. *Awesome taste, Tiff.*

"I'll get right on it," she said, still in shock. But she grabbed her purse and ran to the garage as quickly as her Louboutins would allow. Colin had instructed that someone would take her there and he was waiting. She arrived, only slightly breathless, and when she saw the company vehicle with the driver holding the door for her, she jumped right in. Then they were off.

The black SUV rounded the parking structure with a loud squeal. The driver must have been instructed to hurry. Tiffany waited for him to park, then he raced to the passenger side and held the door open for her. The building itself was ancient but once she got inside, she saw that it had been completely remodeled with a modern flair. Everything was high end, from the smooth marble flooring and spotless glass that allowed the Seattle morning sunshine to bathe the walls. Stunning was an understatement. This was the kind of place where only one type of people lived — *rich*. Not that Tiffany wasn't aware Colin was loaded, but this place reflected his expensive taste that much more.

She took an elevator to the penthouse. Using the key that had been given to her by the driver Tiffany unlocked the door. She didn't know what to expect. A scared little boy, for one thing, and her heart ached for this child Tiffany hadn't even met yet. Maybe it stemmed from the absence of her own father. He had worked so much that he'd hardly been home. She knew that he had just been trying to provide for their family, but Tiffany would have loved to have spent more time with him. She grew up before either of them really had a chance to establish a relationship.

"Hello?" Tiffany called out once inside.

Much like in Molly's studio, she was greeted with a wall of floor-to-ceiling windows. There was a black baby grand piano and even more spotless glass. The gorgeous inside of this home screamed *filthy rich*. This was no place for a child, even with the proper care of a nanny. It was cold, sterile and way too elegant.

There was no answer and Tiffany's stomach sank. *Where is this kiddo?* She began to venture farther inside the spotless and expensive living room. There was no evidence of a toddler living here — no stray toys in bright colors or sippy cups left about. Tiffany decided to move to the left toward a dimly lit hallway. Perhaps the child was in a bedroom hiding. Tiffany wanted nothing more than to be a mom. Maybe when the planets aligned and she met the right guy, not just some sperm donor, then Tiffany would have her chance at motherhood. Tiffany thought she possessed natural mothering instincts. Sure, there were things she needed to work on—and it was true that she wasn't smothering like Mackenzie—but loving a baby was not one of them. Panic started to grip her as she called out again to no answer. She peeked into a room off the hallway, a guest room that was no doubt professionally color-coordinated by a designer—gorgeous and inviting. Tiffany went as far as taking a quick look under the bed. Not even a dust bunny. Closing the door, she moved on to the next room. It was an office, fairly standard and actually quite boring, nothing grand or exquisite about that room. Tiffany looked everywhere—up and down, in and out, high and low. She crossed back into the living room and walked down the opposite hall to the right. There was a room with stacked boxes, all lined up neatly against the cream-colored walls. Probably from his recent move, she gathered. Tiffany checked the bathroom, even behind the glass shower door and there was no toddler hiding. *Where is he?* Now she was terribly worried. 'What if's started to sprout in her mind. Tiffany began to pray that he would appear or make some kind of sound so she could locate him.

At the end of the hall there was a large door, Tiffany opened it and called out again. Nothing. Then her eyes locked with a droopy pair of chocolate brown ones. He howled at her, his bottom lip jutted out a little along with several teeth from his under bite. Tiffany pulled out her cell phone and immediately called the office—more specifically, Colin's desk.

"Hello?"

"Colin, I think we have a problem. There's no child here, just some sad looking dog."

"How is he?" Concern was heavy in Colin's voice.

"The dog? I don't know. Fine, I guess. But your son is not

41

anywhere to be found."

What the hell is Colin's problem? Why isn't he freaking out? He should be here instead of her. Tiffany's blood began to boil. She was more than just mad. She was disgusted.

"That *is* my boy."

"The dog?" Okay, now she was confused. *The dog is his son?* Tiffany felt like she was missing a very large piece to the puzzle.

"Yes, that's Sir McCartney."

"Um, so there's no two year old here?" Tiffany needed verbal confirmation for her brain to process what was going on. This man had acted like his son had been left unattended. Now, she'd come to find out, it's a friggin' dog.

"He's two."

"The dog or the boy?"

"Sir McCartney."

Tiffany squinted as she looked at this brown and white wrinkled creature that was now pancaked on the bed. An enormous flat pink tongue was visible and loud snoring began, drowning out her thoughts. "So there is no boy?"

"*He's* my boy," Colin answered.

"I mean like a real child, Colin." Now she was annoyed. This must be some sort of prank or game to him. Well, she was not interested in playing. "This is ridiculous. You made it seem like you had a *son,* Colin, not some dog."

"He's more than just some dog. Now kindly please escort him back here." Colin hung up.

Tiffany didn't hate dogs. Well, maybe she did a little. She was definitely more of a cat person. Just ask Mr. Sprinkles, her overweight and cranky old cat. All he expected was his food bowl to be full and for her to change his litter box. In exchange, she was rewarded with an occasional snuggle or purr. It was a simple relationship.

Dogs were gross. Cats were independent and clever. Dogs were always jumping on you and chewing on things, right? The one before her didn't look like he could jump at all, but the slobber that was dangling from his loose flaps was icky. How exactly was she supposed to take this dog back to Colin? He expected her to bring this chunky thing into their office? Had he lost his mind?

"Hey you," Tiffany started. The brown eyes looked up at her, but the dog didn't move. "Sir McCartney, you need to come with me." *God, am I really saying this? Is this even in my job description?*

She noticed a furry little nub wiggle on his back side. *Where is its tail? Don't all dogs have a tail that wags?* This was not a normal tail and Tiffany was starting to think that this might not be a normal dog, either.

* * * *

"There he is, my little Pauly. Who's a good boy?" Colin cooed.

Something was very wrong with this picture. He was a grown-ass man and speaking to this stubborn animal with such worship.

Tiffany rolled her eyes. No, this dog was a complete pain in the ass. It had taken forever to get him off his bed and to finally come with her. This flat-faced pup was a brat and now Tiffany could see why. Colin was on the ground scratching Sir McCartney's—or Pauly's, whatever the heck his name was—meaty sides.

"I thought his name was Sir McCartney?" Tiffany asked. Not that she needed to know or even cared. It was more to break up this ridiculous love fest.

"It is. Sir Paul McCartney."

"But you just called him 'Pauly', right?"

"Yeah." Then Colin looked at her and it was like a light bulb went off in his head. A gentle smile replaced the smirk he he'd just been wearing. "You don't know who that is, do you?"

"The dog?"

"No, Sir Paul McCartney."

"Um, isn't that the dog?" Tiffany bit down on her bottom

lip. She started to feel stupid.

Colin rose off the floor and dusted himself off. "Paul McCartney? You know, from the Beatles?"

Tiffany wasn't so great at trivia or names. She had heard of the Beatles but couldn't name a song by the band. It just wasn't her style of music — or at least she didn't think so.

"Wow, seriously?" Colin put his hand over his mouth then rubbed his jaw. The speckle of growth was apparent on his face — dark, shadowy and incredibly sexy.

Tiffany shrugged. "So your dog is named after some singer. That's cool, I guess."

Colin shook his head and seemed about to explain when Tiffany started for her office. She peeked back and saw Colin look down at the dog and say something under his breath. She would have loved to have asked what he'd just said, but why? It was probably some snide remark about her having no clue about the origin of his name. Right now, she just wanted to wash her hands after handling the yucky mutt.

* * * *

Sir McCartney, aka Pauly, became a regular fixture in the office over the next few days. He would lay spread out next to Colin's desk. He'd quit howling at Tiffany every time she passed, which was greatly appreciated. So, not only was Tiffany trying very hard to avoid Colin, but now she had to not make eye contact with this dog. His big brown eyes always looked sad. They would follow her each time she had to pass by. It sort of creeped her out that he was always watching her. He was beyond lazy — never moving, just sleeping. And he snored, loudly.

It was now Friday, which meant Tiffany could let off some steam with her girls as they celebrated *Friendship Friday*. It was this thing they'd always done since forever. The girls would meet at one of their homes, the hostess would provide lots of lovely carb-infused snacks, one of them would pick out a cheesy romance movie and one would bring the booze. It was a grown-up slumber party with all the trimmings. It was all about lounging around in pajamas with no makeup, messy hair and getting drunk while gorging on forbidden foods. Basically, it was the best day of the week. Even with Molly wrapped up in everything Owen, she still managed to set aside time for her besties and that even included their special Friday nights.

If she could just get through the day, Tiffany knew that there were drinks waiting at the finish line for her. After this nightmare of a week, it couldn't come quick enough. She eyed her cell phone and saw that it was only ten in the morning. Tiffany groaned out loud and a few seconds later her office door was nudged open and in strutted Sir McCartney.

"You...get out," she ordered. He plopped down on the floor, letting his hanging jowls fan out on her floor. His chocolate eyes looked up at her and his fat tongue folded out. Nope, he wasn't going anywhere. She huffed. *How am I expected to work when this dog just waltzes in and does whatever he wants?* To be fair, he wasn't doing a whole lot of anything. In fact, he did nothing at all. It was all the heavy breathing and snoring that annoyed her, as well as the simple invasion of her personal space. This creature was an extension of Colin and she wanted nothing to do with him or his master.

Tiffany crinkled up her nose as a foul odor released into her office. "You are just plain nasty, you know that?"

Tiffany rose from her chair and stepped over the brown lump to get through to Colin's office. She saw him bent over his desk, his eyes trained on some papers in front of him. He had his reading glasses on, which meant he was fully focused and was not to be disturbed. The glasses only added to his sex appeal. Tiffany had to admit the nerdy black frames only made him look more intelligent and hotter. *Damn.*

She cleared her throat and begged for the butterflies in

her stomach to go away. He frowned then looked up. Colin slowly peeled the glasses from his eyes, holding them loosely between his fingers. *Well, that is wickedly hot.* It took everything inside Tiffany to not shove those papers off his desk and attack him. *Settle down, girl.* She was going to have to rely on her trusty battery-operated boyfriend to get her through.

"Yes?"

"Your dog is in my office."

"So?" He shrugged and threw her an annoyed glare.

"Well, I'm not quite sure how I'm expected to work while he keeps…um…well…passing gas." There was no nice way of putting it.

"His farts are awful, aren't they? I'm terribly sorry. I tried switching him to different food hoping it would be a little gentler on his belly," Colin explained like a concerned father. Tiffany could care less about his diet. She wanted the dog out of her space. *Now.*

"Do you mind removing him?"

"Oh, Tiffany, come on. Pauly likes you." Colin motioned toward her office. She turned and looked to see little brown legs fully extended behind him as he rested in a comfortable position. "Look how happy he is there." The tiny nub of a tail had started to move at the mention of his name.

"Why don't you make him your assistant?" Tiffany offered sarcastically.

Colin rolled his eyes and placed his glasses back on his face. "Was there anything else?"

"Yeah, you removing that little stink bomb from my office," she said with a bit more bravado than she'd intended.

Colin huffed. "Come here, Pauly. This mean lady doesn't want you in her office anymore." The dog didn't budge. Colin returned his focus on the papers in front of him and said, "See? I told you he likes you. He doesn't want to be out here with me."

"That's not my problem."

"Take it up with Sir McCartney."

Seriously? There had to be something in the employee handbook that said something about this type of nonsense. Employee abuse, maybe?

Tiffany stomped away and went back into her office that now smelled like nothing but foul dog farts. She fished through her purse that was hanging behind the door to see if she had some perfume or body mist to try and neutralize the air. Nothing. Now she had to tolerate the stench. *Note to self…purchase air freshener, immediately.*

She looked down at the sleeping English bulldog and tried to nudge him with her toe. "Hey, you, Sir McCartney. Time to hit the road, pal."

He opened his eyes briefly, then resumed his snooze. He had no desire to move or be bothered by her.

She tried again, this time a little more forcefully. "Wake up, you." Slowly the dog rose from the floor, pausing to stretch in some sort of weird canine yoga pose. He then shook with total excitement, wiggling and shaking his entire stubby and fat body. Tiffany pushed him away and he looked at her again, a pained expression in his eyes as he strolled out. She was hit by a brief moment of guilt, but then Tiffany shut the door and was glad to be rid of the stinky pest. *Or am I?* She kind of missed him the moment he was gone. A teensy part of her had to admit Sir McCartney was so ugly that he was cute.

Chapter Six

"I will gladly take another, my dear," Tiffany replied as she held up her empty glass to Molly.

"These mudslides are pretty amazing." Mackenzie slurped more from her glass, draining it of the chocolate concoction then handing it off, now empty.

"They go down so easily, too," Tiffany commented as she enjoyed her growing buzz.

They were inside the large living room at Molly's. Well, it had been Owen's place first. The home was gorgeous. It was rustic, comfortable and had enough of a modern flare for Tiffany's taste. She remembered how afraid Molly had been when it had come time to decide whether or not to move in.

Tiffany watched as Molly poured more of the chocolate goodness from a thick glass pitcher into each of their tall glasses. The kitchen and dining room were part of the living room. It was a large space, but the flow was easy and great for entertaining. She couldn't help but notice how relaxed Molly was in the space, just fluttering about in the kitchen barefoot. This was definitely her home now.

"Have I mentioned how much I love this house?" Tiffany said when Molly returned to the table.

"Only like a million times," Molly replied as she handed Tiffany a drink. "Hey, why don't we take this party outside to the deck?"

Mackenzie and Tiffany agreed. A little cool air would be lovely. That was the thing about summers in Seattle. They were glorious and absolutely perfect, a reward for putting up with all the crummy rain the remainder of the year.

Once outside, Molly lit a few candles and they all sat around a glass patio table. The stress and frustration from the entire week melted away as her drink slid down her throat. God, she needed this. She needed her girls. They were the one constant in her life.

"You are totally avoiding the elephant in the living room. What's up with Murphy?" Mackenzie asked playfully. "I know I haven't had to post bail money yet, so I'm assuming things are better."

Tiffany nearly choked on her beverage. "Ha! Far from it. Mac, I still might be hitting you up for that bail."

"How is he that awful?" Molly asked with a confused expression on her face. "Such a shame. From the way you describe him, he sounds super-hot." Molly fanned herself as she took another sip.

"He's hot, but you wouldn't believe the crap he pulled on me this week. So he tells me to go and get his *boy*…" Tiffany started to tell the story, but both Mackenzie and Molly stared at her in surprise.

"He has a son? How did I not hear about this until now?" Molly asked.

Tiffany laughed and took a large gulp of her drink. "Oh, you just wait. It gets much better."

She proceeded to explain the whole encounter with Sir McCartney, every last detail about how she scoured that plush condo high and low for a toddler that didn't exist and how she had to entice the stubborn bulldog to follow her back out to the car. Tiffany went on to tell them how much Colin doted on Sir McCartney and what a little stinker that bulldog was. Both were too busy laughing by the end of Tiffany's tale.

"Oh dear, that's crazy. I love the name, though." Mackenzie giggled and shook her head, her blonde hair swinging against her tan shoulders. "This Murphy fella is rather clever. You gotta give him that."

"I still don't get the whole Paul McCartney thing, but whatever floats his boat."

"The Beatles, Tiff. He must be a huge fan. Plus, Paul McCartney kinda looks a little like an English bulldog," Molly explained.

"I personally thought he looked more like Angela Lansbury," Mackenzie added with a wink.

"Now that's funny, Mac." Molly covered her mouth as she laughed hard.

"I still don't get it. Evidently, I live under a rock. Who is Angela Lansbury?" Tiffany asked.

They both looked at her like she was crazy.

Molly grabbed Tiffany's arm and said, "Seriously, Tiff? You're joking, right?"

Tiffany shook her head. "I don't have the faintest idea who she is."

"*Murder She Wrote*? *Bedknobs and Broomsticks*? *Beauty and the Beast,* for Pete's sake," Mackenzie rattled off. "Any of these ring a bell?"

"Maybe." Then she shook her head. "Nope, not really."

"How do you not know who she is? She's a friggin' legend, Tiff," Molly added.

Tiffany felt dumb and out of touch. Usually she was the one that knew all the latest trends.

Mackenzie shoved her large cell phone under Tiffany's nose. "Here, look. That's her."

"Oh, I know who she is," Tiffany answered. "So Paul McCartney looks like her?"

"Gimme my phone. I'll show you." She slid her finger across the screen. The light from the phone washed her face in a blue light. "Here." She handed the phone back to Tiffany.

"Oh shit," Tiffany let out, then burst into laughter. "He totally does."

"Told ya." Mackenzie seemed quite satisfied with herself.

"He does look like Sir McCartney," Tiffany stated frankly.

"That's because he is," Molly said.

"No, Colin's bulldog. It's the jowls." Tiffany grabbed her cheeks to emphasize her point.

None of them could hold it together and started to break out into hysterical laughter, something that happened every Friday night without fail. Thank God for *Friendship Fridays*.

* * * *

The weekend sailed by far too quickly for Tiffany's liking. It was Monday and her office smelled like Sir McCartney — aka Angela Lansbury, when Colin wasn't within earshot.

"God, you smell," Tiffany informed the snoring dog as she sprayed more air freshener. She looked at the meaty lump that refused to leave her office. "What am I going to do with you?"

She returned her attention to a series of emails that needed to be answered. Fully absorbed by an inbox of countless messages, Tiffany was startled by the knock on her door. Colin popped his head in.

"Tiffany, you have a moment?"

"Sure, feel free to join us." She pointed at the bulldog that was deep into his nap.

"Aww, he adores you," Colin said, a smile on his face as he stepped carefully over his dog.

"Yeah, lucky me."

"It is kind of foul smelling in here. You should probably get that sorted," he suggested as he pinched his nose.

"Me? I have a solution. Get your dog out of my office." She smiled at him sweetly.

"Oh, you'd miss his company," Colin teased as he leaned back in the chair, crossing one leg over the other, making himself comfortable.

Tiffany was surprised how at ease she was beginning to feel with him. Maybe things wouldn't be so terrible after all. It would help matter if she weren't so damn attracted to him.

"I can't even close my door because he moans when I do. Have you found him a baby sitter yet?"

"Actually, that's why I needed to speak to you. I need to

fly out for a business meeting and I need you to look after our wee lad while I'm away."

"Excuse me? Um, Colin, I know I'm your assistant, but dog-watching is not something I'm interested in doing."

"You get along famously with him. You two won't even notice that I'm gone. Besides, it's only for a few days. I can't be away from my boy for too long." Colin looked down lovingly.

"Colin, maybe I have plans. Did you ever consider that?" she complained.

He gave her a knowing look. "Then change them."

Tiffany rolled her eyes then thought of an idea. "My apartment building doesn't allow pets," she lied.

"Like Mr. Sprinkles?" He raised his eyebrows at her.

"Cats are okay, but not dogs. I could lose my apartment if they catch me with Mr. Stinky over there."

"Well, you can stay at my condo."

"I don't want to."

"Why not?"

Unable to think quickly on her feet, she waved the proverbial white flag. "Fine. I'll watch him."

"Good. I'll have a car bring you by tonight."

"Wait, what? Tonight?"

Colin smiled as he rose from the chair. "Yes, tonight."

"I'll drive myself. And thanks for the ample notice, Colin," she said.

"Anytime, love." Just like that he left her office, leaving her with a snoring Sir McCartney.

Tiffany released a huge sigh. "So it'll be me and you for a few days. Think we can keep the farting to a minimum?" As if right on cue, he let out a small toot. "Gross." Tiffany reached into a drawer and retrieved the air freshener. She hesitated after spraying the scented mist. "Might as well leave this out, buddy."

* * * *

She pressed the doorbell button. Even that looked expensive. Tiffany smoothed out the imaginary wrinkles on her skirt. Her feet were killing her as she stood there waiting, but that was a small price to pay. The shoes were gorgeous. Her outfit might very well be on point, but she knew her hair was anything but. It had started out in a perfect French twist, but by lunch it had been hanging loose and now it was in an awful sloppy bun. She hadn't had time to change or make herself cute before picking up her stinky bundle of joy.

Why did I have to get roped into watching this dog? It really was quite a bit to ask of her. If this dog was Colin's pride and joy, why did he trust her with him? Tiffany gritted her teeth as she pressed the doorbell again and waited. She heard movement this time and when the door opened, there stood Colin and she melted, just a little. *Why does this man have this effect on me?* He was dressed casually, jeans and a plain, gray-cotton T-shirt. His hair was damp and she could smell the light hint of soap. It all brought her back to the hotel suite. So much had happened recently, Tiffany began to question if she'd even ended up in that room with this same guy. *Was any of it real?*

"Tiffany, I was worried you might have tried to skip out on us," he teased. Colin moved to the side and ushered her inside.

Something smelled delicious and Tiffany's stomach gurgled. *That's embarrassing.* It dawned on her that she hadn't eaten anything since lunch.

"It smells wonderful in here. I didn't realize you could cook," Tiffany commented as she stood awkwardly in the entrance of the condo. She noticed even more of the elegant details of the home as she waited for Colin to get Sir McCartney. Tiffany wished he would hurry so that she could be on her way.

"Glad you think so, because I cooked dinner for us." Colin moved past her and motioned for her to follow him into the kitchen that was just off the living room.

"Oh, that's okay. I'm not hungry," she lied as her nerves went wild.

"That's not what your stomach said a moment ago."

"Yeah, but remember what you told me about mixing business and pleasure," Tiffany countered with more sass than she'd intended. Colin pointed toward some stools and she took a seat on one that was in front of a breakfast bar topped with granite. She watched Colin peek in the oven, looking very domestic with an oven mitt and completely unlike the man she was getting to know as the new CEO of Blue Moose Coffee.

"Tiffany, this is dinner—food, nothing more." He closed the oven and grabbed two glasses from a cabinet. "Wine?"

Is that really such a good idea? Obviously, alcohol was what had gotten her into the mess she was in with him.

"Maybe just water. I really can't stay long."

Colin threw her a sly grin. "Why? Do you have plans?"

"No." She couldn't help but feel like she had walked into a trap. "I just think that maybe—"

"We're not thinking. We're eating." He opened a bottled water and poured it into one of the wine glasses he had set in front of her. Colin then poured himself some red wine. Its rich and robust scent wafted toward Tiffany.

"Colin, can we talk?"

"Isn't that what we've been doing?" he teased as he swirled his drink and sniffed at it.

"Well, not really. I really want to discuss—" she started and he held his hand up.

"Nothing happened." His eyes, dark and smoky, suggested that something had, but the slight frown told her that Colin was being completely honest.

"Really? So we didn't...you know?" Tiffany asked.

"Nope. Your virtue is fully intact, as is mine. Well, from that night, anyway." Colin grinned and gave her a sexy wink.

"But how did I end up in your room?" Tiffany was quite relieved and now more curious than ever to know what in the hell had happened.

"Well, simply put, you were pissed," Colin explained.

"Yeah, I know. I had just fought with Mac, my best friend."

"No, I mean, you were drunk. So drunk, in fact, that you nearly fell overboard. I caught you and the rest is ancient history." Colin smiled sweetly at her then he took a drink.

"The kiss?"

"Oh, that. Yes. Now that *did* happen."

"But how did we go from there to the hotel?"

Colin grinned. "Well, you did try to seduce me. You were nearly successful, too. That is until you started snoring."

"Oh, God, really?" Her cheeks grew hot. Mortified? Yes, that's what she was. Only Tiffany would miss a golden opportunity like that. She wanted to kick herself.

"I won't lie, love. That first kiss was quite something. The second? Well, that started us on our journey to the nearest hotel."

"I'm so sorry. I'm not like that at all," Tiffany apologized.

"No need. You saw something you wanted and you went after it. There's nothing wrong with that at all." Colin raised his glass to her. "I think that's what turned me on the most."

Tiffany hid her face in her hands then Colin stroked her arm. She looked up at him and asked, "So what changed when you saw me on Monday?"

Colin pulled his hand back as though he had been burned by touching her. He explained, "To be honest, nothing. But I didn't know you were employed there and you know my rule." He watched her with a deep, intense stare and continued to speak, "Trust me, Tiffany. I still am interested in you, especially after getting to know you this last week. But nothing can ever come of it."

Well, that is that. If there is no possibility of exploring whatever this is, why am I here?

Tiffany began to get off the stool. "You know, I really should go," she said before he could speak. *There. Problem solved.*

Colin set his glass down, and in a swift movement that

took them both by surprise, he lowered his mouth on hers. He cupped her face delicately, as he took ownership over her lips. She let out a moan and reacted. A pool of warmth developed in her belly. Tiffany needed more of him. Her built-up craving needed to be satisfied. She wrapped her arms around his neck and deepened the kiss. A war was waged inside their mouths, a battle of wills and control. Colin appeared more than eager for this battle to begin and seemed to take great pleasure in challenging her. His lips formed a smile against her mouth. He'd said that the very first kiss they had shared had left quite an impact on him, and Tiffany planned to push this one to a completely different level.

Tiffany's brain was not quiet when she made out. It was obnoxiously busy and filled with thoughts. It was shooting off random facts and details, all things she could care less about at the moment. She thought about unimportant items such as, was her gas tank still near empty, did she need to buy coffee and other worthless bits. Then it would sneak in tiny suggestions like bite his lip, lick his neck and nibble on his ear, all which she put into action. Colin moaned then tried to mutter something that she couldn't quite make out.

How is this supposed to fix things between us? How is this a good idea? Who kisses their boss? Evidently Tiffany. Maybe this would fix the problem. *Oh, who am I kidding?*

The problem was far from solved and things were now more complicated than ever.

Chapter Seven

Tiffany stared at her ceiling, exhausted and not eager to face the day. She'd slept like crap. Was it because of the constant snoring by her new four-legged roommate? Possibly. Or maybe it was because last night Colin had left her more confused than ever. *That kiss.* She could still feel his lips on hers. It was as though he'd left a permanent burn on them. But as she recalled how awkward things had gotten when it was over and how quickly she'd fled the scene, her heart sunk. Colin was the one that had kissed her this time, unlike at Molly's engagement party, so this was all his fault now.

The one good thing that did come out of the previous night was that Tiffany had learned she hadn't slept with him. The bad news was that things had escalated to the point where she'd found herself in a hotel suite with no recollection of the night before or the man who was with her. Tiffany was still rather disgusted with herself. To think that she had been so drunk or maybe even a little bit jealous of Molly finding happiness that she had left with a strange man, almost sleeping with him, and the only reason she hadn't, had been because she had fallen asleep. Tiffany should be thankful to some degree that Colin was a decent enough man to decide not to take advantage. The whole scene was just bad. *Really bad.*

What is my problem? This was not her. Mackenzie was always warning her about making poor decisions and this was another example of her friend hitting the nail on the head. Tiffany felt lost and like a complete screw-up. How did things get so twisted and jumbled? She was in her mid-thirties and wasn't some naive kid. *When am I going to grow up?*

Today was a new day. *I can start over, right?* Take the world by the horns, show it who's boss and all that jazz? Why didn't she feel like it was possible? Coffee, that's why. She hadn't had any yet. Life began after coffee. Any coffee drinker knew that. One can't be expected to conquer the world without having at least one cup.

Tiffany padded barefoot to her kitchen and began her morning ritual, but she wasn't alone. She'd almost forgotten about her visitor. He'd followed her and plopped down on the floor. His chocolate-brownie eyes watched her go about making survival juice, aka coffee.

"Let me get this started and I'll take you outside."

Tiffany quickly ground up the dark-roasted beans. The small grinder made a tremendous amount of noise. Apparently, Sir McCartney was not too fond of it and started barking frantically.

"You better get used to it, pal," Tiffany said to him as she poured the freshly ground beans into the coffee pot filter and pressed Start after filling her machine with water.

"Let's do this," Tiffany called out to the dog as she grabbed the leash Colin had given her and clipped it onto his harness.

The sun was making its way into the sky, creating a tangerine glow against the purple from the leftover night sky. The early morning air was cool, and even the bulldog shivered as he quickly did his business. Tiffany wrapped her sweater tighter around her body and tried to let the newness of the day envelop her. Her mind instantly went to Colin. She wondered what he was doing right now. *Is he drinking coffee? Or maybe staring at the sunrise? Why did he kiss me?* Too many questions and not nearly enough answers. Tiffany exhaled and followed Sir McCartney back to her apartment.

The coffee was ready by the time they came back inside. Sir McCartney looked at her with a longing. *Food.* He was probably hungry. Colin had packed all the essentials for his furry pride and joy. Tiffany set out his dishes on her dining room floor. She added some water to the stainless bowl then watched as he started to go to town on it. When he finally did come up for air, water dripped from jowls, leaving a good-sized puddle on her floor.

"You're gross, you know that?" Tiffany grabbed some paper towels and began to clean up the mess.

She poured some food into his bowl and he attacked it with excitement. Tiffany had no idea he had been so thirsty or hungry and she instantly felt guilty. *Why did Colin leave him with me?* She obviously had no clue how to care for a dog. Dogsitting was way out of her league and not something she'd signed up for. Tiffany prayed she could keep Colin's little precious pup alive until he returned then she planned on asking for a raise.

Tiffany doctored her coffee while Sir McCartney licked his bowl clean, pushing it around with his flat face. Tiffany couldn't help but giggle as she watched him. He was such a character. She took her coffee to her dining room table and leisurely sipped from her mug while Sir McCartney finished his breakfast.

Colin had instructed her not to come to the office but to focus her attention on Sir McCartney until he returned. To think he was so concerned about this dog that he was willing to sacrifice any work that actually needed to be done was a little crazy. It didn't make too much sense to Tiffany, but then again, nothing did of late. *Whatever.* Tiffany looked at it like a mini-vacation and planned on making the most of it. The coffee was starting to kick in and she was nearly ready to grab those horns. Maybe after another cup or two.

* * * *

Showered, caffeinated and bored, Tiffany decided to call Mackenzie.

"Mackenzie, what are you up to?" Tiffany asked after her

friend answered.

"Hey. Nothing much. Just got off the phone with Molly. You have something in mind?" Mackenzie paused. "Wait. Why aren't you at work? It's Tuesday, right? Or have I just completely lost track of what day it is? This happens to me every summer." Mackenzie laughed.

"No, it's Tuesday. You haven't lost your mind. My boss gave me today off," Tiffany started to explain, but Mackenzie cut her off.

"Really? Why? Oh, God, did you get fired, Tiff?"

Tiffany could hear the panic in her voice.

"No, no. It's nothing like that. Why don't you and Molly come over and I can explain better."

It was time to tell them everything. The weight of this whole mess had proved to be too much. She was torn between hating and lusting after Colin. Maybe they could help her figure out what to do.

"Ooh, juicy details. I can't wait! I'll go get Molly and we'll bring lunch."

"Great, see ya in a bit." Tiffany hung up and looked over at a sleeping Sir McCartney and her heart squeezed a little. *Am I starting to fall in love with this stinky but adorable chunk?* It would seem so.

Tiffany hummed as she went about straightening her apartment. Molly and Mackenzie would be there soon. Sir McCartney seemed rather annoyed at the cleaning and kept plopping his fat body down in different places.

"Am I interrupting your nap time?" Tiffany teased as she wiped down her dining room table. "My friends are going to love you," she told him. His only response was looking up at her with sad, heavy brown eyes.

Tiffany had moved onto cleaning the living room when she heard a knock at the door. She hurried to answer it. A slobbering bulldog followed her.

"You're such a good guard dog."

She opened the door and there stood her besties.

"Oh my God, he's the cutest thing ever, Tiff," Molly

squealed. "Let me grab my camera. I have got to get some shots of this cutie pie."

Well, her besties were now officially in love with the wrinkly Sir McCartney, who had finally stopped wagging his little nub of a tail and was now in a deep coma on the floor.

"So why exactly is he here?" Mackenzie asked with a happy grin. "If you don't want to watch him, I'll gladly babysit."

"Does Colin come as part of the package deal?" Molly added as she started snapping pictures of the bulldog. His pink tongue looked like a pale red carpet, rolled out perfectly. "He's so precious." She wrapped up her mini photo shoot and joined Mackenzie and Tiffany at the dining table.

"Who's precious, the dog or Colin?" Mackenzie laughed.

"Neither," Tiffany lied. "Actually, I do need your help — your advice, really."

They were gathered around her table with tall iced coffees and enormous burritos in front of them. Molly and Mackenzie exchanged looks then stared at Tiffany with concern.

"Everything okay, Tiff?" Molly asked first.

"You know we're here for you and you can always tell us anything, right?" Mackenzie eyed her suspiciously. Her friend was the most perceptive out of their bunch. It had surprised Tiffany that she'd been able to hide this from Mackenzie for as long as she had.

Tiffany took a deep breath then began the difficult task of explaining things. She started with the fight she and Mackenzie had had on the boat and concluded with the previous night's kiss. When she finished, the look on their faces were exactly what she'd expected. Tiffany dropped eye contact and picked at the flour tortilla in front of her. She hated when things got uncomfortable. Tiffany inhaled deeply again and bravely looked to her friends, to see their reaction.

Molly stared up toward the ceiling as if she was trying to find just the right words. "I'm trying to place who this guy is and why he was at the engagement party."

"I figured he must be a friend of yours or Owen's." Tiffany shrugged. *Does it really even matter now?*

Molly sighed in mental defeat. "Tiff, why didn't you tell us that morning?" Molly asked.

"Because the day was meant to be about you and finding the perfect dress. Besides, I was in too much shock, I think."

"I knew something was off. I didn't know quite what, but now it all makes sense." Mackenzie smiled softly. "Tiffany, you should have told me. It must have been scary to just wake up in some stranger's bed. I know you don't want a lecture, which is probably why you didn't want to tell me in the first place, but you know I only voice my concerns because I love you. I cannot tell you how thankful I am that nothing happened to you." Her voice started to crack and tears were forming in her eyes.

"So, what now? I mean, this gives a whole new meaning to 'it's complicated'." Molly still looked stunned as she grabbed her burrito and took a bite.

"Oh, I don't know. It's annoying. First, he tells me one thing then he kisses me. How am I supposed to decipher these mixed messages?"

Mackenzie clasped her hands and looked thoughtfully at her and Molly. "Well, I can see he doesn't know what to do."

"Wait, what? You're on *his* side?" Molly asked with a scowl.

"No, it's not about whose side I'm on, because the answer is obvious there. No, what I mean is, look at it from Colin's side. He met this girl, almost slept with her—but didn't. She leaves and he probably doesn't think he'll ever see her again. Then, low and behold, she walks into the office of his new company. Awkward. He doesn't know what to do. He probably finds himself very attracted to you, but it's like he can't have you. But by making you his assistant, that allows him to look but not touch. Now, in all honesty, how long can a person actually do that? That kiss was bound to happen, Tiff." Mackenzie paused and took a long sip of her drink. "Then there's the whole wild chemistry between you two."

"That makes sense, I suppose," Tiffany agreed.

"No, it doesn't," Molly argued. "I think he's playing a stupid head game, if you ask me. Colin's making her watch his dog—who is the cutest thing ever, by the way—but talk about a lot of mixed signals. He's not playing very fair here."

Molly had a point, but so did Mackenzie. *Ugh.* Now Tiffany was even more conflicted.

"Colin wants his cake and to eat it, too," Molly said.

"I know, but imagine the frustration he must be feeling. That's why he kissed her last night." Mackenzie wiped her mouth and took another sip from her giant iced coffee.

Tiffany watched as her friends debated this topic. She was waiting to interject, but as the conversation grew a little louder and heated, she decided it was best to just sit this one out. *Been there, done that.*

"It doesn't make it right or fair to Tiffany. If anything, that's the worst thing he could have done. Why are you so quick to defend him?"

"Wait a second. I'm not defending Colin," Mackenzie countered.

"Sure seems like it. Tiffany is the victim here. First she has some man nearly take advantage of her—" Molly began.

"But he didn't," Mackenzie interjected.

"Yeah, he didn't, but he took a drunk woman—who he didn't know—to his hotel suite. Real upstanding gentleman. Then, when he finds out Tiffany works for Blue Moose, he completely disrupts her life. He doesn't even consider how that would affect her. He literally has given no thought at all to her feelings. He gave her no say in the matter when he stole her from Patty, remember? That still sort of pisses me off."

"I do see your point there," Mackenzie relented. "But I don't think his intent was nearly as malicious as you make it out to be."

"You both are right," Tiffany finally said. "It's not completely Colin's fault that he took me to that hotel. I obviously kissed him first then things sort of went from there. I instigated that. That's my fault," Tiffany admitted. "As for the whole work thing? Yes, that's all on him. He didn't let me have any say. The guy I saw last night was very different than the Colin at work. Not that he's a monster there, but he's all about business and getting his way."

"I think he's like that outside of work, too, Tiff." Mackenzie motioned toward Sir McCartney, who was now trying to sneak onto the couch to snooze.

"Hey, you, down. No couches for you," Tiffany ordered, only to have the saddest brown eyes look back her. He crawled up anyway. *Stubborn-ass dog.* Tiffany went over to him and dragged him off. "I told you 'no'."

Sir McCartney wiggled and rubbed against her legs. She reluctantly petted him. He was sweet, but he needed to stay off her furniture. Even Mr. Sprinkles only stayed on the windowsill. Tiffany looked over to her large and very annoyed cat. He yawned and stretched. He had no interest in their visitor.

"He likes you," Molly said with a soft smile.

"I know, but I don't want him on the couch. He's such a brat."

"Not much different than his owner," Molly added.

Tiffany went to sit back down. "You know, I would have expected Mac to be the one to discredit Colin and for you to be his champion. See? Nothing makes sense anymore."

* * * *

Tiffany survived an entire day with Sir McCartney. Two things she'd realized quickly were that there was no arguing with a bulldog and that he was the biggest snuggle buddy ever. She'd waved the white flag of defeat and had surrendered. Now a happy and content bulldog was cuddling next to her on the couch. Molly and Mackenzie had eventually smoothed things out by the time they had finished their burritos. It was still funny to Tiffany that Mackenzie was rooting for Colin. Never in a million years would she have seen that one coming. Molly was now more domesticated and all that playing house with Owen had started to make her protective motherly instincts surface. Either way, the weight of having held onto that secret, as small as it was, felt good to be off her shoulders. She had always told her friends everything. But sometimes, especially when Tiffany found herself acting like a bumbling idiot, she wasn't so quick to share.

Tiffany tried to focus on the movie that was playing in front of her, but her mind kept wandering—Colin, the kiss, work, Sir McCartney, just everything. Her phone was next to her and it vibrated. Apparently, it had disturbed Sir McCartney. He let out an annoyed huff. He looked up at her then went back to sleep. Tiffany shook her head. This dog cracked her up. He was full of personality, which came as a surprise considering all he ever did was sleep. Tiffany peeked at her phone. It was a text message from Colin. He explained that he was checking in on them both and would be back in a day or so. Tiffany could hear his accent as she read his words. *God, I love his voice. And the feel of his lips.* She'd probably like a lot more, too, but Tiffany knew it was out of the question. *What if it doesn't have to be?* She started to sort out a solution. Maybe they could both have their cake and eat it, too. If Colin wasn't stubborn like his bulldog, it might just work.

Chapter Eight

"Oh, how I've missed you."

"I know. It had to be so incredibly hard to be away from me these last few days," Tiffany teased as Colin rubbed Sir McCartney's ears.

Colin looked up at her. He was not amused. There wasn't even the slightest hint of a smile on his face or in his eyes.

"Well, thank you again. I appreciate you looking after my boy." Colin unclipped the leash that was on the dog's harness. Sir McCartney ran inside Colin's condo. He didn't even look back at Tiffany.

"It was no trouble. He was well behaved — stinky but well mannered," she joked.

Tiffany stood there. Things were definitely different between them. She wondered if she should say something, to address the elephant in the living room, that darn kiss — the same one she'd been thinking about nearly every day since it had happened.

"So —" she began when Colin stopped her.

"It's late and I'm exhausted. I'll see you at the office tomorrow." Colin began to close the door. "Thanks again, Tiffany."

She remained frozen for a moment, stunned and a little sad, after the door had been shut. Maybe Colin was indeed tired. Tiffany tried to shake it off and look at the positive, and right now, she could only see one. Tomorrow was Friday, which meant *Friendship Friday*, which meant booze, carbs, a cheesy movie and her girls.

Screw boys and bulldogs. Who needs them anyway?

As she walked back to her car, the brightly lit parking

structure seemed eerie. Tiffany felt very alone as she picked up her pace. Her compact car was only a few feet away, thankfully. Once safely inside her car, she was even more aware of the loneliness. She missed him. Despite his constant assault of smells, the dog was sweet and had kept her company. Tiffany missed Sir McCartney a lot more than she should.

* * * *

The next day all was quiet at work and Tiffany wasn't so sure she liked it. This whole loneliness thing was starting to really get to her. For starters, Colin and Sir McCartney weren't there. He hadn't called her directly but had left word with the receptionist, who'd given her an annoyed look, pretty much questioning why she had to handle a message if Tiffany was his assistant. The message itself was simple enough. He wanted her to complete a few random tasks and take the rest of the day off.

After quickly doing everything he'd wanted, she'd tried to text him to get confirmation on a few things that needed his attention but he ignored her. *Screw it. Screw him.* If he wanted to act childish about a kiss—an incredible kiss, but it was still only a kiss—then so be it. Tiffany had no desire to play any stupid games with him. There was no reason to avoid her and to act as cold as he had last night—or to leave a damn message for her with the company receptionist. It was his fault, anyway. He'd done the kissing, not her. He didn't want to mix business with pleasure, yet *he'd* done it, not her. *Practice what you preach, buddy.*

Tiffany sighed. She'd forgotten how complicated things could be with the opposite sex. She hadn't dated in a while, but then again, none of the men that had been in her life had ever made her feel this way, either. Thank goodness, she was off work now and could go eat, drown her sorrows and laugh her worries away. *Happy Friday.*

Seattle traffic was usually a bumper-to-bumper nightmare.

Thankfully, the universe was working in her favor and it was a quick and easy drive over to Mackenzie's place.

"God, it smells amazing in here, Mac," Tiffany commented as she entered Mackenzie's house.

"Fajitas tonight!" Molly cheered as she hugged Tiffany. "Oh...and mojitos," Molly added as she raised her glass. Smashed bits of mint leaves were floating in the otherwise-clear beverage.

Yes. Tiffany was suddenly very thirsty.

"Right on. I *so* need this," she said as she accepted an offered sip from Molly's glass. "Wow, that's awesome."

Tiffany walked to where Mackenzie was frying up colorful bell peppers and onions. 'Heavenly' was the only way to describe the scrumptious dinner they were about to feast on. Strips of lean steak, seared and juicy sat ready to add to the peppers and onion mix. A large stack of flour tortillas were being warmed by the side of the stove top. Tiffany's tummy growled and begged for food.

"Tiff, can you grab the guacamole and *pico de gallo* out of the fridge? The chips are over there." Mackenzie pointed toward the opposite countertop.

Tiffany went to the fridge and pulled out two large glass bowls of delicious-looking dips. The guacamole was bright and chunky. The *pico* just screamed, 'Eat me!' Without waiting a moment longer, she opened a bag of corn tortilla chips and dug in. The guacamole was refreshing and creamy. It was *perfect*. She plunged another chip into the *pico de gallo*. Best thing *ever*. Now add a mojito and they were in business.

"This is *so* good," Tiffany said in between bites.

"I just felt like tonight called for some serious Mexican food." Mackenzie added the strips of steak to the hot cast-iron skillet. It sizzled loudly.

"Great choice, because I need some serious comfort," Tiffany whined.

"Uh oh, I know that look. What happened?" Molly asked as she handed Tiffany her own mojito. "Let's go sit. We want to know everything."

"Not a whole lot to tell, sadly. Basically, Colin came back, I dropped off that cute li'l bugger and Colin acted kind of distant."

"Well, maybe he realized what a mistake it was to kiss you. He went against his whole principle of not mixing business with pleasure. So, was he weird to you at work today?" Molly asked as she grabbed a chip and shoveled some *pico* onto it.

"No, he didn't even bother to come in."

"Really?" Mackenzie added from the stove. "Did he call and tell you why?"

"Nope. He left a message with the receptionist." Tiffany smirked and sipped her minty drink.

"That's kinda dumb. I mean, you're his assistant." Molly raised her eyebrows.

"Yeah, I know and, trust me. The receptionist gave me the most annoyed attitude."

"That's kind of cowardly, I think," Molly commented as she sipped her drink.

"You know, that's not even the worst part. I actually miss Sir McCartney."

Both Mackenzie and Molly released a dramatic sigh.

"He is the cutest thing ever. I will give you a couple prints from those shots I got of him," Molly offered.

"I'm not the biggest fans of dogs, but he's downright precious," Mackenzie admitted as she turned off the stove and brought the food over to the table.

"This is so good, Mac," Molly said with a content and happy look on her face.

"I'm feeling these mojitos." Mackenzie took another drink.

"Heck yeah, everything is awesome. I brought dessert and a movie," Tiffany said cheerfully.

Molly threw Tiffany a serious look. "So, what are we going to do about this whole Colin situation?"

"Not a whole lot to do. He's my boss and that's it."

Mackenzie questioned with a knowing look on her face, "So, the next time he kisses you?"

"She'll sue him," Molly said happily. "Then she'll own Blue Moose Coffee."

Tiffany laughed. "There won't be a next time."

"Sure. I used to act like that with Owen. Now look at me." Molly held up her hand, a sparkling engagement ring staring back at Tiffany.

"Yeah, but that's different. How are things going, by the way? Are we going to try again to search high and low for the perfect dress?" Tiffany asked, her attempt at steering the conversation away from her.

"Yeah, Tiff's right. We need to be planning, Molly," Mackenzie agreed.

Molly rolled her eyes in disgust. "I know. I know. I just hate shopping."

"Well, we don't mind it one bit," Tiffany said as she drove another chip into the *pico de gallo*.

"Nope, we are totally down to help. You just need to be willing," Mackenzie said as she tucked some meat and peppers into a warm flour tortilla. "Do your part, Moll."

"I am. Well, okay, maybe I'm not as willing as I like to believe that I am. I'm still holding out hope that we can pull off some kind of wedding in the tropics."

"Either way, we need to be planning." Tiffany raised her glass. Feeling the increasing buzz from the drink, she toasted, "Here's to Molly. May she find the perfect dress or swimsuit for her dream wedding."

"Amen," Molly and Mackenzie said in unison.

"What about you, Mac?" Molly turned her attention to Mackenzie, who seemed a little caught off-guard.

"What about me?"

"Jason. What's up with Mr. Vegas?" Molly asked as she assembled a burrito out of the steak and peppers, dolloping some guacamole on top.

"Well, since you asked. I'm planning to fly out soon to visit him."

"Whoa, really? I don't know, Mac. Is that such a good idea?" Molly asked.

"I really like him. He's very sweet, and it might be fun to see where this goes."

"It can't go that far. He's so far away and you're not allowed to *ever* leave Seattle. You do know that, right?" Molly teased.

"I wouldn't dream of leaving. If anything, Jason is kind of interested in seeing what job opportunities are in the Seattle area. He was here, as you know, right before you got engaged, and he put out some feelers. So, you just never know," Mackenzie explained with a bright expression.

It would be fantastic if Mackenzie were to get involved with a great guy, but what about her? She'd be the only one single, and that would sort of suck.

* * * *

Mondays were never pleasant, but they were even more crummy when a gorgeous Irishman was ignoring you. Colin hadn't spoken a word to Tiffany all day. Well, there had been that curt nod earlier that morning. *Does that count?* Then there was Sir McCartney, who was lying next to Colin's desk. Apparently, they were in solidarity. He, too, was ignoring her. *Ugh, men.*

This was getting ridiculous. Tiffany'd had it. His childish behavior was grating on her last nerve. The least Colin could do was explain that the kiss had been a mistake. Hell, he didn't even have to do that. They both knew now that it had been. He could be decent, civil and professional, but he wasn't offering her that courtesy.

The most difficult part about this entire thing was that Tiffany hadn't meant for any of it to happen. It had been the end result of fighting with Mackenzie, drinking too much really good champagne and gobbling down too many crab cakes. He was the one who had caught her. He should have just let her fall, then things would have wound up differently and neither of them would have to deal with this confusing mess. *So, why is it that every time I look over at him my heart caves in a little?*

Monday took its sweet time coming to a close. Tiffany shut down her computer, grabbed her purse and decided this evening she was going to set fire to her muscles and troubles. She only hoped her girls were down for some serious running, because it was about to be on.

* * * *

"I hate you," Molly yelled from behind her.

"Catch up," Tiffany called back. She pumped her legs and forced herself to go faster. Her pink running shoes pummeled the sandy shore. She could feel her legs working overtime. Powering through the burn, Tiffany celebrated the endorphin rush as it surged through her.

"Tiff, slow it down a bit," Mackenzie pleaded.

Mackenzie was a natural athlete and this running should be a piece of cake for her, so to hear her asking for mercy caused Tiffany to smile.

She was taking pleasure in putting her body through this pain. It helped to erase the awful lonely feeling of today.

"You guys, come on," she shouted back.

Tiffany picked up her pace even more and sprinted farther ahead of them. Her lungs grabbed at the air. Sweat was pouring out of her pores and her legs were calling for her to slow. *Not gonna happen!* The sand made running more of a challenge. It required more skill and amped up her endurance. The waves that splashed on the sand misted her, a welcomed relief as her body was heating up. Tiffany prayed she would just spontaneously combust — be reduced down to a pile of ash on the sand and get pulled out to the sea. All the issues with her lovely boss would be gone forever. *Problem solved.*

Finally, she spotted a giant log ahead — decrepit driftwood, bleached from the sun and elements. She aimed for it. That was her finish line. Tiffany pushed even harder, generating more power through her frustration. Victory was hers when she made it to the log. She stretched and waited for Mackenzie and Molly to catch up. Their faces were red but more importantly, they were angry.

"What the hell?" Molly tried to ask. She panted and tried desperately to catch her breath.

"You okay?" Mackenzie stretched, breathing heavy. "Tough day at work?"

"Sort of. I mean, we didn't speak or anything."

Molly frowned. "Tiff, you need to handle this. Just lay it out and tell him how you feel."

"I don't even know how I feel. I just know that it hurts not talking to him," Tiffany answered. Tears burned her eyes the moment she admitted to herself and to her friends that she might very well have feelings for Colin. There was no *might*. She *did* have feelings and they were driving her bonkers.

"Oh dear," Mackenzie said as she wiped the sweat from her forehead and took a seat on the log next to Molly, who was perched on the decaying wood.

Tiffany stood in front of them and saw them looking back with sympathy.

"You like him, don't you?" Molly asked.

"I don't even think it's a question, more like a fact," Mackenzie added.

The tears started streaming down her face. "How can I have feelings for someone I don't even really know? This is so stupid." She wiped her cheeks and her nose started to run.

"Love is stupid. I know this first hand." Mackenzie raised her hand and frowned.

"Yeah, it can drive a person crazy. Look how it was for me and Owen. Hell, he still drives me nuts," Molly said.

"But you love him, right?" Tiffany smiled.

"Love makes us do very strange things," Molly added. "We put up with so much. Owen could testify to that."

"Yeah, but I don't love Colin," Tiffany countered. *Or do I? Is it possible to be in love with someone I hardly know and kind of hate?*

Chapter Nine

It was hot, like the pit-of-hell kind of hot—scorching and baking the earth, unleashing its rage onto the land. Okay, just the city. Seattle could get extremely warm. It wasn't always raining, regardless of what people thought.

Fourth of July was coming up that weekend and an icky heatwave had decided to pay the area a visit. Owen had suggested they take his boat out and spend the day on the water. With this awful heat, the idea had sounded splendid and Tiffany was super excited, but it was still days away.

Tiffany was sweating. She even had gross boob sweat. Her whole body was wet. Every crease and square inch was perspiring. She sat in front of a fan in her apartment. The window was open, but there was no breeze coming in. It was downright miserable. Even the ice-cold water that she had been nursing was doing little to cool her down. Tiffany had tried reading, but her concentration on the story just wasn't happening. She attempted to watch a movie but that wasn't much better. She considered calling her besties to see if they were suffering, as well. Of course they were. No one enjoyed this kind of sweltering nastiness.

Maybe I should write? It had been ages. Tiffany had tinkered with the thought of starting a funky little blog, blending her love of fashion and knowledge of the latest trends into something fun. Right now, though, it was too damn hot to even think about cute shoes or sexy clothes. Her brain was stewing in its own juices and any motivation she'd had quickly shut down.

Her apartment was quiet. There was only the sound of the oscillating fan as the motor churned with each movement.

Sometimes it sucked to be alone. *Maybe couples stay together to keep boredom at bay?* It would be wonderful to have someone there, even if only to complain with about the awful heat. Tiffany thought about all the prospective mates she'd dated. She had kissed plenty of frogs and none of them had turned out to be a prince. But how was it possible not to land at least one guy that she was more than willing to just deal with? Someone she could tolerate enough to have in her life, someone to waste their time together — just someone she could *like*.

Then she thought of Colin. *Why? What is the point of him even invading my thoughts?* Today at work had been more of the same silent treatment she'd been privy to since he'd returned from his trip. However, Colin had snuck glimpses of her when he'd thought she hadn't been looking. Little had he known she had been looking, a *lot*. No matter how irritated she was with Colin, Tiffany was still attracted to him. *Why does he have to be so incredibly hot?* His assortment of suits was enough to make her head spin, but the way he carried himself, down to his stride, all did funny things to Tiffany. Hearing him talk on the phone was murder. His voice oozed charm and she hung on to his every word. *What the hell is my problem?* This guy had made it quite clear that he wanted nothing to do with her. Yet that didn't stop her from fantasizing about him. Oh, the many ways she'd allowed him to take her. Tiffany wondered if he thought about her when he stroked his cock. Was Colin's mind as dirty as hers?

Tiffany wondered if he felt this intense, magnet-like pull, or was he completely oblivious to it all?

Tiffany had considered putting her résumé out there to see if she'd get any bites. She wasn't sure how much longer she could endure this torture at work. It was beginning to take a toll on her outside of their corporate skyscraper.

Her poor body could testify to that, since she was using over-exercising to release the feelings and frustration. Her friends even refused to run with her now. As much as Tiffany loved Carkeek Park, she wasn't sure she should be running anywhere alone. Sit ups—those had been her latest obsession. It wouldn't be long before Tiffany had abs of steel at the rate she was going. Mackenzie had suggested she take up yoga. *Yeah, meditation isn't going to cut it.* The only time she could almost get Colin out of her mind was when she physically pushed herself to new limits, inflicting grueling tests of endurance and strength. It allowed her to focus her energy on just not dying during the workout.

Tiffany could see why her friends were concerned but not wanting to take part. At least her body was getting toned, and in a way, that satisfied her a great deal. Somehow Tiffany believed it was making Colin suffer. Maybe she should flaunt the new and improved Tiffany more—invest in some short skirts that showcased her great legs and ass, or maybe some wickedly plunging blouses. God knew that seeing Colin prancing around in his perfectly tailored suits was slowly killing her. The worst was when he would roll up his dress shirts to reveal well-toned, tanned forearms or when he fussed with one of his expensive cuff links. Murder, absolute *murder.* He deserved to suffer. Maybe a shopping trip was in order.

* * * *

Survival. Tiffany now wore the badge proudly for enduring an entire week with Colin without killing him. She'd accepted the silent treatment, the cold shoulder and even a brush of rudeness. Sir McCartney, however, had only kept it up for so long. At one point, he'd tried to sneak into Tiffany's office and Colin had retrieved him. It had nearly broken Tiffany's heart.

But that didn't matter now. Tiffany had a lovely three-day weekend that she planned to enjoy with visions of drowning her sorrows. Granted, that was sort of what had gotten her in this whole mess to begin with, but she'd at least stay away from any crab cakes or sexy Irishmen.

This was her reward for tolerating far more bullshit than she should have. Day one of what was going to be a killer Fourth of July weekend included being on a boat with her friends, celebrating America in the best way possible — fireworks, beer and her brand-new bikini. Maybe Owen would bring one of his hot fisherman buddies. Tiffany strutted her stuff as she found Owen's boat down at the harbor.

"Oh my God, look at you!" Mackenzie's brown eyes nearly popped out of her head. "Wow, you are all about them stars and stripes right now."

Her bikini was patriotic, to say the least. Wait until she removed her jean cut-offs and revealed the red-and-white bottoms.

"Mac is right. You are killin' it, Tiff," Molly added. "Now I feel like a beached whale, thank you."

"Oh, stop. Besides, you know you can come work out with me any time."

"Um…and die. No thanks. I do plan to get married to that guy over there," Molly shot back playfully as she pointed to Owen, who was busy chatting with someone Tiffany didn't recognize but thought was very attractive.

Mackenzie had her blonde hair up in a loose bun and was wearing large white sunglasses that shielded her eyes from the bright sunshine. She wore a navy-blue bikini with a white cover-up that showed off her tan skin nicely. Molly's dark hair was down in loose waves. She sported a modest but bright-red one-piece swimsuit with white board shorts. But with her large boobs, Molly looked very much like she was straight out of an episode of *Baywatch*, giving Pam Anderson a run for her money.

Tiffany took in the scene. There were various people milling around, carrying drinks, mainly bottled beer. Conversations were floating in the air along with music that seem to be pouring mysteriously out of the boat. It looked different in the day. She'd only been on it at night and only that one particularly awful night. It was only late afternoon and night was still hours away, Tiffany planned on making new memories on this boat, sending the other ones away forever.

Well, the idea was good in theory until she saw him. Right smack next to Owen, laughing and talking with that distinctively sexy Irish brogue. Tiffany looked over to Molly and Mackenzie, then turned back and connected with Colin's dark gaze. They had already lifted anchor and were headed out of the harbor. She was trapped. *Is jumping overboard considered bad manners? Am I that good of a swimmer?*

Tiffany turned away and released her breath slowly in a feeble attempt at steeling her nerves. Mackenzie and Molly followed her to the side of the boat. Tiffany gripped the railing until her knuckles were white. *Why is he here?*

"Okay, what the hell is going on?" Mackenzie demanded, her face etched with concern and confusion.

Tiffany turned slowly to Molly and asked, "Moll, how come you didn't tell me?"

"Um, tell you what? I'm so lost right now." Molly shrugged and shook her head.

"Colin. Why is he here?"

"What? Where? Who?" Molly started looking around frantically.

"Wait. What?" Mackenzie asked. She stood on the tips of her toes and tried searching over their heads.

"Colin. You know, that guy you all think I may be in love with." Tiffany released the rail and planted her hands firmly on her hips.

"No, we know who you mean, silly. I just don't know who you are talking about," Molly said. Her chocolate eyes were hidden behind large shades, but it was obvious she was trying to locate the man in question.

"There." Tiffany pointed to Colin as discreetly as possible.

"Him?" Molly said, a little too loudly for Tiffany's liking.

"Yes, *him*."

"Let me look," Mackenzie said. "We talking about that

tall guy next to Owen or the shorter one?"

Tiffany groaned. "The tall one."

"Ooh, he's kinda hot. Now I see what all the fuss is about." Mackenzie gave her an approving look. "He's gorgeous, Tiff," Mackenzie commented as she continued to admire him.

Molly had grown a little too quiet, which meant that she knew exactly who he was.

"Just please tell me how you know him and why he's here?" Tiffany pleaded. So much for an awesome weekend on the ocean with her friends. *Damn.*

"Well, that's one of Owen's buddies," Molly finally answered. It was like pulling teeth getting her to respond.

"What? So, you *do* know him?" Tiffany looked hard at Molly. Tiffany was hoping that she was wrong and maybe Molly would have no clue as to who he was.

"Uh, I guess so."

"How did you not know that was Colin?" Mackenzie asked Molly.

"I guess I didn't put two and two together. I mean, I have said hello to him before and stuff, but I don't like *know* him, know him. Does that make sense?" Molly asked hopefully.

Tiffany was furious. How could Molly not put it together?

"So, what do we do now?" Molly asked Tiffany.

"Um, better think of something quick because Owen and Colin are headed this way," Mackenzie said as she held her bottle to her lips.

"Hey, pretty ladies," Owen greeted them happily. He had a beer in his hand and a megawatt smile. He looped his arm around Molly, who was now avoiding Tiffany's stare.

Colin stood there quietly. He likely also understood that there was not much either of them could do with this situation. Tiffany was thankful that Colin looked every bit as uncomfortable as she was and that he didn't want to cause a scene.

"Have you met my buddy Colin, yet?" Owen asked Mackenzie and Tiffany.

Colin tried to speak, but Owen stopped him. "This guy here is one of my best buds. I have known him forever. He just moved to Seattle a few weeks ago."

Tiffany listened as Owen continued to tell them how he'd met Colin. It had been during his photography days on a trip to Ireland and probably with that bitch of an ex of his. During a pub crawl many years ago, they'd wound up sitting next to each other at a bar. Both loved fishing and had hit it off over more than a couple of pints. They'd stayed in touch over the years, becoming the best of friends and even investing in several businesses together. Owen went as far as to announce that Colin had agreed to be the best man at his wedding.

Oh, this day only keeps getting better.

Finally, Owen dragged Colin away. He sent Tiffany an apologetic smile. That was the first glimmer of a smile in over a week. The butterflies that erupted inside her from just the simple flash of kindness made Tiffany angry at herself. *Why can he make me feel like this? Don't I have more control over myself? No wonder I wound up in his hotel suite.* Tiffany lacked self-control, and obviously, her brain was broken. Her heart was an entirely different story. It was more confused and stupid than her brain.

"I'm so sorry, Tiff. I promise I didn't know." Molly hugged her.

"It's not your fault. How could you have known?" Tiffany gave her a tight-lipped smile.

"Um, because he's Irish and his name is Colin Murphy?" Mackenzie added fuel to the fire that was finally starting to cool inside Tiffany.

"Seriously?" Molly glared at Mackenzie

"Well, it doesn't look too good, Molly. We all know you're a lot brighter than that."

"Thanks, Mac," Molly snarled at Mackenzie and stomped away.

This boat was proving to not be a lot of fun, *again*. The first time she had fought with Mackenzie and thrown up. Now

Molly was fighting with Mackenzie and Tiffany wanted to throw up.

"Screw this. Let's grab a drink." Mackenzie reached for Tiffany's hand and led her away from the railing.

After several, Tiffany and Mackenzie could have cared less about who was on the damn boat. Molly had come over and joined them a while later. She apologized again, then Mackenzie had said she was sorry and all was forgiven.

The sun had started to dip into the horizon, Tiffany and her two very best friends in the whole wide world twirled and shimmied as music played. Tiffany tried to ignore Colin's gaze. It had been trained on her all afternoon and well into the evening. *Nope, there will not be a repeat performance of our last encounter on this boat.*

The sky grew darker, more drinks flowed and the vibe was a happy one. The anchored boat bobbed gently on the calm waves. Tiffany needed to find a bathroom and decided to set out on her own. She told the girls to send out a search party if she didn't return soon and off she went.

"Tiffany."

She stopped. The boat was dimly lit, but Tiffany definitely knew who had said her name.

"Can we talk?"

Now he was standing in front of her. He lightly gripped her bare arms.

"Nope, not interested," Tiffany said, her buzz quickly fading away. She gathered up all her strength to keep her wits about her.

"Please. I need to say a few words," Colin pleaded.

Tiffany sighed as she looked at his half-naked body. It was hard to concentrate on what he was saying. His torso was tan and muscles were etched into his stomach. His swim trunks were sitting low on his hips, revealing far too much of the mystery Tiffany would love to explore. Sex-starved and a tad tipsy, Tiffany bit her lip as her eyes stayed on his body. He stood nearly a foot taller than her and she was at the perfect level to view his abs. It was doing many silly things to her. It would definitely give her inspiration later when she was all alone back at home. Her poor battery-operated boyfriend had been getting worked overtime lately.

Colin waited patiently, and when she didn't answer, he continued, "I know things have been awkward, to say the least. I just wanted to say that I'm terribly sorry for my behavior."

The sincerity of his words hit her. She believed him. There was no doubt he was sorry, but where did that put them now?

"So, what does that mean, Colin?" She looked up at him. His brown hair was messy from the ocean wind.

"For starters, I need to be more pleasant to you. You don't deserve that kind of treatment. I plan to be a better boss from here on out."

Boss? So, not boyfriend? Her fuzzy brain tried sorting out his words, but her confused heart was telling her to kiss him. Tiffany' had twisted it that somehow that would right everything.

"Tiffany." Colin's voice was quiet and she felt that magnetic pull again. It was even stronger in the darkness, bringing her closer to him. *God, I just want to feel his arms around me.*

"Tiffany," Molly called out.

Mackenzie and Molly had rounded the corner and stood only a few feet away. *Damn, cock blocked by my besties.*

Well, Tiffany had told them to send out a search party if she didn't return soon. This was the one time Tiffany wasn't so sure she was glad that her friends had her back. If they'd waited just a few more minutes, she would have had her lips on Colin's. Then again, maybe it was best that they had come to her rescue. Tiffany couldn't seem trust herself around him.

Chapter Ten

What is wrong with this picture? Everything. A gourmet coffee sat on her desk, a snoring bulldog rested next to her and Colin was seated across from her. He'd brought the coffee in that morning as a peace offering and had even nailed the exact preparation Tiffany loved. She'd recognized the extra shot of espresso the moment it had touched her lips. Tiffany had been impressed, to say the least, but that was nothing compared to them laughing together for the last hour. True to his word, Colin had acted more pleasant, and as welcomed as this was, it was also killing Tiffany. Though she had to admit that she liked this Colin a whole lot more. Colin was naturally charming, but he was also damn funny. Intelligent was an understatement.

Over the next couple of days, there was coffee on her desk then Colin and Sir McCartney would enter. Then they would spend the next hour talking about everything. Tiffany found herself enjoying these little morning chats, probably far more than she should, considering that Colin had wanted their relationship to remain solely professional. Could they maintain this level of friendship or whatever it was? Tiffany wasn't so sure, at least from where she was standing. Things were becoming more cozy and a whole lot friendlier than a boss and employee relationship. Plus, she was now calling Sir McCartney Pauly. So even they had leveled up in their relationship. Well, at least things at work were easier. Life was just better when a fat bulldog was around.

* * * *

"I fly out next week," Mackenzie told them on Friday as they were all sitting around Molly's large table in her studio. The night lights of Seattle glittered just outside her windows and stained the floor with their beautiful colors.

They had decided to do *Friendship Friday* there tonight since Molly was working late on some important edits for a bestselling author. White cartons of remaining bits of Chinese food surrounded them. Tons of fortune cookies were scattered among the soy sauce packets. Usually Molly would gobble down those cookies with reckless abandon, but not tonight. She just seemed a little off and it concerned Tiffany.

"Do you think you'll be okay going there all by yourself? Shouldn't one of us go with you?" Tiffany asked. She loved Vegas, but had had her fill when they'd visited last time. Tiffany could never look at a hot dog the same way again.

"Nah, I'll be fine. I'm super excited, you guys." Mackenzie's eyes sparkled as she spoke.

Molly was quiet. She was pushing her noodles around and hadn't eaten very much at all.

"Moll, what's going on?" Mackenzie finally asked as she expertly scooped up fried rice with her chopsticks.

"Nothing."

"You're lying." Mackenzie stared her down.

"You do seem rather quiet tonight. You sure everything's okay?" Tiffany asked.

Molly looked at the ceiling, as though she were searching for the right words. Her eyes were wet and Mackenzie and Tiffany exchanged looks. *Something is definitely wrong.*

"Oh shit, you guys broke up, didn't you?" Tiffany got up and hugged Molly. She pushed her away and shook her head.

"No, we're fine," Molly managed between sniffles.

"God, what's the matter then? Someone die?" Mackenzie pressed.

Molly got up from her seat and walked across the room to where her purse was hanging. She retrieved a white box and brought it back to the table.

Mackenzie's eyes grew wide and her mouth hung open. Tiffany snatched the box. It was a pregnancy test.

"Well, um, let's see here," Tiffany tried to speak. She hadn't been expecting this to be the issue. That was for sure.

"How late are you, Moll?" Mackenzie asked.

"Late," Molly said, wiping the tears from her eyes. "Very late."

"It's okay. Why are you crying? This is a wonderful thing," Mackenzie assured her.

"Yeah, if it were either of you two. I wasn't so sure I wanted kids and we aren't even married yet. I'm barely getting used to that idea," Molly babbled as tears streamed down her face.

Tiffany handed her a rogue napkin that was left over from dinner. "Have you told Owen?" Mackenzie asked as she took Molly's shaking hands into hers.

She shook her head. "I wanted to take the test with you guys. You know, just to be sure."

"Let's do this. Go pee." Tiffany cheered. "Molly, you and Owen are going to be fabulous parents. Besides, your kid will have the best aunties."

"You mean besides their real aunts?" Molly teased now.

"Yes, Mac and I are way cooler. No offense."

Molly reluctantly got up from her seat. "I'm scared, you guys."

"Don't be. This is all good stuff. Hell, if anything, I'm super jealous right now. Not only are you marrying one helluva guy, but you might be preggers. It doesn't get much better, does it?" Tiffany playfully rolled her eyes. "Get on in there." She handed Molly the test kit and pointed in the direction of the bathroom.

It drove Tiffany crazy as she watched Molly slowly open the box. Tiffany snatched it from her hands and tore it open. "Here." Tiffany handed her the white plastic test. "Now, go." Tiffany wanted to do a little happy dance and was eager to learn the news.

Molly vanished behind a door. Mackenzie and Tiffany looked at each other.

"Wow," Mackenzie said first.

"I know, right? The one of us who isn't baby crazy is the one that might be expecting one."

"It's always that way, isn't it?" Mackenzie laughed. She reached for the instructions as they waited for what seemed like an eternity for Molly to pee.

"Did you fall in? Come on, Molly," Tiffany shouted loudly.

Tiffany was anxious and wanted to see the results. Did her friend have a bun in the oven? When could she start buying little outfits and spoiling the cutie pie?

Molly emerged from the bathroom holding the tester.

"Well?" Tiffany asked.

"I haven't looked yet," Molly answered.

"This says it could take three minutes for the results to appear," Mackenzie read out loud.

"It's been even longer than that, hasn't it?" Tiffany questioned as she peered down at her cell phone to check the time.

"At least," Mackenzie agreed. "Come on. Hand it over."

They huddled around the plastic stick that would determine Molly's future. These lines could change everything — and they did.

* * * *

Tiffany drove Mackenzie to the Sea-Tac airport and was envious her friend was escaping. She stood next to her while Mackenzie checked in and got her ticket information.

"Please keep a close eye on Molly."

"Yes, Mom," Tiffany answered.

"She seemed a little freaked out over the weekend."

"Molly should be thrilled. I have no idea why she isn't." They stood by a row of seats and visited for another couple of minutes before Mackenzie had to go through security.

Mackenzie frowned. "I'm not sure. I think it's a lot for her to digest. As she pointed out on Friday, she's barely handling the whole marriage idea. They sort of got swept up in this crazy whirlwind romance."

"Isn't that what you're trying to do right now? Mr. Vegas is probably excited to see you."

"I'm excited, too. Jason's a nice guy, Tiff. I really like him."

Tiffany hugged Mackenzie. "I'm glad and I hope you have fun. Please, just be careful."

"I will. I'm not crazy like you or Molly."

"No getting hitched at one of those drive-thru chapels, promise?"

"God, no. I definitely promise not to do anything stupid." Mackenzie laughed.

"You better go. I'll be here to pick you up when you get back," Tiffany confirmed. "I'm going to miss you."

"Me, too. Look after our girl. Love ya." Mackenzie kissed Tiffany's cheek and hugged her once more before she set off toward the growing line of passengers to be scanned.

Mackenzie wheeled her rolling luggage toward security. She looked back and waved. Tiffany watched her friend get in line. It was never easy saying goodbye, even knowing full well that she would be returning soon, but anything could happen.

She quickly got into her car and waited for a chance to get into the lane. Tiffany looked over shoulder and stepped on it.

Tiffany drove away from the airport with an unexplained heaviness in her heart. Colin had told her that she could take the day off, but being home alone would only make her more miserable. She continued on the freeway until her exit came up for Blue Moose Coffee headquarters. Tiffany weaved through the quiet streets. It was early still and most of Seattle was still asleep. The sky was barely starting to turn light and Tiffany sighed. It was going to be a long day.

After turning into the parking structure, Tiffany found a spot and sat for a moment. She dialed Molly's cell and waited.

"Hello?"

"Moll, how's it going?"

"Fine."

"Come on. You okay?"

She heard Molly huff loudly. "Yeah, I'll be fine. Owen is flippin' tickled pink."

"Of course, he is. If he wasn't, we'd hunt him down and do bodily harm," Tiffany teased.

Molly giggled. "Oh stop. That would be more of a punishment for me."

"Well, then it's good that he did the right thing. What did he say, by the way?"

"Just that he was so immeasurably happy and that he wants to get married as soon as possible."

"Probably before it looks like a shotgun wedding. So, can we all go to Hawaii and do this?"

"Ugh, I don't know. But Owen is down for whatever *now*."

"Yeah, that's because you are carrying his precious little offspring. So, let's use this to our advantage. Hawaii, here we come," Tiffany squealed.

"Not so fast. I haven't even picked out a stupid dress," Molly complained.

"Uh, bathing suit. Problem solved."

"I know, but I have to wear something for the reception. What about my family and his?"

"Hmm. Maybe offer to do another ceremony later on? Or like a crazy party for everyone to celebrate. They're going to be so thrilled you are expecting that you can do no wrong. Use this, Molly. I want to go to Hawaii."

Molly laughed and asked, "So, you dropped off Mac? It's wild she's going there by herself. You think she'll be fine?"

"Yes. Now look who the mother of our group is. I swear, you got a bun in the oven for like five minutes and you've gone full maternal on me. I love it," Tiffany teased.

"Oh, give me a break. I'm the last one that should be

having a baby. I'm scared absolutely shitless."

"Moll, you are going to be a great mom."

"I don't know about that," Molly whispered.

"Woman, you have two friends that will be right there with you along the way. Trust me. You got this, because *we* got this."

Funny how confident Tiffany could be when it came to matters that didn't concern her life. She sat there in her car and contemplated going inside her building. *Nope, not today.* She could only handle one major life moment a day and today Tiffany had *adulted* plenty already.

* * * *

Tiffany dragged her feet going into work the next day. Maybe it had to do with the fabulous weather that summer was now delivering to Seattle. Or perhaps it was the relaxing day she'd had after she'd gotten off the phone with Molly. Either way, she had bills and this place paid them.

While taking the elevator up to her floor, her cell phone buzzed. It was Mackenzie.

"Hey you," she answered happily.

"Hey, Tiff, I'm just checking in. Everything's great here."

Whew. That's a relief.

"So how are things going with Mr. Vegas?" Tiffany's phone kept cutting out as she was trying to listen to Mackenzie. "Hang on. Let me get out of this elevator."

"You out yet?"

"Yes. Good grief, the reception is crap inside those things. So, okay, tell me. How's it all going?"

"Well, I had dinner with Jason and saw some of the sights with him."

"Mac, did you get what you were going there for?" Tiffany was dying to know if her friend's dry spell was over.

Silence. This had Tiffany more than a little confused. "Don't tell me the drought is still in effect?"

"Yeah, it kinda is."

"How is that possible?"

"I don't know. Is it me? I mean, I'm totally willing." Mackenzie giggled.

"Yeah, but are you putting out that *vibe*?" Tiffany had to keep from laughing. God knew she was trying to keep that vibe out front and center. She'd even hoped Colin would take notice, but so far…nothing.

"I thought so, but maybe he's not into me."

"I doubt that. So, he just like dropped you off at your hotel?"

Mackenzie answered, "Pretty much. We always have a great time together. We have kissed and stuff, but for some odd reason, we never can get to that next level."

"Weird. Crap, I'm about to head inside my office. I'll call you later, okay?" Tiffany and Mackenzie said goodbye and she noticed the doors were closed. It wasn't completely out of the norm, but Colin usually kept them open.

Tiffany was trying to open one of the doors as she juggled her oversized fake Prada bag and her travel mug of coffee. The door opened. Colin stood there, not much expression on his handsome face. He gave her a curt nod as he went back behind his desk.

Seriously, are we back to this nonsense again?

"Tiffany, after you have put your things down, can you come back in here?" His tone was even and quiet.

"Sure. Where's Pauly?" she asked as she opened her adjoining door.

"I have him at a doggy daycare today." Colin cracked a smile.

"You can't be serious? What will I do without my little chunky monster?"

"Tiffany, can you please hurry?" The sense of urgency in his voice bothered her.

Now Tiffany's nerves were on edge. Whatever it was that he needed to tell her must be pretty serious.

Tiffany hurried to hang up her bag and she decided to take her coffee with her. She noticed that there was no coffee waiting for her on her desk. Something was definitely up.

"What's going on?" she asked, trying desperately to seem cool and casual.

His smoky eyes weren't giving anything away. "Tiffany, I feel like we need to really talk."

"That's what we're doing. Right now, in fact," she joked, hoping it would break the ice. Things felt very chilly. He didn't laugh. This was not a good sign.

"I've tried my best to make this relationship work."

What is he saying? Does he want to start dating? If so, she could totally get behind that plan.

"It's been lovely, but I agree it's been hard." Tiffany smiled sweetly at him. He fiddled nervously with a silver cuff link.

"It has been brutal, actually."

"Now, I wouldn't go that far," Tiffany argued as she searched his face for some sort of clue as to where this was headed. Colin was holding his cards close, not letting her read what he was thinking.

"Tiffany, I'm sorry, but I'm letting you go."

What the hell?

If Colin was bluffing, he was damn good. If not, he was a major jerk. Tiffany rose from her seat and stomped away to grab her bag. She didn't need to hear another word. She'd just lost her job, but worse he'd broke her heart.

Chapter Eleven

Tiffany dug her spoon into the chocolate brownie ice cream.

"I can't even believe this. Can't we sue or something?" Molly asked as she stuck her own spoon in the half-eaten carton.

Tiffany's stomach hurt, not just from the insane amount of ice cream she'd just consumed, but from crying all afternoon. She had no job. *How am I going to pay my bills? How could he do this to me? What did I do to piss him off so badly?* Things had been fine just days ago. This was a nightmare. It had to be.

"Gosh, Molly, I can't even think right now. I don't know what to do."

"Well, you can bet that I'll be telling Owen. He can have a little chat with his leprechaun buddy. This has to be some sort of prank or something. Otherwise, that ass has completely lost his mind."

Tiffany was still in shock. "I don't know what I'm going to do, Moll."

"Don't worry about all that. I got you. I would say we first need to figure out what his grounds of termination are then we need to speak to an attorney. I have several friends and I'll contact them. No one messes with my bestie and gets away with it," Molly stated firmly as she shoveled more ice cream onto her spoon.

"Aren't you sick of it yet?" Tiffany motioned toward the spoon.

"God, no. I'm stress eating. That's something I am *very* good at."

"Yeah, what about your wedding? Don't get fat on my account."

"Tiff, I'm already there. Besides, I'm pregnant. If that's not a good excuse as any, then what is?" Molly scooped another heaping spoonful.

"Valid argument."

"It's going to be okay. I promise."

Tiffany's cell phone rang.

Molly smiled. "Maybe that's the jackass now."

Tiffany glanced at the screen of her phone. He'd tried calling her several times, but she'd sent his calls to voicemail then had ignored them. *What more can he have to say? The damage is already done.* She never wanted to talk to him again. Thankfully the number that flashed on her phone wasn't his. It was Mackenzie.

"Hello," Tiffany answered as she dug another spoonful of ice cream out of the carton, despite being on the verge of vomiting.

"What's wrong with you?" Mackenzie asked.

"Just everything."

Molly scrunched her face up and asked, "Who is it?"

Tiffany whispered, "Mac."

"Oh, is Molly there? What happened? She okay?" Mackenzie rapid fired questions at Tiffany.

"She's fine."

"Let me talk to her, please."

Tiffany handed her phone over to Molly.

"Hey, Mac. Yeah, I'm fine. No, she isn't. Well..." Molly said then paused. Her gaze held Tiffany's. "Can I tell her?" she asked Tiffany.

"Might as well."

"Well, Mac, Colin fired her," Molly said.

Like a bandage, sometimes it was better to do it quickly, but damn, it still hurt. Just hearing the words again, hearing them said out loud made Tiffany's stomach bottom out. She had been *fired*.

Molly nudged Tiffany. "Here. She wants to talk to you."

Molly handed the phone back to Tiffany.

"Yes, Mac?"

"Hey, I don't want you to worry. We got your back. Screw that slimeball."

"Thanks. I appreciate it."

"I have an idea. Why don't you guys fly out?" Mackenzie suggested eagerly.

"Um, did you not hear? I'm destitute."

"I'll pay for you."

"Nah, I can't do that." Tiffany waited a moment. "Wait, is everything okay there?"

"Yeah, but it's not going quite how I imagined," Mackenzie replied.

Molly looked at Tiffany with full-blown concern and asked quietly, "Everything okay?"

Tiffany nodded and whispered, "She's asking if we want to go there."

"You should. I won't be any fun," Molly said as she rubbed her belly.

"Of course, you would be."

Molly smirked. "Really? I can't drink and I highly doubt Owen will want his pregnant, soon-to-be-wife going to Vegas."

Again, another valid point. Tiffany nodded in agreement.

"Well, Tiff, you want to meet me out here?"

What do I have to lose? Definitely not my job. Why the hell not? "Vegas, here I come, baby."

Molly laughed and said, loud enough for Mackenzie to hear, "Do *not* let her around any hot dogs."

* * * *

Tiffany sipped her coffee from the paper cup. It was strong, but considering how wicked early it was, she should be grateful for the jolt of caffeine. The airport was nearly empty. Leave it to Mackenzie to get her on the earliest flight possible. Why had she even agreed to go to Vegas? Because she'd been in an ice-cream-induced coma. No one makes sound decisions when strung out on sugar.

The security line had been quick. It had been her and maybe two or three other passengers. She'd learned her lesson since the last time she'd flown to Vegas. No cute studded jeans. Today she was rockin' yoga pants and a hoodie. Even her hair was in a sloppy bun. *Depression is not cute.*

Tiffany boarded the plane and was lucky to snag a window seat. Not that it mattered because she intended to sleep the entire time.

Oh, how quickly plans change. A man with golden hair, happy green eyes and a toothy smile sat next to her. He was chipper and fairly handsome, but Tiffany was not in the mood to be nice. Her coffee had not kicked in yet and, honestly, out of all the empty seats, why would he want to sit next to her? She'd figured her outfit—a cross between 'homeless chic' and 'GAP depression'—would be a deterrent. She shouldn't have showered. Maybe her fruity body spray had attracted him?

Tiffany looked out of the window. They hadn't taken off yet and she flagged down the flight attendant. She politely asked for a pillow and blanket. Tiffany wasn't even cold, but figured she could use the blanket to hide under. Tiffany wanted to die when Mr. I-could-have-sat-anywhere-on-this-stupid-damn-plane-but-chose-to-sit-right-smack-next-to-you started to make chit-chat.

Kill me now. Better yet, kill Mac.

He took the hint, kind of. He even offered to buy her a drink and asked if flying made her cranky.

Seriously, dude. Shut up.

Tiffany tucked the pillow against the window and finally pulled the blanket over her head. Safe under her shelter, she napped. At some point, the plane arrived in Vegas. Her lovely seat companion had decided not to disturb her and Tiffany woke to the flight attendant gently shaking her.

A little dazed and not nearly as refreshed as she should be

from her nap, Tiffany shuffled her way to the baggage claim to get her single piece of luggage. Mackenzie was waiting for her by the rotating conveyor belt that was sparsely covered in various suitcases and duffel bags. It didn't take long to retrieve hers.

"Rough flight?" Mackenzie asked. Her gaze traveled down the length of Tiffany's body.

"I know. I look like shit. You would too if you'd just gotten fired."

"Well, I bet you didn't set off the machines when you went through them. Last time, you and those damn jeans… It drove me crazy."

"Yeah, but at least I was cute. Today, I look like this. Please tell me you didn't bring Jason with you." Tiffany panicked.

"I thought about it but decided we need to just chill and leave your Seattle troubles behind us for a bit." Mackenzie grabbed Tiffany's rolling luggage from her. "I'm thinking poolside and cocktails?"

It wasn't anywhere near noon. Hell, it wasn't anywhere near nine in the morning yet, but cocktails and being in the pool sounded wonderful.

* * * *

Okay, Vegas is hot. Yes, it's in the middle of the desert, but damn. Tiffany thought Seattle got hot. That was nothing compared to being sizzled in Vegas. It felt as though they were in the center of the earth—a sick oven of heat, but everyone assured her it was a *dry heat. What the hell does that even mean, anyway? How is a* dry *heat good?* Heat was heat and right now it was yucky.

"How have you been dealing with this, Mac?"

So much for hanging outside by the pool. They'd tried, but now they were in Mackenzie's room sipping cocktails and staring longingly at the swimmers and sun-worshippers below.

"Barely."

"Look at those brave people down there," Tiffany commented as she looked outside their large window. It gave a great view of the vast pool area. Tons of families were in the water, splashing and slowly being boiled.

"Brave? Um, no. Insane? Yes."

"So, what's the game plan here? Am I meeting this Jason fella again?"

Mackenzie frowned. "I don't know. Maybe? I mean, you were pretty darn intoxicated the last time you did."

"That I was. So, no hot dogs tonight?" Tiffany joked.

"Tiff, I don't think any of us can ever eat another one, thanks to you."

Tiffany laughed. "Yeah, sorry about that."

"Hey, they aren't good for us anyway. What would you like to do while we're here?"

Tiffany looked at her half-empty glass and raised it. "This."

"Solid plan. But you want to maybe get some food? Or catch a show?"

"Didn't we just talk about me and food don't mix when I'm getting my drink on?" Tiffany winked.

"Well then, slow down on the drinks and let's grab some food. Unlike you, I don't puke, but I need food."

"Okay, but once you eat, more of this is happening." Tiffany shook her glass at Mackenzie and already had a bit of trouble forming her words.

"Maybe you should take a little nap. The heat and all this may not end well," Mackenzie suggested as she finished her own drink.

"That sounds like a good game plan." Tiffany downed the last of her cocktail of vodka and soda water. She threw herself on the enormous bed and melted into the mattress. And just like that, she drifted off but was plagued by alcohol-induced dreams, most of which included Colin. She wasn't really sure she'd even really slept when she began to stir.

"You want to wake up?"

Tiffany opened her eyes, expecting to feel a massive headache and was surprised she felt amazing.

She yawned and stretched. Tiffany was still in her clothes. "I'm up."

"How do you feel?"

The room was darker than she remembered, so she must have slept. Mackenzie was sitting by the table with only one lamp turned on.

"Great. But gosh, how long was I out?"

"A while, but you needed the rest. Now you can party like a rock star," Mackenzie joked.

"Oh yeah, that's me." Tiffany giggled. "Did you eat yet?" Tiffany asked as she got off the bed and took the empty seat across from Mackenzie.

"I went down to the lobby. They have a small café there and I got a sandwich. I'm still hungry and I thought we could go out if you are up to it." Mackenzie smiled.

"How about we check out things out and go have a little fun. But tomorrow, let's take in a show. Sound good?"

"Oh yeah, they have this Beatles one I'm dying to see."

Just like that, Tiffany's heart broke. She didn't even really know who the Beatles were—wasn't sure she'd even recognize one of their hits—but it made her think of her beloved Sir McCartney. Her thoughts went to a dark place—a forbidden area—and she thought of Colin.

"Oh shit, I'm sorry, Tiff. I wasn't thinking," Mackenzie apologized.

"It's fine. You know, on second thought, maybe we can just hang out here tonight." Tiffany got up and crawled back onto the bed.

When am I going to get over the man who ruined my world — not once, but several times now?

* * * *

Breakfast consisted of delicious pancakes and scrambled eggs. Those alone were almost worth the trip. Tiffany stabbed into a sausage link and gazed out of the window. It was early and already Vegas was coming alive with tourists.

"Now that we are properly fueled and rested, let's make the most of our day," Mackenzie said, lifting a small glass of orange juice to her lips.

Tiffany bit into a sausage and agreed. "Yeah, I'd like to attempt to go for a swim today."

"Let's do that early."

"I know. It's already kind of hot. I don't know how people can live here," Tiffany said in amazement.

"It's awful. That's for sure. Hey, I spoke to Jason. He'd love to grab dinner with both us tonight. You cool with that?"

"Fun. I'm totally down. I can finally see what's up with this guy." Tiffany winked at Mackenzie.

"Like I said, he's nice, super down-to-earth and the only thing wrong with him is—" she started to say.

"Is that he won't help end the drought. That's a bit of a red flag for me, Mac," Tiffany said.

"Nah, maybe he's worried it'll ruin everything. Or maybe he's more traditional...or religious?"

"Come on. He's a bouncer at a nightclub. I don't think this a moral thing. Maybe his equipment doesn't work. You know, we're middle-age now. You may want to look for a young buck."

"Shut up. That's terrible." Mackenzie was laughing hard.

"Just sayin'."

* * * *

They were seated around an enormous rustic table at an Indian restaurant, dining on some of the best curry Tiffany had ever eaten. Mackenzie was right. Jason was nice, down-to-earth and, more importantly, very sweet to Mackenzie. He was incredibly funny. That was always a good thing. Tiffany enjoyed looking at him, too. His arms were huge and covered in skillfully applied ink. Yeah, Mackenzie could do a whole lot worse.

After Jason paid for their meal, Mackenzie realized that she'd forgotten her purse back at the hotel that contained the tickets for the show they'd all decided to see together. Jason drove them back in his Jeep to pick it up. It had no top and it was great to have the warm night air touch them as they headed down the busy streets of Vegas. The lights, sounds and energy surged around them. Tiffany absorbed it all.

Tonight was going to be great. Tiffany felt fantastic. That was code for a little drunk. She was even okay with going to that Beatles show. Tiffany had made an internal promise to herself to not even think about Colin—or her precious Pauly. Tiffany also figured if she downed enough cocktails, she wouldn't even know it was a Beatles show. Mackenzie had Jason for her date and Tiffany was with the Captain. Captain Morgan, that was, and he was treating her very good tonight.

Mackenzie and Jason held hands as they entered their hotel only minutes later. Mackenzie stopped suddenly in her tracks, Jason looked confused and Tiffany bumped into Mackenzie's back. *Ouch.* Her reflexes weren't nearly as sharp as they should be.

"Hey, why'd you stop?" Tiffany asked. She wobbled a little and leaned on Mackenzie for support.

Nothing sobered her up quicker than seeing the man she hated—and loved.

Colin stood there with his hands in his pockets, not in a suit but wearing jeans and a cotton T-shirt. An olive green that was definitely his color, she decided. *Damn you, sexy Irishman.*

What Tiffany couldn't understand was why he was there. How in God's name did he even know she was in Vegas?

Tiffany looked down and noticed a furry lump that she loved sprawled out on the marble floor. His tongue was out and his jowls were fanned on the cool stone.

"Pauly...there's my precious buddy." Tiffany squatted down, which was not an easy feat for someone that had eaten her weight in curry and had drank more rum than she probably should have. But it was worth the risk to get some love from the adorable Sir McCartney.

The bulldog dragged his body along the floor to reach her. He was too lazy or too hot to fully lift himself. Tiffany petted him and felt eyes on her. Mackenzie stared at her in complete shock. Jason had no clue who Colin was or why Tiffany was on the ground with a bulldog. Colin was just looking at her with a quiet expression.

Tiffany tried to get off the floor with some grace. She met Colin's gaze and shook her head. "So, who told you? Molly?"

Colin looked away briefly. "Owen."

She hadn't even considered that option, but it made perfect sense. Molly had probably talked to Owen and, unbeknownst to her, they'd both gotten sold out. Now, here was Colin.

Yeah, thanks, Owen. This isn't the least bit uncomfortable.

"Tiffany, can we please talk?" Colin tried reaching for her hand.

She pulled away. "The last time we talked, you fired me."

Jason puffed up his chest and balled up his fist. "This is the guy?"

Mackenzie placed her hand on his chest, holding Jason back.

"Tiffany, it's because I can't work with you. You know my rule."

"Oh, that stupid shit about mixing business with pleasure. Yeah, yeah, yeah. Who cares?" Tiffany teetered and Colin caught her.

"We tend to do this a lot, don't we?" he whispered as she remained in his arms. Tiffany could smell his expensive aftershave and she closed her eyes. His hands felt good on her. There was no denying that. Tiffany couldn't open them. If she looked into his, it would be too much. It took everything she had to not kiss him.

"Tiffany, I'm so sorry, but I need to explain everything." Colin got Tiffany upright, but didn't remove his hold.

Tiffany looked over to Mackenzie and Jason as they stood watch. Jason looked like he was ready to pounce.

Mackenzie smiled encouragingly at her. "Maybe you two should talk. But I do have tickets for a Beatles show, Colin, if you'd like to join us. You guys need to make this quick."

Seriously? Do I have a say in anything anymore?

Tiffany turned back to Colin, who wore a cheesy grin.

"Thanks, Mackenzie. Just give us a moment then we'll join you two."

He led them away, his hand on the small of her back. Sir McCartney trailed after them as Colin steered them to a quiet seating area. It was intimate and perfect for talking. Tiffany's head cleared. Rationality was invading the numbness she'd put her mind under.

Colin helped her into one of the plush seats then sat down. "I know it's shocking that I'm here."

Tiffany rolled her eyes. "Ya think? I'd say so."

"Oh, Tiffany, I don't even know where to begin. I had to let you go…professionally."

"Colin, you could have talked to me instead of blindsiding me like that." Tiffany glared at him. It was hard to be angry at him when he gave her those sad eyes, but she'd sure as hell try.

"You're right. But I needed to end that relationship before we could start another," he explained.

"Um, yeah, firing someone does not make them want to date you. Just an FYI," Tiffany said with sarcasm.

"I deserve that. Again, you're right. I went about it the wrong way. I should have just told you how I felt."

"Which is?" Tiffany waited for him to answer. She was tempted to forgive him, but then she remembered she had no job. That instantly fired her up and made her mad again. "You know, I'm not sure why I'm even having this conversation with you. You fired me, I have no job and I'm bound to lose everything. Thanks for that." Tiffany rose from her seat and he pulled her arm so she'd sit back down.

"I was an utter jerk, but, Tiffany, you didn't stay long enough for me to explain what I meant by letting you go. You simply bolted out of the office."

"Oh, is there a better ending to, 'You're fired'? I wasn't aware."

"Stop. If you'd stayed, you would have learned that I was giving you back to Patty," Colin huffed.

"Giving me back? You make me sound like I'm a *thing*," Tiffany shot back.

"I didn't mean for it to come out like that. I just knew that the only way for me to explore whatever this is between us would be if you weren't my assistant," Colin explained softly. "Tiffany, I really like you."

"So, you flew down to Vegas to profess your undying love for me? Just making sure I got all the facts straight here."

"I brought Pauly along. He misses you terribly, and besides, I figured you couldn't stay mad at me if he was here," Colin teased, then right on cue the chubby bulldog placed a paw on Tiffany's leg. "I know you're livid with me, but let's join your friends and have a good time."

"Colin, I don't think you get why I'm upset," Tiffany complained, but then Pauly looked up her and the coldness melted from her heart. *Damn, Pauly and all his cuteness.*

"Trust me, love. I do."

Hearing him call her 'love' made the butterflies come alive inside her. *Damn Colin and all his sexiness.*

He stood then reached for her hand, acting every bit the perfect gentleman and knight in shining armor. Tiffany sighed.

She accepted it and he pulled her up and close to him. Tiffany almost felt like her feet weren't even on the floor.

Colin looked down at her, his focus trained on her lips, and she ran her tongue across them nervously. It must have proved to be too much for him and the next thing she knew, he'd fused his mouth to hers.

She loved the way this man tasted. The softness and power behind his kiss was propelling her to want more. She had wanted — no, needed — this since their last lip-lock. And from the way Colin was holding on to her, he must have needed it just as badly.

Tiffany nearly forgot they were standing in a crowded hotel lobby in Vegas. The distant sounds echoed around them — mainly chatter from visitors, tiny wheels from luggage carts as they rolled against the smooth floor and the jingle of slot machines in the background — but Tiffany didn't care. Hell, she would have been willing to strip down and make love to Colin right there if he had asked. Tiffany would give everyone an eyeful and a much better show than that Beatles one they were supposed to watch.

Chapter Twelve

Tiffany knew who the Beatles were. *Gosh, I feel like a moron.* Of course, she'd heard their music. The show had been fantastic and she'd had a good time. She wasn't sure if it was because of the holding hands or the sneaky kisses that Colin kept leaving on her neck. Mackenzie and Jason seemed thoroughly in love, as well.

Like the song lyric said, love was all you needed and tonight was proving that.

Not wanting the magic of the night to end, Jason suggested they hit up some casinos, do a little drinking and a whole lot of dancing. Tiffany liked the way this guy thought. If nothing else, Jason was fun. But he was so much more and Tiffany hoped that Mackenzie and he could find a way to make this work. Long-distance relationships usually never did, but there was always the hope that perhaps Jason would move to Seattle. He'd mentioned it several times and seemed eager to explore his options to relocate there.

This was the best double date ever—lots of laughter, dancing and plenty of drinks. Jason and Colin had gotten along really well after the whole mess of Colin's firing her had been cleared up. Even Mackenzie—who was as protective as a pit bull—was now dazzled by his charms and the magic of the night. *This all just feels right—like this is how it's supposed to be.* It was funny how things could change so quickly.

It was one thing to win at a sparkly nickel machine, which was the only level of gambling experience that Tiffany had, but to watch Colin engage in the real thing, like blackjack, was a rush, watching him bet and win serious money. She could never drop that kind of cash, but then again, she wasn't a multimillionaire either. The flurry of activity was wild beyond compare. Cheers erupted as people started to gather and watch her man win. *Her man.* The luck o' the Irish was with Colin as he raked in chips, game after game. It didn't matter if it was roulette or some other dice game. He avoided the slots and stayed close to the tables.

Tiffany was tucked next to him. "For luck?" Colin held up the dice he cupped in his hand for her to blow.

Another win.

He pulled her to him and kissed her hard. Tiffany's world spun. She forgot people were hovering all around them, but the hooting and whistles brought her back to reality. Colin refused to let her go. He'd traveled all these miles, endured the last three days of her not taking his calls and now he was making sure that she wasn't going anywhere. Tiffany was perfectly okay with that. Maybe that was the rum talking. *Shouldn't I still be upset with him for ruining my life?* Then she remembered he'd said he was giving her back to Patty and that made her a little sad. No more Sir McCartney snoozing and farting next to her. Tiffany was convinced she was more bummed out about not being around that chunky bulldog than Colin, and that made her laugh out loud. She had fallen in love with that dog—smells, slobber and all. Tiffany smiled at the thought of him probably snoozing on the plush bed in Colin's suite.

Colin gazed up her. "Thinking about Pauly?"

"How did you know?" Tiffany laughed.

"Because he has that effect on people."

"I've missed him a lot," Tiffany admitted.

"But, love, it's only been about three days," Colin said soothingly, pulling her closer to him. "I'd think you'd miss me more."

"Nah, Pauly has you beat."

They both laughed.

After some cocktails, Tiffany's bladder was about to explode.

"Mackenzie, wanna hit up the bathroom? I'm seriously about to piss myself," Tiffany leaned over and whispered in Mackenzie's ear. She nodded and they excused themselves. They followed a neon sign that led them to a ladies' restroom not too far away.

Tiffany and Mackenzie giggled once inside in the bright room. Mackenzie had dropped her purse and the contents rolled across the tiled floor. They laughed some more. *Why? What's so funny?* Not a damn thing. They were drunk — like they were one more cocktail away from the room-spinning kind of intoxication. But it was freeing and wonderful. All Tiffany's compressed troubles were gone. Tonight was all about fun and throwing caution to the wind. It was about kisses, sneaky butt grabs and basking in the joy of a new romance. Because they were officially a couple now, right? Tiffany wasn't completely clear on that, but she was pretty sure they were green light on the dating front.

"So…you and Colin. God, he's amazing, Tiff," Mackenzie slurred.

Tiffany was bent down and collecting the stray items from Mackenzie's purse.

"Isn't he? So hot, too." Tiffany grinned.

She handed Mackenzie her treasures. Tiffany dug into her own bag. Tonight it was her prized possession, a real Louis Vuitton. The classic brown and tan with the famed initials was one of her favorites in her collection. Tiffany pulled out a tube of lipstick. Colin had kissed off her earlier-applied color.

Puckering up, she spread on the red tone. It created a wet sheen and she rubbed her lips together to mash it around.

"So, are you guys like a couple now?" Mackenzie held out her hand for the lipstick then started adding some to her lips.

"I think so. I'm still a little unclear, but it kinda seems like we are. Wouldn't you say so?"

"Yeah. He's seems totally into you," Mackenzie commented.

Mackenzie started to fix her hair and Tiffany stared at their reflections in the mirror. *Not too bad for some old broads. We're both still sort of hot.* Maybe it was the rum talking, but Tiffany didn't care. Blame it on being more than a little tipsy, but she felt confident and beautiful. Maybe it was all the affection being lavished on her by Colin or the glittery magic of Vegas, but tonight had a special air about it.

"Thanks, Mac."

"For what?" Mackenzie looked confused but still wore a drunk, goofy smile.

"For making me come here. And for being my best friend."

Mackenzie slapped playfully at her.

"No, I'm serious, Mac. You and I haven't always seen eye to eye, but you have always been there for me. I love you for that."

Why is that alcohol has a tendency to make people in mushy, sentimental, whiny bitches?

"Hey, Tiff, I love you, too, but you're killing my buzz." Mackenzie wrapped her arms around her.

She and Mackenzie hugged it out in that brightly lit Vegas restroom so far from home, all the past grievances and irritations forgotten. Friendship wasn't always pretty. Sometimes it was ugly, but if you were lucky, like Tiffany, you had friends that genuinely cared, no matter how drunk or stupid you were.

"There's only one way to get that buzz back," Tiffany announced happily and winked at Mackenzie. "Let's go see the Captain."

Mackenzie looped her arm around Tiffany's. "Time flies when you're having rum."

* * * *

"Ugh, my head," Tiffany complained. "Mackenzie, please tell me you have some aspirin."

"Morning, love."

Huh? Why is Colin in here? Where in the hell am I? Déjà

vu hit her hard. Her brain slowly fed her the details of the previous night. She recalled seeing Pauly, Colin and the Beatles. She remembered dancing, but her aching feet helped jog that memory. Dancing, gambling and drinking, then more dancing, more gambling and more drinking.

"Where's Mackenzie?"

"In her room. Tiffany, we need to talk."

Great, another one of Colin's amazing conversations. They either led to her being fired, kissed or something that never ended well.

"Yes?"

"Now, don't get upset," Colin spoke slowly.

"That's how you get someone upset, Colin. If you have to warn someone, it must be bad." Tiffany's mouth was extremely dry and her throat was parched.

Colin sensed her thirst and quickly handed her a bottle of water. She chugged it down and waited as he prepared to speak.

"Please remain calm. It's not all that bad, really. Just don't freak out, okay?"

"Colin, I'm hungover and not in the mood for riddles," Tiffany pleaded. Her head was beginning to pound unmercifully.

"Well, it's not the easiest thing to just come out with. We were having a lovely time. Bloody hell, Mackenzie practically made us do it."

"To do what? Spit it out, Colin," Tiffany demanded.

"To get married."

"I'm sorry. I thought I heard you say…" Tiffany replied.

"You did." Colin held up his left hand. A gold band was on his ring finger.

Tiffany immediately peered down at her own. A shimmering diamond stared back at her. *Oh shit.*

"You can't be serious? Is this some kind of joke?" Tiffany asked.

Colin moved his hand slowly over his hair and he shook his head.

"Why aren't you freaking out?"

"I don't know. I suppose it's not the most terrible thing."

What's wrong with him? Yes, this is terrible, downright awful and completely not okay in and shape or form. Tiffany was in full blown freak-out mode. Her adrenaline surged through her entire body. The headache from her hangover squeezed her brain, and her stomach was a flood of nerves and too much liquor.

Tiffany wanted to bolt out of the room. She wasn't sure what to do. She had really done it this time. *Married? How did Mackenzie allow this to happen?*

"Tiffany, it's okay. We can figure this out." Colin tried to sit next to her, but Tiffany moved away.

What is there to figure out? This was not an easy fix. She had screwed up big time, something she'd kept doing a lot lately, especially with him.

"This is so bad, Colin." Tiffany verged on tears.

"Not all bad. I mean, granted, we've barely begun dating," Colin tried to explain.

"Dating? Is that what you call this? You fired me," Tiffany nearly shouted.

"Yes, but as I explained last night, that was not my intent. I was letting you go as my assistant," he calmly countered. "I never meant to upset you. It was a complete misunderstanding."

"So then, in my drunken state, I married and slept with you. I mean…you're right. I don't see how this is bad at all," Tiffany replied with sarcasm.

"Tiffany, I know it seems a bit dismal, but this can be fixed" — Colin paused — "if you want. Or we could just stay married," he added.

"Colin, I'm sorry, but have you lost your mind? Stay married? That's insane."

"For the record, we didn't consummate the marriage." Colin got up from the bed and turned away.

Great, again I failed at making love with him.

He started to remove his shirt. His slow and methodical

way of undressing was like a strip tease. *Oh Lord, what is about to happen?* Tiffany's nerves stood on end and she began to panic. He unbuttoned his jeans and slid them off. He was down to his underwear, a boxer brief that hugged his thighs and gave hints about the package he had barely hidden behind the fabric. If Tiffany were to be honest, it was a sight indeed and her body stirred. What was he going to do, make them consummate their marriage now to make it somehow legit? *He wouldn't dare.* Then Colin walked farther away after draping his pants and shirt over a chair. He slipped into the bathroom and closed the door. *Oh, he's just showering.*

Tiffany let her head collapse in her hands as she sat there in the oversized bed, thoroughly confused and angry at herself. She felt like Alice in Wonderland and she'd fallen inside a rabbit's hole...*again.* This was not reality. There was no way that it could be. She needed to wake up from this dream. Tiffany closed her eyes and pinched herself hard. *Ouch!* Nope, she was very much awake and this was very real. She needed to find Mackenzie and see what happened, then figure out how could they fix this.

Pauly hopped onto the bed. He placed a paw on her thigh, as if to say *it'll be okay.*

"Oh, but it won't, li'l man." Tiffany stroked his brown leg down to the speckled white paw. "What am I going to do, Pauly?"

She heard Colin turn on the shower and decided it was indeed time to bolt.

"Sorry, buddy." Tiffany frowned and could swear she felt her heart break as the chocolate droopy eyes looked back at her.

Tiffany hopped off the bed and realized she was still dressed in the previous night's outfit. Only her shoes were missing. She passed by a large mirror on her way out and almost gagged. Her makeup was smeared and her hair was a complete disaster. Yeah, if she were Colin, she'd totally stay married to the troll looking back at her...*not.* Tiffany rolled her raccoon eyes.

Oh, Tiffany, you need to get your shit together, girlfriend.

Chapter Thirteen

"Okay, you need to calm *way* down," Mackenzie ordered.

Tiffany was back inside their room. She'd had a hotel key card in her purse and had been able to get in. It was the only thing that was going right so far that day. Mackenzie was still buried under her comforter when Tiffany had barged in only moments before.

"How do you expect me to be calm? Mac, look? I'm friggin' married," Tiffany cried as she held her hand up. The large diamond nearly blinded both of them.

"Well... I mean, yes, that most certainly is a problem. But we can figure this out, Tiff. Don't panic." Mackenzie released a heavy sigh. "That's one helluva rock." She examined the ring on Tiffany's hand.

Easy for her to say. She wasn't married to a guy that had fired her only days earlier.

Snatching her hand away, Tiffany complained, "I mean, where *were* you? How did you allow this happen to me?"

"Me? You guys were all peachy and told me and Jason to go away. You don't remember?"

"All I remember is dancing, gambling and lots of drinking. Then I woke up in a hotel suite with him, *again*."

"That's kind of becoming a running theme with you lately."

Mackenzie's comment hurt. Had she been making a slew of awful choices lately? *Yes*. But she needed her friend's support right now, not a lecture, because she was already disgusted enough with herself.

Tiffany's eyes became blurry as they filled with tears. "Mackenzie, what am I going to do?"

"Maybe we should call Molly and have her weigh in," she suggested as she hugged Tiffany.

"I'm not sure I want to tell her right now. I mean, she's the one that is supposed to be getting married."

"True, but she's our best friend."

"You know she's going to be super pissed off at you, right?" Tiffany stared at Mackenzie.

"Me? I didn't do anything wrong."

"Well, you used to be the mother hen, the one that made sure we didn't do stupid shit, and you kind of failed."

Mackenzie shook her head. "Unbelievable. You're going to blame me for what you went and did? I thought you were going back to the hotel to bone him, not have Elvis marry you."

Tiffany groaned. "God, what in the hell have I done?"

"So, was it fat Elvis or hot Elvis?"

"It doesn't matter. I don't even know if Elvis married us. You are missing the point here. I'm *married*!"

"Colin seems nice."

"Do you hear yourself right now?" Tiffany was growing agitated.

"I mean, in the scheme of things, what does it all mean? Why not, you know?" Mackenzie began to rattle off some philosophical mumbo jumbo that Tiffany had no interest in listening to. "Life is short and shit happens. Maybe getting married to Colin isn't the worst thing?"

"You can't possibly be serious. Mac. He fired me."

"Because he had feelings for you and didn't want to deal with work interfering with that."

"I can't believe you are defending him and that you think this is all okay," Tiffany said. She ran her fingers through her hair. It was tangled and she caught another glimpse of herself in the mirror. She was a hot mess of a wreck, a pitiful disaster. How could Colin even be attracted to her?

"Tiffany, it will be okay. Things have a way of working themselves out. If they don't... Well, there's not a whole lot you can do. Trust me. I know this first hand."

She looked at Mackenzie—like really looked at her. This wasn't her—Mackenzie, the bossy friend that gave unwanted advice but the best. This was someone who had been dealt some bullshit cards and was now flying by the seat of her pants because she knew it didn't matter how tightly you held on or how well you thought you had all your shit together, you never really did. Life made sure of that.

Tiffany stormed out of the hotel room. She needed air. Everything was so utterly messed up. Her guts felt twisted and cinched together by zip ties. Tiffany walked to the pool area and found a lounger that was partially shaded. She plopped down and stared out at the perfect turquoise water. It was inviting, especially as the sun began to roast everything in sight. She still couldn't wrap her head around the fact that she was married or that Mackenzie and Colin were completely okay with all of it. Was she crazy or not seeing something they all saw? Did she somehow venture into some alternate universe? *God, nothing makes sense anymore.*

As Tiffany contemplated all her crummy choices in life, she couldn't help laugh. Of course, this is something that would happen to her. Last night the Captain had complicated her life and led her astray. She might not ever forgive him for this. *Damn Captain Morgan.* She had to blame someone, right?

* * * *

A few hours later, after reality had set in, Tiffany stared at the sandwich in front of her. She had no appetite and was trying to will herself to eat. Mackenzie was trying to sway her to put something in her stomach.

"You need to eat," said Mackenzie.

"So, what happened with you and Jason?"

"You mean while you were off getting yourself hitched?" Tiffany glared at her. "Really? Come on."

"Not ready to joke about your nuptials yet?" Mackenzie cocked her head to the side and laughed.

"It's not funny. That's why."

"Oh, Tiffany, it kind of is." Mackenzie giggled then looked thoughtfully at the open blue sky over the outside deli. "I don't know what's going to happen with Jason. I like him and he seems to like me, but something just isn't there. I can't quite put my finger on it."

"Yeah, it's called *sex*, I know it's been a while for you."

"It's more than that." Mackenzie frowned.

"He's not Gideon."

Mackenzie shrugged. "Maybe. I'm not sure. But we have bigger fish to fry."

"Ugh, I know. What in the hell am I going to do?"

"Well, let's call Molly."

Tiffany shook her head. "Nope. I don't think I want to tell her over the phone. Hell, I don't even want to tell her."

"If any one out of us will understand, it's her."

"I'm not so sure about that. Molly is different now that she's with Owen."

"Yes, but in a good way," Mackenzie countered.

"And she's pregnant. I don't want to add to her stress."

"She'll be upset if you don't say anything. She'd already going to kill me for allowing this to happen."

"Yeah, you're basically dead meat."

"What do you think Colin is doing right now? You think he flew back to Seattle yet?"

"I have no clue. Can you believe he actually wanted me to consider staying married to him?"

"Well, maybe he sees it a little differently. Like, you both aren't getting any younger and the deed is already done, so why fight it? Or maybe he's relieved. He won't have to deal with you being a bridezilla."

"I totally would be, wouldn't I?" Tiffany laughed for the first time that day.

"Hey, you and I both want the big wedding. Molly doesn't. She'll probably be envious you got the wedding she wanted, a drive-thru with Elvis. That's more her style, for sure."

"You should have seen him this morning. He was so miserable."

"Because you guys were married?" Mackenzie took a drink as Tiffany picked at her food.

"No, because I didn't want to stay married. Oh, Mac, here's the real deal. I would love to be with him, just not like this."

"So, live by Molly's new motto, 'Just go with it'."

"Not this way. Like you say, I want the big wedding and the glamorous engagement party. I want it all. I feel cheated."

"You should talk to Colin."

"Gosh, but how? Where do I start?" Tiffany looked down at the mutilated remains of her sandwich.

"Well, you better think of something fast because he's headed this way with Sir McCartney."

"Are you serious?" Tiffany panicked.

"Um, yeah." Then all of a sudden Mackenzie put a fake smile on her face. "Hi, Colin."

Colin smiled politely at Mackenzie, but his eyes searched Tiffany. "Hello, Mackenzie."

"I guess congratulations are in order."

Tiffany kicked her hard under the table. Mackenzie winced as she got up from her seat and hugged Colin. "You mind if I take this little darlin' for a walk?" She looked over to Tiffany and stuck out her tongue.

Colin handed over the leash and gave Mackenzie a grateful smile. "He'd love that. Thank you, Mackenzie."

Mackenzie hightailed it out of there, completely abandoning Tiffany. What kind of friend does that? *My friend, that's who. A friend who allows her buddy to get hitched in Vegas.*

Colin took Mackenzie's seat and he released a heavy sigh. "I was worried about where you had run off to."

"Why? Of course, I would go back to my friend. Granted,

I'm not sure we're friends anymore." Tiffany laughed nervously.

Colin spoke softly, "She's a very good friend and Pauly seems to be quite taken with her. And I know that he's a fabulous judge of character."

"What are we doing here? I mean, how do we fix this?" Tiffany asked.

"Simple. We stay married."

"Um, no. That is not an option."

"Why not?"

"Colin, we haven't even dated yet. You don't know anything about me. Like…what's my favorite color?" Tiffany threw hands up in the air.

"Periwinkle."

"What?" Tiffany was shocked. *How can he possibly know that?*

"Fine. How about favorite food?"

"That's a toss-up. Chinese or Italian." Colin smiled.

"Okay, those were easy. Anyone could know."

"Tiffany, did you think those days when we spent time talking that I wasn't listening? I find you incredibly interesting." His voice got low and a magical light danced in his eyes. "I have been intrigued by you since the moment you fell into my arms on Owen's boat."

"But that's not enough to stay married. This is not how I ever dreamed it happening, that's for sure.

"I can understand that. Imagine my end. Think of how much I stand to lose? I don't recall having you sign a prenuptial agreement."

Damn. "But I would never—" Tiffany started when Colin took her hand.

"How am I to be sure? As you just pointed out, we don't know each other very well."

Tiffany looked down at his hand. His wedding band was still on. It was surreal. The man sitting across from her was legally her husband.

"I think we need to take this one step at a time," Colin

said softly as his thumb rubbed gentle circles on her skin. "I know you feel it, too. There's something here. What it is I'm not entirely certain, but I do think it's worth exploring."

"So, what do you suggest we do, then?" Tiffany looked into his dark eyes.

This man was so impossibly handsome, so out of her league, and yet, she was terribly drawn to him. Tiffany's heart was surrendering. Tiffany was officially way over her head in whatever madness this was.

* * * *

Several hours later, Tiffany and Mackenzie found themselves on the most luxurious private jet. Okay, it was the first private jet they had ever been on, but it was pretty damn amazing. Colin was on the phone with a client and seated diagonally from them. Sir McCartney was snoring in his own seat. It all seemed so weird and that was really the only way that Tiffany could describe it.

Mackenzie looked over at her, holding the flute of champagne that Colin had his flight attendant pass around to ease their nerves. He'd called flying a 'senseless necessity'.

"This is crazy. You know that, right?" Mackenzie said.

"You're telling me." Tiffany slowly sipped her drink, enjoying the flood of bubbles in her mouth.

"So, what are you two going to do?" Mackenzie whispered.

"I'm not sure. I guess he wants us to see where this goes."

Mackenzie smiled and laughed. "Um, yeah, marriage is usually where it ends up and you guys are already kinda there."

"I know, but he wants us to *date* now."

"Really? So, do you have your position back or what's the deal there?"

"I have no clue. I can't imagine that's part of his plan."

Mackenzie looked around the plane. "You know, you could do a lot worse. You probably don't need to work anymore."

Tiffany shook her head. "It's not like I'm really his wife or anything. I mean, hell, I'm not even his girlfriend."

"Tiff, you *are* his wife. Just look down at your finger if you need another reminder."

"Yeah, but we've never even slept together. We've never been on a date or anything. This isn't what it really is, you know?"

"I see what you mean. But no matter how you slice it, you're married." Mackenzie sipped from her flute. "So, you guys haven't done the deed yet?"

Tiffany shook her head in disbelief and quickly rerouted the conversation. "Was it hard saying goodbye to Jason this afternoon?"

Mackenzie frowned. "I don't even know what's going on there, to be honest. He acted strange when we spoke. I think he expected me to stay longer, then he was a little more than confused by your whole situation. Nothing seems to make any sense. Maybe it's just easier being alone, and so I told him that I think we're better off as just friends. I mean he can't seem to make up his mind as to what he wants, and it's too hard to try and figure him out." Mackenzie released a heavy sigh. "I can't stand men. Why do we even bother, Tiff? They just make everything more complicated."

"God, isn't that the truth? Like a few months ago… Things were just normal. We were all single, just doing our thing in Seattle. Now it's like I have no clue what's up and what's down. You're right. Everything is crazy. Sorry that things didn't work out between you and Jason, though."

Mackenzie raised her glass. "Here's to life's unexpected moments and to having no clue how to handle them."

"Cheers." Tiffany clinked her glass with Mackenzie's and closed her eyes. When was she going to wake up from this dream, because it had to be? This could *not* really be her life.

Chapter Fourteen

"Um, *no*. That's not happening, not by a long shot." Tiffany cemented her stance outside the black SUV that Colin was sitting in the back of.

"Get in. We're going home."

"I'm going to *my* home. You're going to yours. It's that simple." Tiffany was not budging on this matter. Colin had already sent Mackenzie off in Tiffany's car when they had touched down from Vegas, and now he was insisting they go home, *together*. His home was not hers. Just because they were technically wed didn't mean they were actually a married couple.

"Tiffany, please, get inside the car."

Tiffany walked to the driver's side and tapped on the dark glass. The driver rolled the window down. "Sir, you may leave now. I'll be taking another car. Thank you." He nodded.

Colin rolled down the back-passenger window. "So, that's it?"

"Yep. I'm going home. We can talk later. I'm exhausted, Colin."

He rolled the window back up. The dark tint hid him as the car pulled away. A part of her already missed him, but it had been the right call. They needed to figure this out, maybe see an attorney. Tiffany wasn't sure how any of this would work, but sleep was all that she wanted right now. She was still slightly hungover from the previous night. She hadn't even been married for a full twenty-four hours and here she was getting into a cab all alone. *Yeah, being married is everything I hoped it would be and so much more…*not!

Tiffany tried to close her eyes and nap as the cab drove her, but her brain wouldn't shut off. A headache was beginning, and she let her head rest on the cool window. She looked outside briefly and took in the glittering lights of Seattle. *God, this place is beautiful at night, almost magical.*

The cab driver announced they were nearing her apartment as he slowed the car.

Home sweet home. Alone.

After paying the driver, Tiffany lugged her bags to the door. She had some difficulty as she fished her keys out of her large purse. She finally located them and held the small set of keys up. *Mission accomplished.* Once inside, Tiffany was slightly out of breath and decided to leave her luggage in the living room. It could wait until tomorrow to be unpacked. She showered and dressed in her most comfy pajamas. Mr. Sprinkles didn't seem to notice or care that she had been gone. He whined for more food then went about sleeping in his favorite spot. It was late—almost midnight—and Tiffany threatened to drop from pure exhaustion. Emotionally worn out and physically tired, she craved the warmth and comfort of her bed. She was going to sleep well tonight. Tomorrow she would get together with Molly and Mackenzie. They could sort this thing out together. Mackenzie had just called a few minutes ago to let Tiffany know she'd gotten home fine and that things would be okay. Tiffany believed her. When they put their heads together, they were bound to come up with a solution. Things would be okay. Maybe it was the sheer tiredness, but Tiffany actually felt positive about all of this. She was back home now, safely away from Vegas, a place she planned never to return to. Tiffany peeled back her comforter, a sunny yellow with black and gray flowers. It was amazing to be in her bed. She closed her eyes and began to be carried away into a deep slumber.

A noise, something had startled her. *What the hell? Is someone knocking? God, what time is it? How long have I been asleep? Have I been asleep?* Tiffany's brain was confused as it shot all these questions. Then she heard it again. Someone was definitely knocking on her door. Tiffany's vision was blurred as she tried to look at her alarm clock. She jumped out of her bed and raced to the front door. Tiffany cautiously peeked out of the peephole. *Seriously?*

Tiffany pulled the door opened and glared at her visitor.

Colin and a very groggy looking Pauly stood there.

"What are you doing here?"

"Well, you didn't want to come home with us, so here we are." Colin seemed quite pleased with himself. He made no excuses for his ridiculous behavior. He just stood there proudly.

"I see that. But, again, that doesn't really answer my question. Why are you *here*?"

"Because, love, no matter which way we look at this, we're married. Do you mind letting me, your darling husband, inside?"

Tiffany turned around and Colin followed her in. He was dragging an enormous suitcase and had a backpack slung on one shoulder. Pauly scampered into the living room and sought refuge on the couch.

"Down," Tiffany ordered. He looked up at her with his sad, droopy brown eyes as he remained seated. "So, you and your dog just think you can move in?"

"I thought you liked him," Colin said as he wheeled his luggage behind the couch. "Well, I wouldn't call it 'moving in'."

"What would you call it, then?"

"A temporary arrangement until you come to your senses." Colin kissed Tiffany on the cheek then surveyed the room. "Where's the bedroom?"

She pointed to the couch where Pauly was already stretched out. Tiffany rolled her eyes. She was in no mood to deal with this. She went into her kitchen and poured herself some water. The cool drink settled her growing irritation. She walked past Colin, into her bedroom and she shut her door. Nope, there was no way Tiffany was going to deal with any more tonight. If he wanted to stay, he and his bulldog could sleep on the couch.

* * * *

The early morning sunlight was splashing warm rays into her room. She stared up at the ceiling. She'd been awake for a little while but didn't want to leave her bed. Tiffany had slept well, a deep and peaceful sleep. It had truly been one of the best she'd had in a long time. Then she heard a soft knock on her door. Her heart skipped a beat and Tiffany panicked for a moment until she remembered that she wasn't alone. She'd hoped that it had been an illusion or some kind of figment of her imagination, but nope, Colin was indeed here.

"Can I please come in?"

Did she really have much say? Could she just hide in her bed all day and hope he'd go away? Basically, *no* was the answer to the questions.

Colin opened the door slowly. Suddenly she heard something bang against it then something heavy was on her.

"Pauly, get down," Colin called out.

The fat English bulldog was rubbing all over Tiffany and burrowing himself deeper into her covers. *Gross.* Tiffany could only imagine the snot and ickiness of her little snuggle buddy. Yet, he oozed nothing but love for her and it softened her heart toward him.

"I'm sorry. I guess he missed you. He has been standing guard by your door all night," Colin explained as he tried to remove his plump fur-baby from the bed. Pauly made himself heavy and was dead weight until Colin released his hold. He scrambled to get closer to Tiffany.

"Probably protecting me from you," Tiffany teased. "Oh, just leave him. There's no use in fighting it. He just wants to cuddle." Tiffany was resolved that there was no point in denying Pauly. At least, not until she'd had her coffee. Only then would Tiffany even attempt to tackle the day, not until she was properly armed with caffeine.

"You sure?" Colin joined them on the bed.

"I didn't say you could," Tiffany swatted Colin away.

"But I'm cuter than him," Colin argued playfully as he kissed Tiffany on her forehead.

"Trust me. The dog is much cuter."

Tiffany gave up then finally crawled out of bed, made coffee and breakfast. She couldn't help but think how strange this all was. She scraped some leftover scrambled eggs into Pauly's bowl and Colin scowled at her.

"You'll be sorry you fed him that."

"Why?" Tiffany asked as she began to load the dishwasher.

"You think his farts were awful before. Oh, sweetheart, you're in for a treat."

Tiffany filled up her mug with more coffee and just stood there staring at this foreign scene. A man—a sexy Irishman at that—was sitting at her table—a man who was now her husband. She swallowed the hot liquid, praying for it to work its magic on her tired brain.

He sat across from Tiffany as she nursed her second cup of coffee and life was starting to make a little more sense. No, it actually wasn't, but her brain was at least able to function. Colin was now reading the paper but had spent half the morning making phone calls. She'd overheard him earlier while she'd been preparing breakfast. He'd been direct and had a commanding presence, yet he'd remained charming and she knew the people on the other end had been eating out of his hand. Colin was damn good at what he did.

"Colin, we need to really talk." She stared at him. For sleeping on a couch and looking rumpled, he was incredibly gorgeous, maybe even more so than ever. He had whiskers along his jaw, his brown hair wasn't perfectly combed and he sat shirtless, wearing only flannel pajama bottoms. He'd had no problem making himself comfortable in her house, but then again, this was a man who was used to always getting his way. Tiffany would be able to focus better if maybe he'd thrown on a shirt.

"I couldn't agree more." He lifted his mug and smiled at her before taking a sip.

"So, where do we begin?"

"Well, for starters, we need to consider other living arrangements. This place, as quaint and cozy as it is, it's not large enough for us to co-exist. I will have your things moved over then we can begin to sort that matter."

"No, that's not happening. First off, you came here. I never invited you. Colin, you are *not* living here, nor am I moving into your place."

"Tiffany, we're married and if we're to see if this will work, we need to be living together." He winked at her. "Think of the benefits of marriage."

She could think of a few, but that wasn't the point. "We can't just move in with each other. I'm not doing it." Tiffany was firm on that. She'd seen first-hand how difficult it had been for Molly to give up all her stuff and move in with Owen and their relationship was completely different. They were actually a couple. Tiffany and Colin, though legally bound, were anything but.

"That's fine. I'll just stay here. I just think we'd be more comfortable at my residence."

"You do what you want, but you're staying on the couch."

"You don't fancy sharing your bed yet?"

The sly smile on his handsome face along with his accent had Tiffany questioning her sanity. *How in the hell do I expect to survive living with this man?* "Colin, couch or no deal."

"Then the couch it is, love," he answered. "So, what would you like to do today as a happily married couple?"

"First off, we aren't a couple, married or otherwise."

"We kind of are, now." Colin sipped his coffee again. "We're married and I intend to make this work—or at the very least try."

"I understand that, but we need to lay down a few ground rules."

"Such as?"

"For starters, let's not act like we're a couple—married or anything like that."

"But we are."

"Why do you care so much about that, Colin? It's only a piece of paper."

He looked up toward the ceiling and answered, "I think it's a little more than that. We said vows in front of God."

"No, we said them in front of Elvis."

"That might be the case, but we professed our love and commitment to one another, to this marriage before God. So, in His eyes, we made a promise. And I keep my promises."

"You can't be serious? We were drunk. This is the result of far too much rum and poor decision-making. I think God can overlook our little lapse of judgment and forgive us."

"Tiffany, I take marriage very seriously."

"You got married in Vegas to someone you barely know. I don't think that says a lot about how much you value the sanctity of marriage," Tiffany argued.

Colin laughed. "Oh, Tiffany.

"What? It's true."

"Hardly, love."

"Care to elaborate?"

"No need to justify it to you. You'll come around soon enough."

"Really, how so?" Tiffany challenged.

"Because things happen for a reason. This has happened for a reason."

"Yeah, rum, remember?"

"Tiffany, I wasn't drinking."

Tiffany blinked hard at him. *What?* He had gone and married her *sober*, knowing full well that she was too intoxicated to make a sound decision?

"Wait. You're kidding me, right?"

He shook his head. "When I want something, I go after it. I wanted you."

"That doesn't make this okay—not by a long shot, pal.

This, in fact, is even far worse than I thought. How could you, Colin?"

"How could I what? Force you to marry me? That didn't take a lot, especially since it was your idea."

"There's no way I would suggest we get married."

"Well, you did and I went along with it. Because, honestly, it wasn't a bad one." There was no hint of a smile on his face. He was dead serious. "I don't regret a thing."

"So you're saying this was all my idea?"

He nodded in agreement. "Yes."

Note to self, no more rum…ever again.

* * * *

"Molly's on her way over. You just sit and breathe." Mackenzie handed her a bottle of water.

"How could it have been my idea?" Tiffany had told Mackenzie everything, that she'd been the one to suggest they get hitched with Elvis. Mackenzie agreed maybe '*no more rum ever again*' was a good idea. Or any adult beverages, for that matter.

"Well, when you're drunk you do come up with some crazy ones, so this is probably just another one of them. I can't believe he's actually at your place."

Tiffany had raced over to Mackenzie's house. She'd needed to escape her own apartment and have some space to think. Her world had imploded when Colin had told her that he'd been sober when they'd gotten married, and she needed to sort through the remaining pieces that still made sense. *Her friends.* They were her solid foundation and she needed them now more than ever.

Mackenzie was tossing a salad and wore a tired expression.

"What's going on with you?"

"Nothing. I just can't believe all this, you know? First, Molly gets hit with a fish, ends up engaged and pregnant. You come to be with me in Vegas, we blink and you're married to a millionaire and we're flying home on his private jet. Where does that leave me? Single and alone—and it just kind of sucks. Where's my awesome love story?"

"Oh, Mac, I'm sorry. Trust me. This isn't how I wanted this to be. This is a mistake, a complete disaster."

"Is it? I mean, do you or do not have feelings for Colin?" Mackenzie looked at her. They both knew the answer.

"But I don't know him, certainly not enough to be married to him. I'd love to date him. I mean, the man is gorgeous, is he not? But to have him want to play house and have him preach about the importance of wedding vows and shit? That is *not* what I had in mind."

"He's hot as hell. I'd be all over him. But let's consider that this man was sober when he married you. That speaks volumes. He wanted you. He saw an opportunity and seized it. I could kill him for doing it that way, yet at the same time, I don't blame him."

"Mac, it still doesn't make it a real wedding or marriage. I don't feel like a wife. We still haven't slept together."

"Maybe you need to fix that. It might change your perspective on this whole thing."

Before Tiffany could respond, she heard Mackenzie's door open.

Molly called out, "I'm here, girls."

Mackenzie looked at Tiffany and smiled. "It'll be okay. I promise." She patted Tiffany's jean-clad knee as she got up to greet Molly.

Would things be okay, or was Molly going to be royally pissed? Tiffany slouched in her chair and waited for her friends to return to the table.

"Hey, girl," Molly said as she bent and kissed Tiffany's cheek a few minutes later.

Tiffany put on a brave face. She was trying to figure out exactly how to tell Molly everything, every awful detail about the terrible mistake she'd made. Tiffany inhaled deeply and pretended she had nerves of steel as Molly listened.

Tiffany hung her head and waited as her friend digested

everything she'd just said.

"Tiff, okay. You need to try and explain this to me one more time—maybe a little slower. For some reason, I'm only hearing that you're *married*." Molly dropped her fork.

Mackenzie sat back and watched, obviously waiting for the moment that she would need to step in and rescue her, but that time had not yet come.

"I know. It sounds crazy, but it's true." Tiffany lifted her hand. The diamond twinkled under the kitchen lights.

"Mac, weren't you with her? I mean, this creep just fired her."

"He explained that whole mess. They asked for me and Jason to leave them be. I honestly thought they were going to go back to the hotel to finally get their lovin' on."

"Nope, nope, nope. This is *not* okay." Molly turned to Tiffany. "We can get this sorted. We can get an annulment or something. You don't worry. I will make some calls tomorrow morning."

"Moll, it's okay. Believe it or not, I was the one that made us get married."

"He was sober, you were drunk, so nope, I'm not buying that for a minute." Molly drove her fork into the salad and speared a mushroom.

"How are you feeling?" Tiffany asked cautiously. She was terrified at how strongly Molly was reacting. She watched her friend tear into the salad.

"How do you think?" Molly glared at Tiffany and Mackenzie. "You guys go to Vegas, and I hear nothing about this mess until now. I'm just shocked that Mac didn't get hitched, too. I mean, why not?" Molly shoved the lettuce into her mouth, chewing then swallowing. "I'm stuck here, trying to wrap my head around my own stupid wedding and this creature that is now growing inside me."

"I didn't mean for this to happen." Tiffany frowned. "I wanted the whole enchilada—the engagement party, the wedding shower, the bachelorette party, the amazing wedding. I did not want a Vegas wedding."

"Yeah, I get that. What about the fact that you don't even like Colin? Can we discuss that you are now married to a man you hate?"

"She doesn't hate him anymore," Mackenzie rebutted.

"Oh, really? Because when you went to Vegas to play with that bouncer, I was sitting with her and scarfing down ice cream because this jerk fired her."

"He didn't mean for it to go like that. He wanted to give her back to Patty. He actually wanted to start dating Tiffany and couldn't do it when she was still his assistant, but she ran out before he could fully explain everything."

"Seriously?" Molly turned to face Tiffany. "So, let me get this straight. He *wasn't* firing you?"

Tiffany shook her head. "Apparently not. Colin didn't want to work with me anymore because he wanted to date me. So, I guess I was getting promoted to possible girlfriend."

"But now you're promoted to *wife*? And you're okay with this?"

"I don't know what I am, to be honest."

Molly chewed on a carrot and looked at both of them. "You know, I didn't tell him where you were. So, I'll be having a little chat with Owen when I get home."

"Don't be mean to that man. He was just trying to help," Mackenzie stated.

"Well, a lot of good that did. Now, look at things."

"Things will turn out fine. I don't think this is such a bad thing, Molly," Mackenzie argued. "You're getting married to an amazing guy and are pregnant with his baby. Tiffany is married to a millionaire, who also happens to be Owen's best man. Life is serving it up pretty darn nicely to both of you. If anything, let's look at how things are for me. Let's see… That's right. I have no one."

"Oh, Mac, please don't feel like that," Tiffany begged. She watched Mackenzie wipe away tears.

"No, it's fine. This is how life goes. We get married, have kids and live happily ever after. I'm just waiting for my turn. I only hope I get one."

Molly sighed. "I'm sorry. You're right. Tiff, if you want to stay married, then you have my blessing or whatever. I'm here for you, no matter what. Mac, quit your shit. Someone will be crazy enough to marry you, the poor, lucky bastard. We got this."

"We're here for each other, because we're like sisters. We have each other's backs and we need one another." Tiffany sipped the iced tea in front of her to calm the emotions that were bubbling inside her.

"I couldn't imagine facing all this without you two by my side," Molly said as her eyes grew wet. She began to fan them in a feeble attempt at drying them. "These damn hormones."

"How did everything change so quickly?" Tiffany asked.

Mackenzie and Molly shook their heads. None of them had an answer because not one of them understood how so much could change in such little time. Just since spring, Mackenzie had tragically lost a sister, Molly had gotten engaged and preggers and Tiffany had gotten fired from her position and married to the CEO. Don't get her started on her love affair with Pauly. If this wasn't all the makings for some ugly-cry-romcom chickflick, she didn't know what was. Yet, this was now their lives.

Chapter Fifteen

"You're finally home. I was beginning to worry," Colin said as soon as Tiffany unlocked her apartment door and came inside.

She was surprised to see he was still there, especially stretched out on her couch. Tiffany huffed, but that was not nearly half as surprising as seeing Mr. Sprinkles laying on top of him.

"I think your kitty is rather fond of me." Colin stroked her cat.

Mr. Sprinkles barely allowed Tiffany to pet him. He never wanted to snuggle, and yet there he was, all cozy and purring loudly on Colin. She would probably be purring if she were on Colin, too. Tiffany covered her mouth as she giggled out loud.

"What was that about?"

"Nothing," Tiffany lied as she headed toward her kitchen.

"Did you eat yet?" Colin asked.

"Yeah, with Molly and Mackenzie." Tiffany returned to the living room after grabbing a bottled water. She handed one to Colin. "You got Owen in so much trouble."

"Me? For what?" Colin looked up at her in confusion.

"For asking him where I was."

"Is that what your friend told you? Clever girl, that Molly." Colin wore a grin.

Tiffany was confused now. She sat as Colin moved to make room for her. There were other areas to sit, but for some unknown reason, she wanted to be near him. Mr. Sprinkles wasn't too keen on her choice.

"So, wait. Who told you I was in Vegas?"

"Well, I was drowning my sorrows with my mate, Owen, and his lovely bride-to-be was quite happy to share the details of where you were."

No way Molly was in on it. There had to be a mistake. As angry as she had been this afternoon, there was no way she would be involved in any of this.

"Did you ask her?" Tiffany questioned him.

She watched as he gently stroked Mr. Sprinkles, who was sending icy daggers toward Tiffany.

"Well, I suppose I didn't have to. That's why I told you in Vegas that it was him. Owen did furnish that information, but he'd been fed it by Molly, in front of me. I don't want you to be upset with her or with Owen. I'm the one who asked where you were."

Okay, nothing made sense anymore.

"She seemed pretty unhappy about this marriage business."

"That's because you beat her to it," Colin said.

"Nah, she's wanting the exact opposite. She's a no-frills kinda girl, and getting her to even plan her wedding has been a nightmare. She and I have very ideas about weddings."

"And what exactly is it that you want, Tiffany?" Colin's voice grew rough and quiet. His eyes didn't blink as he stared at her.

Tiffany looked away. She noticed the bulldog was now watching them. Mr. Sprinkles hissed suddenly and Pauly charged in turbo speed toward the couch, causing the cat to leap off. Colin seized the opportunity of chaos and confusion and pulled Tiffany to his chest.

"Do you know?" he asked again, "because I do." Colin brought her lips to his. He was gentle at first, soft and tender. The wild explosion slammed into Tiffany as Colin wrapped his arms tighter around her.

What do I want? This? Because this feels very nice, but it isn't real. They hadn't earned this yet. They were miles away from this point by any relationship standards. As tempted as she was, Tiffany wasn't ready.

Tiffany reluctantly pulled away. "Colin, do you think maybe you should go home?" She felt flushed and was doing everything in her power to keep it together. Well, to keep from stripping them both naked and showing him exactly what she needed.

"I *am* home."

* * * *

This was technically not his home, yet over the next few days, Colin persisted that it was. He'd even brought over more of his belongings and her living room was beginning to fill up. Tiffany needed to put a stop to this.

"You can't keep bringing stuff here. There's no more room," Tiffany said on the third night that Colin stayed.

"Well, I suggested that my place was bigger."

"Then go there. Simple fix." Tiffany was standing over the stove and watched as Colin brought yet another giant suitcase into her living room.

"No can do. My wife is here."

"Why are you being so difficult?"

Colin walked into the kitchen and leaned against the counter. "I'm not being difficult. You are, and I do love a challenge."

This cat and mouse game was driving Tiffany crazy. Colin was nothing more than a patient wolf. He was waiting for her moment of weakness and she was doing everything to keep her resolve — like him standing there, doing nothing at all. Yet it made her body respond. *Why does he have to be sexy* all *the time?* He had gone to the office briefly, and his pale pink dress shirt was rolled up his forearms. His gray slacks hugged his ass, one that she'd been noticing more each day. Tiffany wasn't sure how much more of this she could take. He was doing this on purpose and was enjoying every little bit of it.

Colin began to remove his tie from his collar. It was like the start of a good strip tease and Tiffany had to keep her eyes trained on the food she was cooking. *Don't watch the hot guy removing his clothes in your kitchen*, Tiffany told herself. But her eyes had other plans as they caught him unbuttoning his shirt. *Lord, help me.* Tiffany began salivating and she was dying to touch his skin. She had no self-control. Tiffany inhaled deeply and attempted to channel her energy to the task in front of her.

"It smells good. What are you cooking?"

Tiffany was not prepared for Colin to be behind her, nor was she prepared for him to wrap his arms around her waist.

"I never thought I'd have a wife that could cook."

"You don't."

"No, I do. Just look at you."

"No, I mean, I can't cook. I pretty much survive on takeout and salads."

He roamed his hands down her sides then squeezed her ass with one hand while the other remained locked on her hip. "Whatever it is that you're cooking or eating is working. You're gorgeous," Colin whispered in her ear. "But I finally got you to admit you're my wife."

Tiffany's knees grew weak and her body was responding to him against her wishes. "It's only a technicality."

"It doesn't have to be," Colin said before his lips found the back of her exposed neck.

* * * *

Tiffany lay there. It was still dark. Her body was programmed to be up at this awful time after years of waking up early. Tiffany was cranky. Last night had been by far one of the most awful nights she'd ever experienced — tossing and turning, dreaming of Colin, mostly naked. It had ravaged her mind all night. While he slept soundly on the couch — she assumed he'd slept well, but she was hoping he'd suffered like she had. Tiffany was being tortured by her body. It wanted Colin, badly. He knew it and she knew it. Hell, Sir McCartney even knew it, which is probably why he was guarding her bedroom door. Tiffany found herself fully aroused, angry at her body's betrayal but horny as hell. She laid her palm on her belly and her body responded. Tiffany's core heated up as she slipped her hand below the waist band of her pajama pants. Tiffany cupped her mound, giving it a hard squeeze. She closed her eyes and tried to imagine Colin was between her legs. Tiffany used her finger to slowly tease the soft and silky folds of her pussy. She hissed as her finger grazed her swollen clit. She was wet—dripping wet, in fact, and throbbing with need. Tiffany inserted a finger, then another inside her. *It feels so good, but it would be even better if it was Colin's tongue.* She'd mastered the fine art of getting herself off years ago and knew what strokes to use. Her imagination worked overtime, conjuring up images of Colin and all the things he would do to her. Tiffany grew needy and her pussy wanted to be filled. This was just supposed to be quick relief, but it was becoming a feverish task. She was getting close to climaxing when she thought she heard something. *Fuck.* She stayed frozen, her fingers deep inside her as Tiffany listened again. Nothing. But now it was ruined. She was too paranoid to finish and she blew out a frustrated breath.

Tiffany swung her legs over her bed and sat for a moment in a sleepy and horny daze. *Why am I even getting up?* It's not like she had her old job back. Maybe she should go for a run or grocery shopping, not that she could afford food since she was unemployed. Perhaps it was time to start the job hunt. Nothing more had been said about her going back to Patty, so that obviously wasn't happening. Tiffany scooched off her bed and opened her door quietly. A snoring bulldog was still standing guard and Tiffany stepped carefully over him. Her heart squeezed. He was the sweetest thing. She should take him for a walk later.

Part of her morning routine was to shower then have coffee. Not wanting to stray from that, she shuffled into her bathroom. Sleep deprived and not thinking, Tiffany opened the shower curtain and there was Colin in all his masculine glory. Tiffany blinked and her brain took snapshots to save later for her lady spank-bank. Lots of toned muscle and suds.

How did I not hear the running water? Maybe that was the noise I heard when I was trying to get off?

"Oh God, I'm so sorry," Tiffany flipped the curtain back.

"Top o' the mornin' to you." She could hear the amusement in his voice. "Care to join me?"

"When *are* you going home?" Tiffany complained as she sat on the toilet.

"I'm not — at least not until you come with me."

"I'm not going anywhere."

"Well, after I come home from the office, we're going out."

"You know you're not my boss anymore, right?"

He laughed. "Good point, but I'm your husband." Colin began to sing.

"Whatever." Tiffany was not in the mood to begin with the whole marriage battle.

She finished peeing and flushed. When Colin let out a yelp, an evil smile played across her lips.

Serves him right.

* * * *

"Tiffany."

She fluttered opened her eyes. She could have sworn she'd heard her name. Something heavy was pinning her legs down and she began to panic.

"Tiffany." It was Colin. He was standing over her. She looked at her legs and saw that Pauly had decided they would make a good place to nap.

She was a little disoriented. Tiffany had tried to occupy herself. She'd gone for a walk with the new love of her life, which would explain why he was now in a coma. She'd searched online for work and had even put a few feelers out there. Tiffany had cleaned every room until it sparkled, washed her linens then sat on the couch completely bored. Her eyes had grown heavy. The snores coming from her little chunky man had lulled her to sleep. "What time is it?"

"A little after seven. I just got home." Colin kissed her on the top of her head. "I'm sorry I'm late. I tried texting you."

"No, your home is across town. This is *my* home," Tiffany argued as she yawned and tried to stretch. The bulldog huffed when she removed her legs from under him.

"Tiffany, let's not do this, okay? We're going out," Colin ordered as he began to turn on a light in the living room then he started to undress. Did this man have any modesty?

"Do you mind?" Tiffany asked.

"Mind what?"

"Not undressing here."

"Babe, you're in my room. You're even on my bed," he pointed out.

"It's *my* couch."

"Hey, we made a deal. I offered to sleep in your bed." Colin winked at her as he delivered that sexy grin that always made her melt into a big puddle of no self-control.

"Ugh, I can't stand you." Tiffany got off the couch and stomped off to her bedroom.

"No, I think you are starting to like me. But not nearly as much as I like you," he called after her.

She smiled as leaned up against her closed bedroom door. Tiffany was starting to like him a lot, but she wasn't quite ready to admit that.

* * * *

Tiffany found herself laughing, not pretty, little lady giggles. No, this was side-hurting, snorting and hard laughing. She was having a really good time with Colin, so much that she was starting to question why she was even fighting this whole marriage thing. This guy was funny, smart and sexy. *What the hell is my problem?*

"So, I spoke with Owen and he invited us over to their place for dinner tomorrow," Colin said as he took another slice of pizza.

She never would have guessed that he loved pizza. When he'd said they were going out, she'd expected some ridiculous place, annoyingly fancy, but no. Instead, he took her to this little hole-in-the-wall pizzeria. It was the best pizza she had ever eaten.

Tiffany put her slice down. Molly hadn't mentioned anything about getting together, but then again, Owen and Colin were buddies and probably had come up with this plan on their own. It dawned on Tiffany that tomorrow was *Friendship Friday*. They had missed the last one and she needed some serious girl time.

"Tomorrow is Friday, right?"

Colin nodded. "Owen was thinking we could maybe play cards or some board games. He got some steaks and thought it would be fun to double date."

"That's lovely of him to offer, but tomorrow is Friday. We girls have plans. Sorry."

"But your friend will be there. I'm sure she's aware you have plans."

"Yes, we get together every Friday and it's like this grown-up sleepover. It's the best, and since I missed last week, for obvious reasons. I'm not missing this one," Tiffany carefully explained.

"Well, you might want to tell Molly that. I spoke with her this afternoon and she said we could bring dessert."

"What about Mac? I need to call Molly and straighten this out."

"I thought you guys had spoken already. I'm sorry." Colin looked down at his pizza.

Tiffany hadn't meant to make him feel rejected. They had just been laughing and getting along so well only moments ago. She extended the olive branch and reached for his hand. "I'm sorry. I didn't mean to act like that. I will call her later and get it all sorted."

"I thought it was quite lovely of her to invite us. I'm so grateful that your friends have been so kind to me."

"It's funny. You are nothing that I expected you to be."

"And what did you expect?"

"I'm not sure."

When Tiffany had first kissed this Irishman, she hadn't known what she was doing. When she'd woken up in his bed—not once, but twice—Tiffany'd had no clue what she was doing. And now, as Tiffany rose from her side of the booth to reach across the table to kiss him, she didn't know what she was doing. *When am I going to finally figure this out?*

* * * *

Colin had already left for work and Tiffany needed to talk to Molly. After taking Pauly out for a little walk to do his business, she'd made her coffee and called Molly. They'd been chatting when she'd decided to bring up the topic of going over there.

"Molly, I was just surprised that we weren't going to do *Friendship Friday*?" Tiffany asked.

"I know, but I invited Mac over here, too. Owen has another buddy he wants to introduce to her."

"Gosh, he's just the little matchmaker, isn't he?" Tiffany laughed and took another sip of her coffee. "Can we bring Pauly?" The bulldog perked up at the sound of his name. "Yes, I'm talking about you," Tiffany cooed to Pauly.

"Huh?" Molly said.

"Not you, sorry. I was talking to Pauly. Do you mind if we bring him? I don't trust him and Mr. Sprinkles together."

"Look who's the maternal one. Of course you can bring that furry ball of meaty cuteness."

"Well, he's grown on me." Tiffany looked over at him and she sighed.

"What about Colin? He growing on you yet?" Molly teased.

"Last night was great. We laughed so much. But it's like I'm in this weird limbo. I'm fighting a war that I have a feeling I won't win. Then, when I really think about it, I wonder why I'm even fighting it?"

"Because you're stubborn and because this didn't go your way," Molly answered.

"I guess." Tiffany sipped her coffee, relishing the dark flavor — it was rich and almost spicy. "I like Colin. Do I love him? I don't know."

"You kind of need to figure that out, especially if you're going to stay married to him."

Molly had a valid point. How much longer could they keep this up? They'd been married now for a week.

"So how are you feeling, Ms. Mama-to-be?" Tiffany didn't want to think any more about herself. It made her brain hurt.

"Like there's a raging sea in my belly half the time. I always feel like I'm going to be sick."

"I'm sorry. Hopefully that will get better soon." Tiffany felt awful for her and had heard that eventually morning sickness did subside. "So anymore thoughts on the wedding?"

Molly laughed. "Owen teased that we should just go to Vegas."

"God, no. Please have it in Hawaii or somewhere wonderful. No fat Elvis," Tiffany begged.

"I'm almost wanting to wait until after I have this baby."

"What? No way!"

"I mean, why rush it?" Molly said.

"Are you having doubts or is this about shopping for a dress?" Tiffany joked.

"Both. Just kidding, it's more about the dress, the ceremony — the whole thing, really."

"That's why you should just have a simple ceremony with your closest friends — so, me and Mac, then we just vacation in Hawaii."

"I'm not completely ruling out that idea. But now with

143

me being pregnant, I feel like I can't do anything. No bachelorette party or anything fun."

"Why, because you can't drink? We don't need drinks to enjoy strippers," Tiffany joked.

"Yeah, we kind of do. Otherwise, it's just plain sad. It helps being drunk when they are grinding on you," Molly explained.

"Who says we have to have strippers?"

"True. Oh, Tiff, it's like everything is moving too fast. I didn't think we'd be pregnant for a couple years, if at all," Molly admitted as she broke down.

"At least you're having sex. I'm the only married one, and I haven't even slept with my husband yet." *Husband.* She hadn't even said it out loud until then. The word felt foreign, but it had a nice ring to it.

"Well, Mrs. Murphy, maybe instead of coming over here, you should stay home and show your husband a good time," Molly suggested.

Tiffany thought about that for a minute. *How shocked would Colin be? Maybe it* is *time.*

"Hey, I gotta go," Molly said.

"You okay?"

"Yeah, just gotta go puke. Bye." Molly hung up.

Being a wife, that was something that Tiffany could probably do. Motherhood? Now that could wait a while.

Chapter Sixteen

What am I doing? Tiffany stared at the candles that were lit. The shadows from the flames danced on the walls. She had taken the rest of the day to primp and prepare. That meant shaving, plucking—lots and lots of hair removal. Tiffany went as far as painting her nails a fire-engine red. She'd wanted something sexy. *What's more sexy than red?* Tiffany had gone shopping earlier, buying wine, fruit and lingerie. She'd gone all out for tonight and now she was having second thoughts.

Pauly was watching her carefully.

"It's stupid, isn't it?" she asked him.

He lifted his eyes.

"This feels dumb. Am I right?"

She looked at his squishy face and plopped on the floor next to him. He moved close to her, raised his paw and patted her thigh. It was as though Pauly understood and was comforting her. She rubbed his ears. They were like little fat pads of velvet.

"Do I love your dad? I'm not sure. I really like him, though." Tiffany continued to explain and Pauly leaned against her. It was as though he couldn't get close enough to her. "Don't worry. I love you more."

"Really?"

Tiffany looked up and saw Colin standing in front of them. It was dark. The only light was from the candles she'd lit. How did she not hear him enter the apartment? Should she add ninja skills to his growing list of qualities?

"Colin, I didn't hear you come in."

"Why's it so dark in here? What's with all the candles?

Planning a séance?" Colin joked.

Tiffany laughed. "No. This is my crummy attempt at trying to be romantic. Even Pauly agrees I'm awful at it."

"Well, he's wrong then." Colin joined her on the floor. He held a flower, just a single red rose. "Happy one-week anniversary."

"It's been a week already?" she said, even though she knew it.

He nodded. Feeling nervous and embarrassed, Tiffany suggested, "We should probably get ready to go to Molly's."

"No need. Owen already called and canceled. Molly isn't feeling too great, poor girl."

No, Molly may have had a bout a morning sickness, but Tiffany knew exactly why her friend had canceled. She wanted Tiffany to get her groove on. *Bless her heart.*

"Pauly been a good boy for you?" Colin asked as he gave some attention to the bulldog. He was trying to crawl on Colin but stayed close to Tiffany.

"He's always good. We even went for a walk again, didn't we?"

"Please be careful. It makes me nervous with you and him going out there alone."

"Oh, Colin, it's fine. He protects me."

Colin gave her smirk.

"Okay, so I'm protecting him while I drag him along for some exercise."

"He's worth a great deal of money, you know."

"Trust me. I'm super careful with him."

"No. I know you aren't putting him in harm's way. I meant, someone might try to steal him from you. I don't want either of you to get hurt. I don't want any harm to come your way, ever."

"Oh." The way Colin had said it, the protectiveness behind his words, it was all male.

Colin traced Tiffany's exposed collarbone with the soft rose, then quickly replaced it with his lips. "You are too precious to me."

Tiffany moaned as Colin started to kiss her neck, while he began to slowly maneuver his hands over her body. It had been her intent to seduce him, not the other way around.

He moved a hand up her bare thigh and he nipped at her ear. "Please tell me you want this as much as I do," Colin whispered.

Tiffany responded in the only way her body would allow. She grabbed him hard and brought him to her mouth. Tiffany needed Colin now. She was tired of playing games and she wanted this man. Tiffany was intent on having him, all of him. Colin wasn't the only one that went after something that he wanted. Tiffany planned to prove to him just how much she wanted this – hell, needed this.

"Bedroom, now," Tiffany ordered. She popped up from the floor and raced into her room. Colin was up in an instant. The confusion on his face was priceless, but the lust in his eyes told Tiffany that he was willing to push any questions aside for now.

Tiffany shoved Colin onto the bed but the plump bulldog tried to climb up. "Down, Pauly," Tiffany scolded him. Usually he ignored her and did what he wanted, but there must have been something animalistic in her voice because he quickly left the room.

She already knew what Colin looked like naked, thanks to the sneak peek she'd gotten when he was in the shower, but Tiffany had never touched him. All the days of teasing, the pent-up need…it was begging to be released.

Tiffany tugged his shirt out of his pants and wrestled with the stubborn belt. Colin cupped her hands and quickly undid his pants. His semi-hard cock sprang out. Tiffany moaned. She'd been imagining it for quite some time now and there it was. Without hesitating, Tiffany took the velvety head past her lips. She swirled her tongue over the tip and could taste a sweet and salty blend as fluid beaded out from Colin. She opened her mouth wider to take more of him and Colin groaned at the pleasure-filled torture she was inflicting on him.

"Baby," Colin said in ragged breaths.

Tiffany stared up at him and watched him smile as she sucked gently. She savored the feel of his rigid member inside her mouth. Colin weaved his fingers through her hair as he urged her head farther down on him.

She gripped his erection and worked her mouth up and down in a beautiful rhythm that had Colin moaning and whispering naughty curses. She almost came just from hearing the words in his accent. Tiffany had sought her wet cunt with her fingers but they were providing little relief.

Suddenly Colin removed Tiffany from him and, in a single motion, put her on her back. With one hand he reached up to her wrists and pinned them to the mattress.

"You sexy little minx," Colin breathed into Tiffany's ear. He flicked his tongue against her skin.

Colin looked down at her and ran his hand down and across her pussy. He dove his fingers into her and Tiffany let out a gasp. She wiggled under his touch then wrapped her legs around his waist to try to pull him closer to her. The sensation of being lightly restrained with his hands holding her wrists was turning her on far more than she'd realized.

"I need you," Tiffany pleaded as she rode his hand.

In a frantic whirlwind, he released her and they both shed whatever clothes remained. Then they became a tangled net of limbs. Colin greedily kissed, licked and sucked every inch of skin he could reach. Tiffany was breathless as a raging heat grew in her center. A frenzy of passion exploded between them as they wrestled for control. Tiffany was determined to win the battle. She rolled Colin over onto his back.

Tiffany splayed her hands across his chest as she straddled him. He looked up at her with lust in his eyes. It was surreal seeing him under her. His skin was warm to the touch and she didn't need to imagine what he tasted like anymore. She'd sampled him. She'd had his cock deep in her throat. Tiffany had taken her time, brought him close to the edge then pulled him back. He had begged for mercy. And, with the combined effort of her hand and mouth, she'd brought him to an orgasm. Tiffany had swallowed every sweet 'n' salty bit of it. Now it was her turn.

Their hasty lust was turning into gentle caresses and deep exploration. Then Tiffany could wait no longer. She raised up, gripped Colin's stiff cock and lowered herself onto it. She was filled in a way she'd never experienced before and her need to come took her breath away. Tiffany gripped the headboard of the bed and Colin anchored her to him, holding her hips. She began to rock, finding the angle that worked her most sensitive areas. They moved in rhythm, as though they'd had years of practice. It was as though Colin knew what she needed, arching his hips and meeting her with a growing intensity when she began to lift off him then plunge back down.

Tiffany had known that when they finally did make love, it was going to be incredible and it was. Earth-shattering and soul-melting was not what she'd expected, but that is exactly what this was turning out to be. It was more than screwing. She knew the difference. There had been plenty of that in her past. This was what it felt like to fuse yourself to someone else – someone you loved.

Then the heat within her reached its peak and she tensed, waves of bliss rolling through her. Colin groaned and arched, gripping her hips and pulsing his cum deep inside her. *Nothing like this…ever before…*

Tiffany remained on top of him after they had both come together. She leaned over, resting on his chest, every muscle in her body limp. The candlelight flickered, creating a romantic glow in the otherwise-dark room. The apartment was quiet and she felt again like they were the only two people in the entire world. Tiffany could feel Colin's heart pounding hard but his hands stayed on her, as though he feared what would happen if they broke apart.

"So, you want to stay married?" Colin asked in a ragged breath.

"I think I need a few more samples before I decide for

sure." Tiffany raised her head and kissed him.

"I think we can arrange that." Colin held on to her as she tried to move off him.

"Let me go." Tiffany laughed, suddenly self-conscious and covering her breasts. The euphoric haze was wearing off and being completely naked was becoming a reality. Tiffany wanted to hide under the comforter, to shield her body from Colin's gaze. "Come on, Colin."

"Nope, not doing it."

"Why?"

"Do you know how long I have wanted this? That first night when you kissed me, I wanted you then. I can't explain the connection I feel with you, but I can say with all honesty that I have never in my life felt anything like this." Colin kissed her again. "Woman, you have ruined me."

* * * *

"Married life agrees with you." Molly smiled at Tiffany. "She's glowing, isn't she?" Molly asked Mackenzie.

They were seated at a small table the next day, sharing a late afternoon latte.

"I have to admit that I wish I would have slept with him sooner," Tiffany said. "Last night was incredible."

It was all she could think about. If she'd thought their first go-around was spectacular, that had been nothing compared to the loving that had continued all night. Colin had lavished her body with more attention than she'd ever experienced with a lover. It was as though he were trying to prove something or maybe make up for lost time. Either way, her husband was quite talented and Tiffany was pleasantly sore today.

"So how are you feeling, Mama?" Tiffany looked at Molly.

"Fine." Molly smiled. "Look, I knew you and Colin needed to sort out that whole *consummating* the marriage business. You did and now normal life can resume."

Mackenzie laughed. "Normal life? That ship has sailed,

ladies."

"Gosh, isn't that the truth," Tiffany agreed.

"I hate to rain on your parade, but have you guys discussed like work and stuff?" Mackenzie asked.

"I doubt she'll go back to work," Molly added. "She's a kept woman now." She winked at Tiffany.

"We haven't discussed it, but we need to. I have been going a little stir-crazy from not doing anything and also not knowing what to do about money. I need to work."

"I get that," Mackenzie agreed. "And it's smart to not rely on him. We don't know how this will all pan out. What if you guys don't make it? You definitely need a backup plan."

"Things are going to be fine," Molly argued. "But you do need to address some of these concerns with him."

"You guys are right, but I think I'd feel better knowing I have a job. Even if everything turns out great, I can't just stay home all day. I need to be doing something."

"It's good to know that all those millions haven't changed you." Mackenzie lifted her latte.

"Here's to our rich bitch," Molly added.

Tiffany shook her head and refused to toast with them. "I'm not a gold digger. That money is *not* mine."

"Oh, babe, we know that. We're just teasing," Mackenzie said soothingly. "Molly is really the rich bitch out of all of us. She made her money. I'm broke because I decided to shape the young minds of our future. You peddle coffee, which is basically like being a drug dealer without all the glamour."

"Good grief." Molly was giggling hard, which became contagious and they all broke out into hysterical laughter.

"Mac, you seriously have been on vacation for a little too long. When does school start back?"

"Next month. I'm ready. I hate being off this long. If I had some hot fisherman or sexy Irish CEO, maybe I wouldn't mind so much."

"We need to find her a man," Molly joked.

"I agree. Maybe we should look into speed dating. Or what's that app they have now?"

"Okay, you two, that's enough. True love will find me. It's taking its sweet-ass time, but it'll show up eventually."

They nodded. She was right. It would, but if anyone deserved to find love, it was Mac. Or, at the very least, she needed to get laid.

* * * *

Tiffany's bed squeaked as Colin gripped the headboard and moved in a steady rhythm. If he wasn't careful, he was going to break it, but it would totally be worth it. She'd read somewhere that it was better for a man to break your headboard than your heart.

They were working together to climb that peak so they could find release together again. Colin had already brought her there twice, but he wanted her to join him when he finally came. Tiffany was panting as the sensations intensified and her orgasm fired. Colin grew rigid as he buried himself deeply inside her. Tiffany's pussy squeezed Colin's cock, milking him as they came together. Their bodies were sweaty and sensitive. Tiffany closed her eyes. *Damn, he's good.* This was beyond some of the best sex she'd ever experienced.

"You still needing more convincing?" Colin asked as he rolled over.

"Convincing for what?" Tiffany was in a post-orgasmic daze and words were difficult to manage.

"About staying married." Colin turned on his side to face her. He stroked her skin.

"I may still need some more test runs on this," Tiffany teased as her hand traveled over his well-defined abs.

Colin laughed. "You can test drive it as much you'd like." Then Colin's face turned serious. "Tiffany, we do need to talk. We can't keep dancing around it."

"I know. I was telling the girls today that I need to have

some purpose. I need to find a job or something."

"A job? Oh, don't be silly. You don't need to work," Colin said.

"I do too need to work. I have no money coming in."

"You don't need to worry about anything like that again, Tiffany. I will always care for you and you'll never want for anything." Colin kissed her on top of her head and she recoiled.

"I don't want to be taken care of. Colin, I want to work, especially if this whole sham of a marriage crumbles. I need to be able to support myself."

"That's my job as your husband. You have your role as my wife. There will be duties that need to be fulfilled." A playful sinister smile crossed his lips as he kissed her again.

"Duties?" Tiffany raised her eyebrows at him.

"Just some work-related duties."

Tiffany was a tad disappointed, then quickly worried what he meant by *work*. Without hesitating, she snapped, "What the hell does *that* mean?"

"It's not as bad as it sounds. For example, I have a few functions in the coming weeks that we need to attend and I'd like you to be by my side," Colin explained.

"I'm not going to live out my days as some trophy wife, Colin. I want to have purpose and do something with myself."

"And being an assistant was doing *something* with your life?"

The arrogance in his tone disgusted her. "I think you need to leave." She wasn't about to be insulted in her own home—heck, in her own bed.

"You can't be serious?"

"Colin, I am. You should go."

"No, I won't, because that isn't how marriage works." Colin sat up, propping himself on the pillows. "So, we don't agree on something—too bad. There will be more of that to come. Trust me, love. You don't have the right to ask me to leave."

"Why not? This is *my* home," Tiffany countered.

"Because you refuse to move into mine. I'm willing to sell it and be here with you if that's what it takes. I'll have you know that you aren't getting rid of me so easily."

Tiffany wanted to scream, but instead, tears pushed their way through. Colin used his thumb to brush them away.

"I don't mean to upset you. If you want to work, then fine, but you don't have to. I do need you to be by my side for certain events and not because I look at you as some kind of prize or trophy. You are worth so much more than that. But I need you there because we are in this together. We are partners now. A team."

Tiffany's anger dissipated. The man had a way with words. He knew how to sell something and he'd just sold her on the idea of their marriage—a partnership.

"Then I want to stay on as your assistant. I have ideas and would love to help this company grow."

"You can't be my assistant."

"Wow, so that whole team thing was just some bullshit line?"

"No, you would be my partner, Tiffany. Equals."

"Oh." She felt like an idiot. Tiffany really needed to think before she spoke. She was getting tired of putting her foot in her mouth.

Colin cupped her cheek and pulled her to him. "I know you won't say it yet, but, Tiffany, I think I love you." He kissed her and Tiffany let herself melt against him.

* * * *

"Okay, so we're doing this…like next weekend," Molly announced in her studio the following day.

Mackenzie and Tiffany exchanged surprised looks.

"Are you sure?" Tiffany asked.

"Yes. Owen and I talked it over. I need to quit putting it off. Hawaii, it is."

"But that leaves us with no time to throw a shower or

anything," Tiffany complained.

"Moll, let's take a breath here, okay?" Mackenzie added.

"Nope, this is the plan. We want you guys there and we plan on having a party for everyone when we get back," Molly stated firmly. "I don't want the fuss, just Owen."

"But the fuss is what makes it so fun." Tiffany laughed. "You are robbing us both. You know that, right?"

"I'll let you guys be in charge of my baby shower."

Tiffany glanced over at Mackenzie. "That works."

"Eek, this is so exciting," Mackenzie squealed. "So, when do we leave and have you guys decided where at in Hawaii?"

"Well, we have made some arrangements. Colin offered his jet for us all to fly out."

"He already knows about this?" Tiffany asked.

"Owen called him this morning and he instantly offered the plane. He's Owen's best man, after all."

"That's really cool of him to do." Mackenzie patted Tiffany. "Must be nice to have a hubby with a private jet. Comes in handy."

Tiffany glared at her.

"We have a lot to do in a short window. But we got this," Molly said.

"Tiff, looks like you'll have a honeymoon after all." Mackenzie winked.

Tiffany rolled her eyes. Then again, Mackenzie was right. Long moonlit walks on the beach, afternoon delights in their swanky hotel room... *Yeah, I can work with that.*

* * * *

Tiffany was typing away, something she hadn't done in weeks, maybe even months. She felt like an open vessel as creativity flowed through her. Tiffany had a jumbo mug of coffee next to her. It was her second cup. The caffeine overdose she was about to experience could have something to do with the rapid typing of words for her new blog. *Or could it be that life was good? Really good.* What a difference a week and lots of hot sex with your husband could make. Tiffany still got the butterflies when that word entered her brain or escaped her lips. There were proving to be more benefits to this marriage than she'd realized. One, getting to hear Colin's voice day in and day out was one of her favorite things. Seeing him get ready for work was basically suit-porn. It sometimes led to Colin being attacked before he was set to leave for the office, not that he ever complained. It was good for your husband to be the CEO. Then there was the regular stuff — eating and just hanging out with Colin and Pauly. They were becoming this little family. All of it combined had spurred a fantastic idea for a new blog. Tiffany was excited to chart her life as a newlywed for the whole cyber world to see.

Her fingers continued to dance on the keys of her laptop as Pauly snored loudly under her feet. He was another huge part of her blog and she decided to title it *Bulldogs & Handbags, The Barely Married Seattleite.* It was there that she'd posted some adorable snapshots of Pauly in his many napping poses. She discovered that Pauly actually adored the camera. Granted, Tiffany did bribe him with treats and used whatever means necessary to capture a cute picture. The blog wasn't just about her precious Pauly, but Tiffany was also able to channel her fashionista spirit. She was loving every minute of it. Okay, truth be told, she'd barely started the blog a few days before, but it was already getting some attention. Tiffany could kick herself for waiting so long to finally do it, but maybe the timing hadn't been right and now Tiffany's creative juices were flowing. She had Colin to thank for that.

Tiffany was deep in thought, stringing sentences together lightning fast, when her cell phone chirped.

Debating whether or not to send it to voicemail, she decided to answer it.

"Hello?"

"Good afternoon, my lovely wifey," Colin playfully

responded.

She smiled and felt her heart tug a little. Tiffany was quickly falling head over heels in love with Colin. She just worried that it was just this wedded bliss or the newness of their romance — the honeymoon phase. *Will I still feel like this in a week, a month? How long before these feelings go away?*

"So, what do you want?" Tiffany was still partially distracted by the blinking cursor on her screen. It was willing her to type more, and she was eager to oblige.

"Nothing, just wanted to see how you and my boys were doing."

"Boys? You mean Pauly."

Colin laughed. "No, Mr. Sprinkles too. He adores me."

"God, he does. I have tried for years to get him to be sweet, but he just warmed right up to you," Tiffany said as she started to secretly type, hoping Colin didn't hear her. She hadn't told him about her new blog or even that writing was a quiet passion of hers.

"What are you doing right now?" Colin asked.

Crap. Could he tell that she was distracted, or had he heard her working the keys on her laptop?

"Um, nothing. Why?"

"I was thinking we could have lunch."

"Oh, okay. Where?" Tiffany watched as the words magically appeared on the screen. They were her words and she was creating that magic.

"Home. In bed."

Tiffany conceived an idea for another article and made a side note as she answered Colin, "Sure, sounds lovely. What time do you want me to meet you there?"

"Wow, that was easy. How about in thirty minutes?" Colin shot back.

"Huh? Where are we going again?" Tiffany was confused.

"You aren't even listening, are you?" Colin accused her. "What *are* you doing?"

"Sorry, I was just reading something. You have my full attention now. So, what is happening?" Tiffany tried to stay focused and the only way she was able to manage that was to close her laptop. *Out of sight, out of mind – for the time being, anyway.*

"I'm headed home for lunch and *you* are supposed to be my lunch," Colin explained again.

"Oh. Does this fall under those wifely duties you told me about?" Tiffany teased.

"You could say that. I'll be home soon. Love ya." Colin hung up.

Tiffany laughed.

This will make a great post on my blog.

* * * *

"So, Tiff, how's married life treating you?"

"It's been less than two weeks, but it's actually going really well," Tiffany answered happily.

It was going amazingly. Her blog was doing well, Colin had asked for Tiffany to join him in one of the board meetings later that week and lots of incredible sex was happening – all the time and everywhere.

Mackenzie and Molly nodded. "That's great. He's a good guy, Tiff. I really hope he makes you happy."

Today was gorgeous, a little warm, but a perfect day overall to sit at the waterfront with her besties and catch up. Late afternoon lattes were a long-honored tradition and Tiffany was never one to give up an opportunity to partake in a little caffeine refreshment.

"He does, and we finally discussed all that work stuff." Tiffany sipped her iced latte.

"Good. How did that go?" Mackenzie asked, swirling the bright pink straw in her large plastic cup.

Tiffany grinned. "He made me partner in the company."

They both stared back at her. The shock on their faces was cemented for some time.

Screw Botox, just tell your friends that you are a partner in a multi-million coffee corporation.

"Are you kidding me?" Molly asked. "That's insane. I mean good crazy, but damn."

"I know. Colin wants us to be equals. At first, he didn't want me to work, but Colin knows it's important for me. I offered to come back as his assistant and he said no. I was pissed, but then he told me why."

"Wow, Colin is really putting a lot of faith in this marriage. No prenuptial agreements and just handing over half of it to you. Wow, that says a lot," Mackenzie pointed out.

"It's wild, but I won't let him down. I want to make Blue Moose Coffee a success. I have always had ideas, just no one to hear them."

"Tiff, this is huge. Do you think it's going to hurt your marriage, though?" Molly asked.

"It shouldn't. He wants us to be a united front, a team."

"Have I mentioned how much being pregnant sucks? I hate decaf," Molly complained as she sipped on her coffee. "So, how much longer until you guys move into his place?" Molly asked. "I know you have really been fighting that."

"I don't want to move."

"Tiffany, come on. That's not fair to him. He's giving you a whole lot," Mackenzie reasoned.

Tiffany rolled her eyes. Did her friends not think she was willing to work hard and that she wasn't putting in her fair share? It gave her a lot to think about. Tiffany needed to reflect on everything. *Maybe I'm not being fair to Colin*.

* * * *

"What is that bloody thing?" Colin turned up his nose, but his eyes were curious as he went to touch it.

"He's awesome, isn't he?" The Fremont Troll stared at them in all his concrete glory. Pauly growled and wasn't so sure he liked this giant sculpture.

Tiffany had taken Colin on a walk and they had planned to stop for ice cream. There was one place she needed to show him in their neighborhood. He was confused when she had led them to where the troll lived.

"He's fantastic. A bit ugly, but quite incredible." Colin was intrigued as he examined the cool stone.

After taking more than enough selfies with the troll, Colin and Tiffany enjoyed some gourmet ice cream from a small shop. The cool, milky treat provided some relief in the wicked heatwave they were experiencing again. Seattle was being cooked but not for much longer. September was right around the corner.

"You live in a very unique neighborhood, Tiffany," Colin said as he spooned ice cream into his mouth.

"Thanks. I love it here."

"Yes, I know that, but can we seriously start considering where we'll live?"

"Not this again," Tiffany whined.

"Yes, this again. What happens when we want children? Your apartment is a one-bedroom."

"They can have your old room," Tiffany teased. Colin had been upgraded from her living room to her bedroom.

"You cheeky girl."

Tiffany swallowed more ice cream and let herself imagine living with Colin — not in her little space, but in his domain. *What if things change?* Unlike Molly, she planned on keeping her apartment for a while, just to make sure she could deal with moving into Colin's place. She knew how hard it had been Molly. Tiffany also felt like she had the upper hand when it came to their living arrangements and wasn't sure she was ready to give that up quite yet. But Colin stared at her with those loving eyes and that sexy smile. She melted.

"Fine. I'm in." Tiffany waved the imaginary white flag.

Colin cocked his head to the side. "All in?"

"Yep. Let's do this."

"You mean it?"

"If this is what you want, then yes." Tiffany smiled at him.

She watched the happiness explode over his face. They were doing well, really starting to get this whole marriage thing figured out, and this was a small sacrifice on her part. She couldn't dismiss the nagging sensation, that dirty feeling of impending doom—or the worry that this might not be exactly what she wanted and that it could very well change everything. Tiffany prayed she was wrong.

Chapter Seventeen

"Molly, you need to try on something," Tiffany pleaded. "Don't be so difficult."

"Here. Try this," Mackenzie ordered. "Tiff is right. Quit being a pain. We leave in like two days and you have no dress for the ceremony."

"I thought that white swimsuit you forced me to buy at the last store was what I could wear."

Tiffany looked over at Mackenzie and they both rolled their eyes. Molly was not making this last-minute shopping excursion easy, not by a long shot. They were all leaving for Hawaii in a few days. Tiffany blamed it on the wedding-day jitters, Molly had been crabby all day, which did not make for a fun one. Their patience was threadbare and their nerves frayed from tolerating her moodiness as they searched high and low for proper wedding attire.

"Are you serious about us all wearing bikinis to the ceremony?" Tiffany asked.

"I think something simple, like this, is worth looking at." Mackenzie held up an ultra-feminine off-white dress. "I thought the whole bathing suit thing was a joke."

"Why do we even have to do this?" Molly complained.

"Because you said 'yes'. This day is meant to be special, Molly — not just for you, but also for Owen. Show a little more enthusiasm, please."

"This coming from the woman that got married in a drive-thru?"

"If I could do it all over again, I would." Tiffany stared hard at Molly. She'd had enough of her attitude.

"Would you?" Molly asked.

"She's happy, even though it wasn't how she would have done it," Mackenzie added.

"It's been an interesting week, but yes, overall I'm happy. I just would have loved to have planned a wedding and done all the fun stuff that goes with it."

"When *are* you going to tell your family?"

Tiffany sighed. She hadn't even breathed a word to them about her nuptials, dating life, unemployment, nothing. Tiffany wasn't nearly as close with her family as she'd like to be, but they did deserve to know she was married.

"I'll tell them soon. Let's give it some more time."

Molly frowned and asked, "So did you go into work yet?"

Tiffany winced. "Yes, I did. It was so weird. People are not all warm and fuzzy now, even Patty was kind of cold."

"What all do they know? Like, do they know you guys got married?" Mackenzie asked, her eyes wide and waiting.

Tiffany nodded. "Colin is obviously not great at keeping secrets."

"Crap. Well, that makes sense then why they weren't so thrilled to see you." Molly accepted another dress from Mackenzie to try on. "Going to Hawaii will take your mind off it."

"Actually, I'm not sure I want to ever go back to Blue Moose."

"What about that whole, '*I want to earn my own money*' and stuff? That was sure quick." Mackenzie laughed.

Tiffany already knew what she wanted to do—her blog. "I'll find something else to do. When we come back from Hawaii, I'll be moving in with Colin. Am I making the right decision, guys?"

"I think so. It was a hard transition for me, but ultimately, I'm glad I did move in with Owen. I feel like I know him so much more," Molly explained.

"I lived with Gideon. It was a little bit of an adjustment, but overall it was nice." Mackenzie looked sad.

Anytime she brought up her ex, that same expression washed over her, Tiffany wondered if it would ever go away. It had been over two years since Mackenzie's heart had been ripped from her chest. Tiffany wished the hurt would go away and that Mackenzie could find the happiness and love she deserved.

Molly disappeared behind the changing-room door. "I hate trying on clothes." She emerged wearing a soft cream-colored dress.

This is the one. Tiffany exchanged looks with Mackenzie. This was definitely it.

"Molly, you look lovely." Mackenzie wiped a tear from her eye.

Tiffany smiled at Molly. "God, Molly, you're getting married!"

Molly smoothed the side of the garment that did wonders for her. "You guys have no idea how much I love him."

"We do," Tiffany said.

Mackenzie and Tiffany wrapped their arms around Molly.

"I have an idea," Mackenzie said happily. "You wouldn't let us throw you any kind of killer bachelorette party."

"Well, for obvious reasons." Molly rubbed her belly that was not yet giving away her secret.

"Let's do *Friendship Friday* early or, heck, while we are in Hawaii," Mackenzie added excitedly. "You guys are having the ceremony on Saturday, right? Let Owen hang out with Colin and we'll have a total girls' night in one of our rooms. It'll be fun."

"I think that's brilliant. We need to do something to celebrate this," Tiffany agreed.

"Oh, guys, it's fine."

"Nope. This is a big deal, Moll," Tiffany argued.

Molly smiled. "It *is* a big deal and maybe that's why I'm starting to freak out. It's one thing to live with him, but this is marriage. I will be with Owen for the rest of my life."

Tiffany grew quiet. Marriage was a big deal. Even though she and Colin were enjoying playing house and exploring the fun physical pleasures of marriage, Tiffany hadn't really taken it seriously. Seeing the powerful emotion behind Molly's words caused Tiffany reconsider this whole arrangement. If she wasn't in love, should she stick it out just because the deed was already done? *Am I in love?* Colin had already expressed that he thought he loved her. That was a little different than actually saying, 'I love you'. *How soon should I say those sacred words?*

"You okay?" Molly asked Tiffany.

"I'm fine."

"You sure?" Molly pressed further.

Mackenzie reached out and touched her arm. "You know, you don't have to stay married to Colin."

"I was just thinking about that," Tiffany admitted.

"Why? Is there trouble in paradise?" Molly asked.

"No, but shouldn't you only be married to someone if you truly love them and they love you back?"

Mackenzie and Molly exchanged looks.

Molly was the first to answer. "Well, yes. Love is funny and can be sort of hard to navigate sometimes."

"So, he doesn't love you?" Mackenzie asked with a sharp edge to her voice.

"Colin said he thinks he does." Tiffany looked away at the other dresses on the rack in front of her.

"Wait. So is it you that isn't sure?" Molly frowned.

"I mean, things are fun right now. I don't want to mess them up. But I haven't said I love you," Tiffany admitted.

"Oh dear." Molly sighed. "It will happen. Just be patient and don't make any rash decisions."

"I disagree," Mackenzie countered.

Molly glared at her and put her hands on her hips. "Oh really?"

"Yeah, if Tiff isn't in love with him by now, then why stay married?"

"Um, because she does love him and she's just being difficult."

"Well, maybe she does, maybe she doesn't. Let's not fight about this, Moll." Mackenzie held up a simple blue dress. "Let's find you something, Tiff. Here, go try this one on,"

Mackenzie ordered.

"She does too love him," Molly said as she crammed Tiffany into a dressing room.

Tiffany wasn't sure and hoped that Hawaii would make everything a little clearer. Somewhere in the dark region of her mind, she feared that seeing Molly get married in a beautiful ceremony was going to trigger something. *Resentment? Jealousy? Regret?* She wasn't sure and wasn't eager to find out.

* * * *

Tiffany busied herself by packing and talking to the one soul that wouldn't offer any solid advice but possessed the best listening skills.

"Oh, Pauly, what am I going to do?" Tiffany examined several shoe options. She was debating which ones would pair nicely with her outfits.

She had resorted to discussing her problems with a bulldog. That's where Tiffany was in her life.

"Why did I let this happen? Is there really a way out? I mean, I like him, but love is such a strong word. I don't think I feel the way Molly does about Owen."

Tiffany had been in love before. *Well, kind of.* More like in lust, and she was definitely in *that* with Colin. Love was a tad more tricky. So much more was involved. There was potential for getting hurt and that was a biggy. She'd seen Mackenzie suffer the worst kind of heartbreak. Hell, two years later and she still mourned a love that had turned sour. Would that be her? Not if she could help it.

She paused to pet the snoring pup. He was stretched out on her bed next to her open suitcase. His needs were so simple—food, water, the occasional walk and love—and lots of sleep. She kissed him on top of his wrinkled head. Loving him was easy. Tiffany would even say it was possibly love at first sight, despite the farting and drool. *Why isn't falling in love with Colin just as easy?*

166

* * * *

Tiffany had never been anywhere so breathtakingly beautiful. She totally understood why this slice of heaven was everyone's honeymoon destination. The slight breeze whispered through the towering palm trees. The sky was the brightest blue and the ocean begged to played in. Maybe Tiffany wouldn't board the plane back home and would just become a beach bum for the rest of her life. She was completely okay with that. This was indeed paradise.

"It's great, isn't it?" Molly asked as they looked out at the water from their adjoining hotel room balconies. "I love it here. The light is amazing and look at how vivid everything is."

Tiffany was glad that Molly was feeling better. Her coloring was back and she seemed normal. Pregnancy was a funny thing and not something Tiffany was sure she wanted to experience right away. She'd always loved drooling over tiny babies with their chubby cheeks and impossible cuteness. With Pauly in her life—for now, anyway—Tiffany wasn't itching to get pregnant.

"It's incredible. I've never seen anywhere so beautiful," Tiffany replied. "You bring your camera?" That was a stupid question. Molly never went anywhere without her trusty camera.

Molly smirked at her. "You know it."

Mackenzie came outside and joined them. She was in her own room and hanging out of her own balcony, next to theirs. The stucco balconies were all divided with a sheet of gleaming glass. Tiffany wished she were sharing a room with her.

"My room is amazing. Thank you, Molly," Mackenzie said as she clung to the railing and was looking out at the curling waves in front of them.

"Yeah, they are pretty incredible," Tiffany added.

The rooms were luxury at its best. Molly had hooked them up for sure. The resort was right on the shore and there was nothing blocking their view of the rolling blue. Okay, there was a palm tree that was slightly in the way, but there were no buildings obstructing the magnificent scenery.

"Owen and Colin decided to check out the golf course since it's still early. You guys want to grab some dinner soon?"

"Gosh, what time is it?"

"Well, there's a time difference of two hours," Molly informed them.

"I think I'm still functioning on Seattle time," Mackenzie yawned. "I might try and catch a nap before we head out, if that's cool?"

"I'm totally good with taking a nap." Molly did look tired.

"So, what about me? You guys are no fun," Tiffany teased. "Here we are in paradise for only a short time and you want to nap."

"Go to the beach or something, then come get us in like an hour," Molly suggested.

Tiffany looked out at the bleached sand and decided that was exactly where she wanted to be. "I think I'll take Pauly."

"You spoil that dog," Mackenzie said sweetly, "but I can see why."

Tiffany looked down at the bulldog sitting next to her leg. He was hanging his head and appeared sad but was probably really just tired.

Tiffany was pretty sure that walking on the beach was the last thing he wanted to do, but she was dying to feel the sand between her toes. Besides, she needed the company since her friends were too tired to hang out. They said their goodbyes and made plans to meet up in a little while. Tiffany grabbed Pauly's leash and they headed out.

The sun was still covering them in a lovely tropical heat. Granted, the bulldog didn't seem to like it quite as much as Tiffany and was now panting hard. Tiffany was amused that Pauly loved the water. He even tried biting several waves that slapped against the shore. She loved this playful side of him. He didn't display it often, but when he did, it was beyond entertaining.

The sand felt just as good as she'd imagined. It was warm and heavy as she dug her toes in deeper. Tiffany's feet were nearly buried as she sat and watched surfers trying to stay on top of powerful waves. The beach itself was quiet. There were couples walking hand in hand along the shore and a few people soaking up the last of the sun's rays before it set for the day.

"Pauly, isn't this place amazing?" Tiffany brushed sand off her furry companion. He was snuggled up tightly against her bare legs. This was peace. The ocean drowned out any noise from the world and Tiffany finally relaxed. Her troubles and any pending thoughts of what the future might hold were floating away. She was here in this moment, just her and this calm.

"Cute dog," a voice said.

The sun was in Tiffany's eyes. The figure in front of her was a mixture of nude, bronzed torso and brightly colored board shorts. She was too blinded to make out anything more.

"Thanks," Tiffany replied as she tried to get a better glimpse of the stranger that was standing near her.

"Mind if I pet him?"

Pauly squirmed under the man's touch. Suddenly, Tiffany thought about Colin's warning. Her protective motherly instincts went haywire. She tightened her grip on the dog's leash.

"Haven't seen you two here before." He took a seat next to her. Pauly was between them.

"Yeah, just visiting."

"I'd remember a pretty girl like you," he flirted playfully. "I'd love to show you around."

Tiffany quickly replied, "Yeah, I doubt I'd have the time. My friend is getting married this weekend."

"Well, it's only Thursday. Maybe tomorrow?"

Damn, this guy is persistent.

Now that he was sitting next to her, Tiffany was able to see him clearly. His hair was the typical, shaggy-surfer length. Pale blond streaks were intertwined with a sandy brown. He was sun-kissed, lean and chiseled.

Tiffany's pulse quickened then another shadowy figure loomed over her.

"Hey, mate."

"Yeah, bro?"

Oh dear.

Colin remained standing. "Can I help you with something?" Colin asked.

"I'm good. Do *you* need something?"

Tiffany watched as the two men stared each other down.

"Well, actually, since you asked. I'd love to spend some time with my wife here. Perhaps you can move along," Colin's tone was authoritative and possessive. Tiffany cringed as she heard him speak.

"Funny, she didn't mention that. Maybe you shouldn't be leaving such a pretty woman all alone."

"Mate, it's time to walk away now."

The surfer rose from the sand and the men squared off. Tiffany held on to Pauly protectively as the two guys towered over her. The bulldog was growing agitated and starting to make low, growling noises.

"Colin, it's fine. He was just curious about Pauly." She wanted to defuse this before it came to blows, which Tiffany was worried was about to happen at any moment.

"I'm sure he was, Tiffany," Colin answered swiftly.

"Hey, screw this," he said to Colin. He looked down at Tiffany. "But I hope to see ya around." The surfer winked at her before he turned and strutted away.

Colin stared in that direction for a moment, then he finally joined her on the sand. "You weren't in the room when I got back."

"Yeah, Mackenzie and Molly were tired. I figured the beach would be a nice place for Pauly and me to kill some time."

Colin patted the dog, who seemed quite pleased to see him. "I just worry about you being by yourself."

"What do you think I did before I met you?" Tiffany asked.

"Doesn't matter. You're my wife now and I want to protect you."

"Colin, I'm a big girl. I can handle myself," Tiffany said.

"Really? Didn't quite look that way when I arrived a moment ago."

Tiffany rolled her eyes and looked away. "He was asking about Pauly, then you showed up," Tiffany explained. She didn't want to admit to Colin that the surfer was sort of hitting on her, even though it had probably been fairly obvious.

"Yeah, looked like that's all he was interested in." Sarcasm oozed from his lips.

"Colin, stop. Nothing happened. Jeesh."

"Would something have if I hadn't shown up?" Colin questioned her.

"Are you serious?" Tiffany glared at him. "Have I ever given you any reason to doubt me?"

"You certainly weren't telling him to take a hike," Colin argued coolly. "You seemed a bit too cozy for my liking. All smiles."

"Colin, just stop. I was being polite, nothing more."

"How do you suppose it looked from my view?"

"I don't know, like I was sitting here and doing nothing wrong?"

"You didn't appear so innocent, my dear."

Unbelievable. On one hand, Tiffany knew that Colin's concerns were semi-valid and on the other, she hadn't been ramming her tongue down that guy's throat, either.

"Then you don't know me too well, Colin," Tiffany spat. She got up quickly, pausing briefly to brush the sand from her bottom, preparing to walk away.

"You know, maybe you're right. How much do we really know about each other? Perhaps we do need to reevaluate this whole matter of being married." Colin shook his head.

Tiffany felt like she'd just been sucker-punched. *But why? Haven't I been thinking the same thing for the last two days?* Maybe she wouldn't have actually gone through with breaking things off, but since Molly had woken her up to the seriousness of her situation she'd certainly been considering that she'd bitten off way more than she could chew with this 'til death do us part' marriage thing. She'd wanted to see how this trip went, then she planned to make up her mind. To have Colin not trust her and to hear those words leave his mouth broke her heart.

The honeymoon was officially over.

Chapter Eighteen

"Tiff, here. Drink this." Mackenzie handed her a glass with an amber-liquid filled about halfway.

"Rum? Because if so, no thanks."

"Whiskey," Mackenzie answered.

"Well, in that case, thank you." Tiffany accepted the glass and took a sip. She winced as it burned her throat. "This is super strong."

"That's kind of the point." Mackenzie grabbed her own and took a sip, also wincing as she swallowed.

They were all in Mackenzie's room. Molly was furious and Mackenzie was oddly peaceful. Then again, this could be just the calm before the storm. You just never knew with her these days. One moment she'd fly off the handle. The next, Mackenzie was all sunshine and rainbows.

"So, he wants to reconsider this whole marriage thing?" Molly asked as she fussed with the plastic top from the bottle of water she had been nursing. "How *dare* he?"

Tiffany had failed to share with her friends that she'd pretty much decided to do the same reconsidering thing when they'd left the boutique — the same shop where they'd ended up buying Molly's dress for the wedding. Tiffany was tormented, but she knew above all else that she didn't want to ruin Molly's wedding. This was Molly's time — her special moment — and this was no place to break that kind of news.

"Jealousy is such a nasty thing. Ugh, men." Molly rolled her eyes in frustration. "He's right. He doesn't know you and too bad, because you're friggin' amazing, Tiff." Molly gave Mackenzie a high-five.

Mackenzie laughed. "Tiff's pretty awesome. But more importantly, she's loyal. You weren't flirting with that surfer, were you?" she joked.

"Nah, but I wasn't being a bitch, either. Colin would have preferred that." Tiffany explained, "He sat down and asked about Pauly. I was more concerned that maybe he was going to try and nab him. Colin has me so paranoid about that now. It's just the way Colin acted like I was his property and that I couldn't think for myself. It was kind of degrading."

"See? That shit pisses me off. Tiffany survived long before she met him and she'll continue to survive after him," Molly added.

After him. So, this is it. The end. Gosh, we haven't really started and it's already over. That was quick.

"You know. Let's just quit talking about it," Tiffany said. "You're getting married this weekend, Molly. This is a happy time. Let's focus on that."

"It's kind of hard to when I'm worried about your marriage."

"Don't be. It's not like it was a real one, anyway. Definitely not like yours. You guys fell in love and he asked you to be his wife. I didn't get any of that." Stinging, hot tears streamed down Tiffany's cheeks.

"You're right. You got Elvis and a drive-thru chapel," Molly agreed. "That's a rip off for someone like you that wants it all. Me? I would have loved to have gone that route."

"But instead, you two get sand, sun and a gorgeous ceremony," Tiffany countered and forced a smile.

Mackenzie yawned. "You know, guys. It's been a long day and things will look better in the morning."

Tiffany crawled into bed next to Molly. "You sure Owen is cool with you staying here with us?"

"Yes. He's probably out getting drunk with your husband," Molly teased.

"I'm really sorry about all this. You should be with Owen

174

and enjoying this beautiful place, not babysitting me."

"It's fine. I promise. Owen understands how important you and Mac are to me. We're sisters, and right now you need me. God knows that you've been there for me." Molly tugged the blanket around her.

"I'll always need you, Moll. And you too, Mac," Tiffany called out to Mackenzie.

"Sure, yet, here I am alone in bed. Look who is snuggling with whom," Mackenzie joked as she turned off the light.

As Tiffany closed her eyes, she could hear the ocean. Its steady song began to lull her to sleep.

* * * *

"I don't think it gets any better than this." Molly released a happy sigh.

They were seated in a row, their feet swimming in a bubbling bath of fizzy water, cucumber slices on their eyes and their hands being massaged.

"It's lovely," Mackenzie answered slowly.

Tiffany wished she were more enthusiastic about getting pampered. Normally this would be her thing, but today the heavy feelings leftover from yesterday were still clinging to her. She wanted to snap out of this mood and had been trying to fake it for most of the day. Tiffany managed to get through lunch without cracking. No tears were shed over her Caesar salad. But now she was exhausted from all the effort of trying to keep a happy face for Molly's sake. Mackenzie knew that she had been struggling and tried to keep the conversation light anytime Molly tried to bring up the subject of Colin.

Today wasn't the day to discuss any of it, nor was tomorrow — or hell, any time after that. Tiffany didn't want to talk about Colin, but she knew that it was a topic that was unavoidable. *But it can be avoided for now, right?*

Plucking off the cucumbers Tiffany looked at her friends. Mackenzie and Molly looked about as comfy in their recliners as one could get. They were fully relishing this treatment. Tiffany sighed quietly. She envied them.

"Does it feel weird knowing that tomorrow you and that fisherman are getting hitched?" Mackenzie asked playfully.

"Yes and no. Like part of me is completely freaked out and wondering what in the hell I'm doing. Then there's the lovey-dovey side that is so excited and can't believe that he's going to be all mine," Molly answered. She wore a happy smile. Molly didn't look like the same woman from a few months before. This one was softer and radiated joy.

"So, what is the game plan for tomorrow, exactly?" Tiffany asked. "Like, what time do we head to the beach for the ceremony? Hair, makeup and all that fun stuff before... Do we have an ETA for that?"

"See? Tiffany would be the total bridezilla, planning everything to the very second. Me? I'm just kind of taking a chill approach with this." Molly sighed. "That's why we are getting married here, no stress."

"Best destination *ever*, by the way," Mackenzie added. "Chill is good. Stress is bad."

"Well, Thailand would've been amazing and that was one of our options, but it was too hard to coordinate on short notice. But you can't beat Hawaii. It's gorgeous. I'm happy and Owen's happy," Molly commented.

"We're all happy," Mackenzie added.

"So, you're not the least bit stressed?" Tiffany asked.

"I wasn't until that whole Colin and you incident that you refuse to discuss." Molly threw her a frustrated glare.

"It wasn't my fault," Tiffany replied. She sat back and tried to enjoy the hand massage, but found herself more annoyed with being touched and pulled her hand away. "Sorry," she apologized to the lady, who looked insulted.

"You guys getting hungry yet?" Molly asked. "It seems like I'm always hungry now."

"You're pregnant. Isn't that what pregnant chicks do? Eat? And well...I guess throw up. Maybe that's why they're hungry all time," Tiffany pondered out loud.

"So, are you starting to get any cravings yet?" Mackenzie asked with excitement. "Like pickles and ice cream or any of that nonsense?"

"Thankfully no. I just want to eat and sleep."

"You're making a human, so eating and sleeping about sums it up, I would imagine," Tiffany agreed.

Molly giggled. "I'm probably making it seem far worse than what it actually is. I'm so barely pregnant. Talk to me when I'm almost due. I'm sure I'll be utterly miserable by then."

"Wouldn't blame you if you were." Mackenzie patted Molly's arm. "Waddling around, eating everything in sight and being in a preggo coma, you poor girl."

"Oh stop!" Molly rolled her eyes. "But I'm going in for an ultrasound next week. You guys wanna come?"

"Oh my God, yes!" Mackenzie squealed.

"Absolutely," Tiffany replied happily. "Will we get to find out the gender?"

"Not from what I read online. That's like closer to sixteen or twenty weeks. I can't remember, but something along those lines. Owen is asking us to keep the gender a surprise."

"No way. That's no fun. It won't only drive you crazy but us, too," Mackenzie complained.

"What about Owen? I mean, will he care if we go to the ultrasound? This is kind of a special moment for you guys." Tiffany wasn't so sure she'd want to share this with anyone but the father of her baby, especially the first ultrasound.

"Oh, please. Owen is quite aware what he signed up for. You guys are a package deal. This is a big thing for all of us. Can you even believe I'm going to be a mom?"

"No, I'm barely wrapping my head around the fact that you are getting married tomorrow. But I'm so happy for you," Mackenzie said. "Okay, and a little jealous."

Funny, Tiffany would have been jealous a month earlier, but not now. Now, Tiffany was wishing more than ever that she could go back to when times were simpler, when hanging out with her besties was the highlight of her week.

She'd even be willing to endure all those nights of them being single in Seattle. Tiffany would do anything to stave off this feeling of impending doom. She glanced at her cell phone—not a single message or missed call.

Maybe those nights of being single in Seattle aren't a thing of the past.

* * * *

"You know, I'm just not feeling well tonight."

"Tiff, come on. You have to deal with this," Mackenzie urged. "The wedding is tomorrow and tonight is the dinner. Molly will want you there."

"I'm sure she'll understand. Besides, I have a bit of a headache," Tiffany lied and Mackenzie saw through it.

"Yeah, a six foot two headache. More like a pain in the ass."

Tiffany laughed. Mackenzie didn't mince words and always told it like was. Sometimes it drove Tiffany nuts, but then there were times when she needed to hear it straight.

"Don't let him ruin this for you. For us," Mackenzie hissed angrily.

Tiffany nodded but wasn't convinced.

"Look. Here's an idea. Why don't we make you look friggin' fabulous, like super-hot and Colin can eat his dumb ole heart out?" she suggested.

Mackenzie was already dressed in a soft, coral-colored strapless dress and she looked incredible. Mackenzie brushed her blonde hair and continued, "That way he can see what he's missing out on. Colin is such idiot. He could have been getting laid in one of the most beautiful places."

"True. You have a point there." Tiffany smiled. She was in a fetal position on one of the beds in Mackenzie's room. She figured if she looked the part of being sick, maybe Mackenzie would buy it. *Yep, not happening.*

"Come on. Let's get you dressed."

"I'd rather not."

"Too bad. You can't sit in here and wallow. Your best friend needs you out there. Regardless of this whole stress-free act she's trying to pull, you know Molly has to be freaking out," Mackenzie argued as she tugged Tiffany from the bed. "I know either of us would be. How can she not be a little nervous?"

With her shoulders slumped, Tiffany looked at Mackenzie. "You know you suck, right?"

Mackenzie winked. "Some say better than others."

Who is this new and improved Mac? The old Mackenzie was a prude. Now she was sassy, and if Tiffany didn't feel like her heart was missing, she'd gobble up this fun Mackenzie. Maybe Tiffany cared more about Colin that she realized. But there was someone else she was missing, *a lot.*

Chapter Nineteen

Now *this* was Hawaii—or at least the one Tiffany had always pictured, thanks to the movies. There were torches flickering in the darkness, the roar of the ocean in the background and everyone—literally everyone—was wearing a lei. Mackenzie walked with Tiffany. She'd give anything to not have to endure this dinner. Tiffany avoided the cold stare coming from Colin, but she could feel it to her very core, freezing her. She looked to Mackenzie, who gave her a tender smile and squeezed her hand.

"It'll be okay," Mackenzie muttered under her breath.

Sure, it will be. The icy daggers that Colin were sending in her direction weren't any cause for alarm. *Everything is just peachy.*

"There you guys are," Molly greeted them happily. She rose from the table, adjusted her enormous lei and hugged them both.

The table was small and the seating choices were limited. Owen was seated next to Molly and across from Colin. There were two remaining seats—one right next to Colin. Tiffany paused, she didn't know where to sit, but Mackenzie winked.

Mackenzie took the seat next to Colin, acting as a wall between them, which Tiffany appreciated.

"Hey, Colin, hope you don't mind," Mackenzie said in a rich and sarcastic tone.

He shook his head and sent Owen an annoyed look. It would appear that he wanted to be there as much as Tiffany did.

"We ordered already, but what about drinks? What are

you guys in the mood for? Rum?"

Rum, yeah, right. That's what had gotten her into this horrible mess to begin with.

"I think she'll pass on the rum, Moll," Mackenzie answered playfully.

The three of them laughed nervously. Owen looked confused and Colin turned his head away, pretending that something more interesting had caught his attention.

A server came by and Mackenzie and Tiffany order drinks that didn't contain the evil ingredient. *No, Mr. Captain Morgan, there will be no more shenanigans.*

This was as awkward and just about as uncomfortable as Tiffany had imagined it would be.

Owen cleared his throat and raised his glass. "I just wanted to thank our dear friends for being here with us. Molly is my lighthouse in the dark, my heart and the love of my life. She's given me so much, and our love continues to grow in ways I never imagined." Owen paused and placed his hand on Molly's flat stomach. "Here's to love," Owen toasted. His stormy-gray eyes were wet and he hastily wiped them. He bent over and kissed Molly full on the mouth.

Molly was not quick to let Owen go. Mackenzie sipped her drink and obviously drowned her emotions.

Then there was Tiffany. That was the kind of man she wanted to marry, one that had a delicate heart and was deeply in love — not the one who had his arms crossed and a sour expression on his face.

The hula dancers were in full motion when Tiffany flagged down the waitress and ordered another drink. *Stress… There was only one way to combat this.* Playing nice and masking all of her feelings was a taking its toll on Tiffany. *This is exactly what adult beverages are made for.*

* * * *

"You can't see the bride. Go away, Owen," Mackenzie said when Owen knocked on their hotel room door the next afternoon.

The wedding ceremony was to take place in just a few hours. Regardless of how completely nontraditional their wedding and entire romance was, some superstitions were meant to be kept, this being one of them.

"I need to talk to Tiffany."

"Why?" Tiffany whispered to Molly and Mackenzie, both shrugged at her.

"What do you want, babe?" Molly called out.

"Just to speak to Tiffany for a moment. Please."

Tiffany went to the door. "I'll go outside and talk to him," she told the girls. "Hey, Owen, I'm coming out now. No peeking at Moll, okay?"

"No peeking, I promise."

Tiffany slipped outside as quickly as she could. Owen looked handsome in a dark floral Hawaiian shirt and khakis.

"What's up? You okay?" Tiffany asked. She was praying he wasn't going to tell her that he had cold feet and was going to cancel the wedding.

"I'm good—a little nervous, but very happy."

That was a tremendous relief.

"Okay, that's great. So why do you need to talk to me?" Tiffany followed Owen as he led her away from the hotel and toward the beach.

It was slightly breezy. The sun was painting the sky orange. It was the perfect backdrop for what was going to be a special union of love.

"It's about Colin."

"What about him?" Tiffany wrapped her arms around herself—not for warmth, but to shield herself from whatever Owen had to say.

"Well, Colin's wondering if he should leave."

"Leave? He's your best man. That's kind of a shitty thing to do." Tiffany was upset. *How dare he trample on this special day?*

Owen nodded. "But I also see where he's coming from.

Last night was really hard, Tiffany."

"On him? Because he's the one in the wrong here."

"I don't know who is right or wrong. Honestly, you both mean a lot to me, so I don't care. I want you to talk to him," Owen pleaded.

"Owen, there's not much to discuss. I'm sorry that he wants to pout and run away. I'm here for Molly and for you. This isn't about Colin or me. It's about my best friend marrying the man she loves." Tiffany hugged Owen. He looked like he could use it.

"You're a good person. Colin is too. That's why I can't figure out what's going on with the both you. I mean, he's told me his version, Molly explained yours, then there's what really happened."

"Owen, it's simple. Colin and I don't have anything near what you and Molly have. You guys love each other, like real love. Colin and I were drunk in Vegas and you know what they say about Vegas. 'What happens in Vegas stays in Vegas'." Tiffany smiled up at him.

"But it didn't stay in Vegas. Heck, I don't think it even started in Vegas. I think it started in Seattle, on my boat," Owen countered. "Sometimes the unexpected is the best thing that happens to us."

"There was nothing unexpected about Colin and I."

"Wrong. Do you think he expected you to kiss him that night on the boat?" Owen raised his eyebrows knowingly at her.

"How did you know about that? Damn, Molly." Tiffany shook her head. *Is nothing sacred between them anymore?*

"Colin."

"*Colin* told you?"

Owen nodded. "That's not all he told me."

"Oh God," Tiffany gasped and her cheeks burned.

"No, no, not that." Owen tried to reassure her.

Yeah, right. Tiffany looked away. She was fully embarrassed.

"Hey, I'm serious. Colin really does care about you."

"He sure has a funny way of showing it," Tiffany replied angrily.

"Oh stop. You know how us guys are. Cut him some slack. When he saw that surfer dude hitting on you, he got a little territorial. Was it right? No, but most of the time men aren't." He looked over his shoulder dramatically. "Now, you didn't hear that from me."

Tiffany laughed. Maybe Owen had a point. Tiffany's heart had been aching. *If not being with Colin is the right thing, it shouldn't hurt this bad, right?*

Owen and Tiffany stared out at the rolling blue as it slapped at the shore. "Just please talk to Colin."

Tiffany exhaled. "It's just because you'll be without a best man. Ah, the things that I do for you, Owen."

"Oh, like making you talk to *your* husband. Whatever you gotta tell yourself... If you want it to be because you're worried that I'll have no best man, then that works for me. Just talk to him before he tries to leave."

"You know, Owen, Molly sure lucked out that day you hit her with that fish," Tiffany teased.

He let out a loud laugh. "Not that again. She was in the way. I swear."

"Whatever you have to tell yourself. I think you hit her on purpose. It'll be our little secret," Tiffany promised then patted his arm.

* * * *

Tiffany stood outside. She'd been staring at a small chip of paint on the otherwise perfectly white door. She was scared to knock. What was she going to say? But she also knew there wasn't much time. The wedding was only an hour or so away and standing outside the door all night wasn't really an option. *Here goes nothing.* Tiffany knocked softly then waited. And waited. *Nothing.* Maybe he'd already left and she was too late. Tiffany balled up her fist and tried again, this time with a little more force—maybe too much force. The door move as she moved in for another strike.

Colin stood there with a confused look on his face. He wasn't wearing a ridiculous Hawaiian shirt and certainly didn't look like he was ready to be Owen's best man.

"So, you were just going to leave?"

"Does it matter?" Colin's eyes were quiet, but there was something brewing in them.

"Yes, it does. Your best friend needs his best man. My best friend needs her maid of honor. They don't deserve to have us ruin their day because we're stupid."

"I know. But what about this?" Colin waved his hand between them.

"We can deal with it later." Tiffany looked up him. His lips were pouted and she suddenly wanted to feel them on hers.

"I'd like to deal with it now." His voice was deep and rough.

"Well, we don't have time right now. Afterward, I promise," Tiffany offered.

Colin stepped away from the door and moved in closer.

"Tiffany, I think we have time." He grabbed her in a swift move and before she could blink, his lips were on hers — right where they belonged.

Time stood still and sped forward all at the same time. Tiffany's heart pounded hard. She was rattled and unexpectedly happy.

"Colin —" Tiffany started once he kiss ended.

"No, let me speak first." He put his finger to her lips to silence her. "I shouldn't have acted the way I did. Then saying that we should reconsider us? What a fool I was."

"I know, but —" Tiffany began. He shook his head.

"I'm not finished. The last two days have been brutal. I've missed you like crazy, yet I continued to be a jerk to you at dinner last night." Colin's eyes were sad and regret was etched on his handsome face. "Look, Tiffany, we may not have gone about this marriage the traditional way, but here we are and that's what truly matters. We are here together."

He wrapped his arms around her and continued, "Some people don't get the chance to be with someone that makes them laugh like no other, to be with someone that terrifies them so much."

"Wait, *terrify*?"

"Because of how much I love you. It scares me to death. I've never felt this way about another person." Colin rested his lips softly on her forehead. He gingerly brushed them against her skin then said, "How is it possible to love someone this quickly unless they are your soul mate."

"Oh, Colin, I have been carrying around this ache." Tiffany clutched her chest. "I thought the easiest way to numb all these feelings was to cut you from my heart. But I realized I can't."

All morning Tiffany had suffered, even when she'd stared out the endless blue and was sipping her coffee, the two things that should have brought her peace. Tiffany's heart was too busy wilting inside of her. She'd missed Colin and Pauly, knowing that they weren't more than a hundred feet away. It had been pure torture—to fight over something so petty and stupid. Tiffany was more than angry with herself. Colin was right. She should have told that guy to buzz off. She was a married woman now and couldn't have guys hitting on her. There was only one man's attention she wanted. Well, two guys.

This trip could have been incredible, full of romance and making love. But instead, it was ruined because Tiffany and Colin were both more stubborn than a certain English bulldog. Tiffany had put on a brave face most of the day. When she'd snuck off into the restroom to cry, no one had noticed thankfully. Molly had been too deep into her own anxiety, constantly dabbing an array of emotional tears. Mackenzie had taken charge, being the bossy one they knew and loved, making sure everything else went according to plan. She'd turned out to be the best of the maids of honor. Mackenzie had even made sure Molly ate, napped and had tissues easily at her disposal when the tears revisited.

Tiffany was doing the bare minimum of her bridesmaid's duties. Her mind was miles away. Colin had been on her mind all day.

But now she was here in his arms and it was too much. Tiffany melted against him. Colin bent down, resting his chin on the top of her head and tightened their embrace. Tiffany began to cry into his chest. These weren't dainty pretty little tears. It was full-on, snot-dripping ugly crying.

"Sweetheart, please don't cry. You'll upset Pauly. He's missed you." Colin pushed her away a few inches to look at her. He gripped her bare arms softly. "But not nearly as much I have."

Tiffany could only nod. Her words were caught up in her throat. She could only imagine how awful she must look. Her mascara and eyeliner were probably ruined. Tiffany desperately tried to smooth any smudged makeup and compose herself.

"Sorry. I must look like a hot mess," Tiffany apologized.

"No, you're beautiful, Tiffany," Colin whispered as he left a trail of feathery kisses where tears had dampened her cheeks. "Pauly and I are the luckiest guys on this island. This planet."

God, I love this man – and his stinky, slobbering bulldog.

* * * *

Tiffany's arm was looped with his as they walked slowly down a makeshift aisle on the sand. It was lined with large tropical flowers, creating a romantic pathway to the sea. Owen stood with his pants rolled up, the tide splashing his exposed calves. Colin took his place next to him. Mackenzie had her arm linked with Molly's. They were only several paces behind Tiffany and Colin.

Mackenzie and Tiffany were wearing identical dresses in a pale aqua. They each wore their hair up with flowers pinned neatly inside and were fighting the ocean breeze to keep them locked into place.

Molly looked stunning. Her cream-colored dress was blowing around her. Molly's dark hair was loose with a single flower tucked behind one ear. She looked like an island princess and Tiffany watched Owen's reaction. His face lit up and pure love radiated from him as he gazed at her. This man truly adored and loved her friend.

The ceremony began, an explanation of what all this meant from a man that wore flowers draped around his neck. The couple exchanged beautiful words and made promises. Tiffany's gaze kept finding Colin's. Her heart was both mended and broken at the same time. Mended because she was healed now from of the love that had gone missing, if only for less than two days. That had been long enough for Tiffany. Broken because this ceremony was simple and beautiful and Tiffany wished that she and Colin had been able to have had something even half as lovely. Deep down it shouldn't matter where or how they'd gotten married. They were two souls that belonged together, but she yearned for it nonetheless.

Husband and wife, for richer or poorer, in sickness and in health. Tiffany had agreed to those terms. Molly had just agreed to those very same ones with a bright smile and tears streaming down her cheeks. They were all no longer single in Seattle, except for Mackenzie, who was taking it all in stride. Tiffany knew the right guy was out there for Mac, but it'd be great if he would just show up.

"You may kiss your bride," the man performing the service announced.

Molly was now a married woman.

Colin smiled at Tiffany and they moved together slowly, following Molly and Owen away from the shore. Love had been declared that day, not by one set of souls but two, each who had found one another in the most unexpected way.

* * * *

Molly and Owen would be staying behind in paradise for

another week to break in their new marriage and enjoy a quiet honeymoon.

It had been hard to say goodbye after breakfast. Tiffany could have stayed there forever, but real life awaited back in Seattle—a new adventure with Colin, her husband. She also had a new secret mission. Find Mackenzie a husband.

Colin helped Mackenzie into the cabin of his private jet. Tiffany walked the other love of her life, Pauly, up the stairs. The little chunk should be used to traveling by now, but he wasn't eager to leave this little slice of heaven, either. It finally took a lot of gentle coaxing and a nudge on his cute bully butt to get him to go up the stairs.

Once they were all boarded and had taken their seats, they were able to relax. The mood was quiet, except for Pauly's snorts. Even the jet engines could hardly drown out his hard breathing.

"That poor creature probably has sleep apnea," Mackenzie said as she tried to snuggle deeper into her chair. "You should get him one of those sleeping masks."

Tiffany glanced down at Pauly then looked over to Colin. "Is that possible, Colin?" Can we get him one?"

Colin laughed. "I don't think they have one that would fit his face."

"Well, I'm going to find out. Good thinking, Mac," Tiffany said.

"Who would've thought that you, a non-dog lover, would care so much about one?" Mackenzie commented. "Not that anyone can blame you. He's super cute. I mean, just look at him."

Pauly slowly turned around in the seat, knowing full well they were talking about him. He stared at Tiffany and lifted a paw.

"He's not just any dog. He's Sir Pauly McCartney, the cutest bulldog ever."

"I swear the only reason Tiffany likes me is because of him," Colin teased.

"Probably true." Tiffany laughed. Pauly put his head on

her lap, his wrinkles scrunched up on his meaty face and he began to snore.

They had been in the air for a few hours, Mackenzie was curled up and napping, the gentle hum of the jet engines and Pauly's snoring was enough to lull anyone to sleep. Tiffany was watching the jet wing slice through the clouds when Colin spoke.

"You know he was miserable those last couple days without you," he started.

"Just Pauly?" Tiffany winked. She already knew that Colin had suffered as much as she had, if not more. Last night they'd made up for lost time and today Tiffany's body was proof of just how much. She was a little sore and even had dark circles under her eyes from barely sleeping.

"Pauly wouldn't eat or anything. He just stayed by the door, waiting for you. It was quite sad."

"Aww, my poor li'l man," Tiffany cooed to Pauly, who wiggled his tiny nub of a tail. "I'll never leave you again."

"Tiffany, I really want you to move in with me when we get back. I want to make this work." Colin's eyes followed hers. "We also need to tell our families."

Then there was that. Tiffany hadn't even mentioned Colin to her family — not that they spoke a lot, but they did deserve to know. *How am I going to tell them I'm already married?* It would be easier to say they were dating or that they had just gotten engaged. Explaining that they had already been married for nearly a month was going to be difficult. Then there was his family. Tiffany knew next to nothing about them. *What if they hate me?*

"Well, I guess we can hold a dinner or something to announce it, just get it done all in one shot," Tiffany suggested.

"That may prove to be a tad challenging as mine are back in Ireland, love," Colin said with a wink.

Tiffany considered that for a moment. That meant they weren't likely to tell his family anytime soon and now she needed to muster up the courage to tell hers.

"We can fly out to see mine maybe in a week or so. We do have that fundraiser event that we need to attend, since we skipped out on that last function," Colin explained.

"That's because when I was getting dressed, you couldn't keep your hands off me."

"You shouldn't have looked so delicious." Colin's voice grew deeper and he had the burning in his eyes.

Tiffany gave him a sly smile and she peeked over to where Mackenzie was.

"Fancy becoming a member of the mile-high club?" Colin asked with a devilish grin.

He'd read her mind.

Chapter Twenty

Moving sucked. It didn't matter that Tiffany was relocating or upgrading to a wonderfully new place with her lovely husband. Packing was not a fun task. However, it helped to have a bottle of wine and one of your besties to suffer along with you.

"So, you're totally good with this, right?" Mackenzie ran packaging tape along another cardboard box.

"Yes, I actually am. I mean, I'm a little bummed to be leaving here. Colin told me he wants us to start looking at houses."

"Wow, that's crazy. He's probably eager to fill it with lots of babies."

"I know. It's funny. He actually mentioned how lovely it would be if we could get pregnant soon so that Molly and Owen's baby could have a little friend." Tiffany laughed.

"Oh dear. But that would be kind of adorable."

"I want to enjoy being married for a minute before we start adding babies into the mix."

Mackenzie paused and gave her a thoughtful glance. "I'm glad things are working out for you two. You were downright miserable for those couple of days."

"You were right. You said it would work out and it did."

"I'm usually right, but no one ever wants to listen to me," Mackenzie teased.

"That's because you're bossy and no one wants to be wrong."

"Not my problem." Mackenzie taped another box and laughed. "So where is your dear hubby today?"

"Work."

"What's up with you and that whole scene?" Mackenzie asked. She stacked the freshly taped box on top of another.

The growing line of boxes proved that Tiffany owned far too much junk. And they had thought Molly was a hoarder.

"I'm not really sure. Anytime I go in, I'm treated so weirdly now."

"That's because who really likes the boss's wife?"

"But I was one of them first. Me being married to Colin shouldn't change that."

"Doesn't matter. You crossed over to the dark side, pumpkin. No one ever likes the head honcho," Mackenzie explained as she grabbed her wine glass. "We need more," she said as she raised her empty glass. "You want some?"

"Please." Tiffany sighed. "It sucks because, believe it or not, I did love working there."

"I know. But now maybe you can do something you really want to do. What about writing? You used to love that."

"Yeah, I actually have been getting back into it. I sort of started a blog," Tiffany admitted. The wine was making her lips loose.

"Is it about designer bag knock-offs and how to properly store booze in them? I'd read that shit for sure." Mackenzie handed Tiffany a glass.

"I have some of the best booze-smuggling bags." Tiffany giggled. "Actually, I do talk about bags, Pauly and being married. I kind of like doing it," she added sheepishly.

"That's really awesome. I'm so proud of you, Tiff."

They sat on the floor surrounded by towers of cardboard. Pauly was on his favorite napping place, her couch. That dog had no problem taking what he wanted. He was so much like Colin. They both had burrowed their way into her heart.

Feeling a surge of love pass through her as she looked at the sleeping bulldog, Tiffany asked, "Mac, so what about you?"

"What about me?" She took a long sip from her wine glass.

"You need a man."

"Ha, they are a lot more trouble than they are worth. I've seen it with you and Molly. Granted, it all worked out, but jeesh," Mackenzie joked. "I'm good, thanks."

"It wasn't that bad," Tiffany countered as she swallowed the tart wine.

"Oh, it was. Trust me. I was the one watching it all go down."

"Whatever. But I was thinking it might be fun to go to one of those speed dating things. I could be your wing woman," Tiffany suggested.

"How much have you had to drink?" Mackenzie gave her a concerned look.

"Stop. It might be fun."

"Painful is more like it." Mackenzie leaned back against a large box and sighed. "The right guy is out there and I do want to meet someone that's wonderful. I just don't want to force it, and speeding dating or trying to pick some psycho offline is forcing it."

"Well, it's my personal mission to get you married off."

"Don't make it be. Love doesn't work like that. You should know. Both you and Molly met your respective husbands in sort of unusual ways. Something strange will happen for me when the time is right."

"Or watch, you'll meet him like in the most boring way, like at a grocery store or something cheesy," Tiffany teased.

"I'd take boring to being hit by a fish or nearly falling overboard off a boat. I'm a little scared of how I'd meet someone with the way things have been going for us." Mackenzie laughed.

"I don't blame you. But, boy, what a story for your grandkids someday."

* * * *

"Please, just take it," Colin asked again.

"No, I can't. It's too much, Colin."

Colin placed the black plastic card in the palm of Tiffany's hand. "I want you to take it. We have that function this weekend. Buy whatever you want, maybe something in red." He wiggled his eyebrows at her.

Tiffany rolled her eyes. She'd have thought she'd jump at the chance of being handed a credit card with no limit. But no, there was something that was keeping her from wanting to spend his money. *Pride, possibly?* She wasn't quite sure. Normally, Tiffany had no problem spending money. Her fabulous shoe and handbag collection was proof of that. Maybe it was because this money was not really Tiffany's, despite how many times Colin told her that it was now.

The past week had been interesting, to say the least, professionally speaking. Tiffany had visited the corporate office again. The reception had still been a little chilly, even from Patty. She had attended another board meeting and found herself literally bored out of her mind. Tiffany wanted to do things, to share ideas, not look over graphs and projections. But Colin had insisted that she learn the business. Colin hadn't been kidding when he had said that he wanted her to be his partner. It was Tiffany that wasn't so sure that this is what she wanted now. Being a trophy wife was looking a lot more inviting.

Married life? That too had been interesting, but in a much more fun way. The chemistry between her and Colin was unmatched to anything she'd ever experienced. Their bodies were attuned to one another and their affection was on a deeper level. Everyday life was more entertaining with Colin around. Even packing and bringing over some of her belongings had proven to be fun. Colin had been helpful and accommodating. He'd told her he wanted to prove that this was the best plan for them. Colin had made the work of moving easy. He'd encouraged her to add her personality to his place. Tiffany had to admit that it did need something. It was so sterile. Colin had claimed it did need something, *her*. He was giving her complete freedom to come in and change things up. But it was really the little things that were proving to be quite wonderful, like sharing dinner, watching a movie together with a fat bulldog tucked between them. This marriage thing might not be so bad after all.

Tiffany stared into his dark eyes and spied the dusting of whiskers on his jaw and around his mouth. "Colin, I just feel funny about it."

"Babe, look. What's mine is yours. Don't be bothered by it."

"Have you seen my hoard of handbags?" Tiffany asked playfully. She pulled the sheet up closer to her neck, hiding her nearly naked body. She wore nothing but a sexy pair of panties.

Colin used one finger to pull the sheet back down. "You're gorgeous. You know that?"

She blushed. The way he looked at her made Tiffany feel special. His skin was tan against the brightness of the sheet that was gathered at his waist, barely covering him. They were in his bed, tangled up in the sheet, and it was like heaven.

Colin moved forward. "I can't get enough of you. What spell have you put me under?" He began to kiss her and as Tiffany returned the kiss. She bit his bottom lip, tugging it gently. Colin groaned.

"The same spell you have over me," Tiffany teased.

"I agree that it's some kind of magic." Colin went for her neck, sucking it lightly.

Tiffany's body hummed and she wrapped her legs around him. She ran her fingers along his skin. It was warm under her touch.

Colin ventured lower, stopping along the way to kiss and lavish attention on each sensitive spot on her body. When he dove under the sheets, he used his mouth to remove her red panties and he came up quickly, the lacy fabric held in his teeth.

"Definitely buy something in red," Colin ordered after he'd dropped the panties and before he ducked back beneath the sheet and in between her legs.

* * * *

"We need to tell them, love," Colin said from across the table.

They were eating dinner at home. It was a quiet evening. Colin was still dressed in a slightly rumpled dress shirt and slacks from the day's work. Tiffany watched the muscles in his exposed forearms move as he reached for more sushi. Damn, she loved his arms. She loved all of him, but just that flash of skin…its fine, dark hair and olive skin against the expensive fabric of his shirt did funny things to her insides.

"I know. I just don't know how to tell them."

"I suggest we take them to dinner and explain what has happened," Colin offered as he expertly used chopsticks to pick up a rice-covered piece of tuna.

"Then they'll think I'm an out-of-control drunk."

"You kind of are," Colin teased.

Tiffany gasped. "You took advantage of this out-of-control drunk girl, mister."

"I'd do it all over again." Colin winked at her. "Figure the first time you were pissed you kissed me on Owen's boat. I was an innocent bystander, simply minding my own business." Colin chewed his bite of sushi. "Then that bit of rum in Vegas. I should write a check to Captain Morgan as a token of my gratitude."

Tiffany laughed. "You're terrible. You know that?"

"But you love me," Colin countered with a sly grin.

"That I do." Tiffany exhaled. That still didn't solved how she was going to tell her family.

* * * *

"See? That wasn't too bad," Colin said as he held open the black SUV back passenger door.

"I think my mom adores you. My dad? Not so much."

"Well, give him time. I think he's more upset that he

wasn't able to walk you down the aisle."

Colin had pulled out all the stops. He had reserved the top of the Space Needle for her family. Her mother and father had been shocked, to say the least. Her mother had fallen under Colin's spell quickly, no real surprise there. Her father, however, had worn a stoic face and refused to be impressed. He was a hard man to please to begin with and he hadn't been a fan of all the showy flashiness that Colin had presented. From the amazing meal to the yacht ride around the harbor, none of it had amused her father.

They had left out several key details of their getting together to keep her father from killing either of them — such as her being drunk at the time of their nuptials, them not really knowing each other but for a second and anything else that didn't sound remotely good. They'd kept the story simple. Tiffany had done most of the talking and Colin had added his bits here and there. The story was that they were thrown together by two of their incredible friends at their engagement party. That wasn't too far from the truth. Answering her parents' questions about them getting married had been a little trickier. Colin explained that he'd never met someone so beautiful and amazing and that he hadn't been able to imagine spending another second without her. Tiffany's mother had been dazzled by their whirlwind romance, but her father wasn't buying it. He had been somewhat polite, but Tiffany could tell he wasn't thrilled with this new arrangement.

The evening had ended with hugs. Her father had shaken Colin's hand and had whispered something in his ear. Tiffany had asked later what was said, but Colin refused to share. Something man to man is what Tiffany had gathered and Colin wasn't about to break the guy code.

One family down, another to go. They were leaving for Ireland at the end of the week. Tiffany prayed it would go half as well as tonight had.

Colin interrupted Tiffany's thoughts. "I'd be upset too if our daughter robbed me of that."

"Then you should be ashamed of yourself," Tiffany teased as she stopped to kiss Colin before getting inside the car.

"Oh, he'd be even more upset if he knew what I'm about to do to his precious little girl," Colin growled, his voice thick with lust.

"Best to keep that between us then." Tiffany giggled as Colin slid his hand up her thigh.

The car ride home was going to be fun, full of teasing and driving each other crazy. *That's what being a newlywed is all about*, Tiffany thought.

Chapter Twenty-One

Colin had also failed to mention just how large his family was. They had all—most of them, anyway—been waiting to greet them as they landed in Galway, Ireland. Tiffany was overwhelmed as arms wrapped around her and many voices proclaimed in thick brogue how happy they were to finally meet her. This was only the beginning of what the next few days would bring. Sitting around a table and eating was a favorite activity. Sharing stories of the past and being asked a million questions took up most of their visit. But Tiffany really liked his family. They were warm and welcoming. The female members of this family—aunts, sisters, cousins and his mother—all treated Tiffany as though she'd been one of them for years. There was no cattiness or awkwardness. They were genuinely happy to welcome her into their lives. Tiffany was now one of the Murphy women and they were thrilled to share all the secrets on how to survive being married to a Murphy man.

Then there were the men in the Murphy clan. Each had an outrageous personality and she could see how they had influenced Colin to become the wonderful man that he was.

Humor was huge in this family. Laughter filled the cottage for the days that Colin and Tiffany spent there. Love was proudly on display and now she was a part of that.

Tiffany had not been prepared for this visit to go this well or to fall in love with a family on the other side of the globe.

Galway was a harbor city and home to the cliffs of Moher. The place was rich in history. All those magical things she'd heard about Ireland were all true, except leprechauns. Colin teased that Tiffany wasn't looking hard enough. Green?

Yes, it was indeed as green as Americans portrayed it to be in movies. Storybook didn't even begin to describe the charm of this wonderful place.

Then they traveled to Dublin. All Americans knew that name. Tiffany got to experience the incredible energy and vibrancy of the large city before they departed for home. It was a rushed trip and Colin wanted to squeeze in as many of the sights as possible. He wanted Tiffany to get to know his country, but Colin teased that he was more content spending their time at the inn, cuddled beneath the covers.

As they boarded the plane home, Tiffany was crushed to leave. A week was not enough time. She could have spent months there — maybe even years — taking in all the beauty, both rugged, natural and refined and to spend more time to get to know his amazing family. No, a week hadn't been nearly enough time. They would definitely need to come back.

* * * *

Mackenzie had offered to babysit Sir McCartney, aka Pauly, the bulldog that was wiggling hysterically at Tiffany's legs. He was in a frenzied state, rubbing against her and whimpering.

"God, he missed you," Mackenzie said as they stood inside her living room to pick up their precious pup.

"And I missed him, too. Yes, I did. I missed my little man," Tiffany cooed to Pauly, working him up further. Slobber hung off his jowls and his pink tongue waved as he struggled to catch his breath in all the excitement.

"Glad to see he missed me," Colin said. "There was a time when I was his favorite, you know."

"Well, sorry to say, but that time has passed. He loves me best now." Tiffany stuck her tongue out at him.

"Come and sit, you guys. Tell me everything," Mackenzie demanded as she led them to her couches.

"Oh my God, Mac, it was incredible," Tiffany started.

"His family is so great. Ireland is just as beautiful as you'd imagine. We are *so* going back and I'm bringing you guys next time," Tiffany gushed as she sat next to Colin, opposite of Mackenzie.

"I love America. I have a love for Ireland. It's home. But America is incredible, a land full of opportunity," Colin argued.

Tiffany shooed him playfully with her hand. "Nah, it has nothing on Ireland. Mac, trust me. That place is spectacular."

"That's great." Mackenzie listened while Tiffany went over more details of their trip.

Tiffany was aware that she was probably boring Mackenzie to death, but she couldn't contain her excitement. Tiffany wasn't much better than Pauly, just minus the drool and heavy breathing. Colin watched her with amusement and rolled his eyes as Tiffany described everything she'd seen.

"Well, we better get him going," Colin spoke of Pauly like he was their child. Tiffany and Mackenzie giggled.

Tiffany hugged Mackenzie and said, "Thanks again for watching him."

"He was a doll. Anytime."

Colin loaded a very happy bulldog into the back of his car. He opened the door for Tiffany and they headed home.

After Tiffany buckled her seat belt, she released a happy sigh.

"I'm glad that you really enjoyed meeting my family," Colin said as he started the car.

"They are amazing. I miss them so much."

Colin leaned over and let his lips brush against hers. "You're amazing, and I can't wait to get you home."

Tiffany giggled. "I'm serious."

"Me too." Colin pulled away from the curb and smiled at Tiffany. "I plan on showing you how serious I am."

* * * *

Tiffany stared in wonder at just how damn sexy Colin

looked. He'd curled his hand around his cock and trained his dark eyes on her. She sat across from him with her legs spread wide. She was completely naked except for her black Manolo Blahnik heels. Tiffany used her fingers to trace her silky folds and Colin grunted as he watched her pleasure herself.

"God, you're so hot," Colin growled through clenched teeth as he stroked himself faster.

Tiffany gave him a sly smile and tickled her swollen clit. Fingering herself in front of him was incredibly erotic and she was so close to coming. Tiffany had managed to put on quite a show and wasn't sure how much longer either of them could hold off before each of them finished with mind-blowing orgasms. She didn't want this incredible feeling to ever end. Colin swirled his thumb over the tip of his member as he instructed Tiffany what to do next. Tiffany happily obliged, enjoying every bit of the torturous pleasure she was creating. This naughty game had been going on for quite a while.

Colin moved his hand up and down his hard cock. It strained in his strong grasp and he moaned deep in his throat right before unleashing a string of pearl glaze that shot onto his naked stomach. She was tempted to crawl over and lick him clean. *God, my man is delicious.*

"That was so good," Colin said as he caught his breath. "Did you come?"

Tiffany shook her head and he frowned.

"Let's fix that, baby," he said. Colin grabbed her legs and brought Tiffany toward him.

She squealed and before Tiffany knew it, Colin was pleasuring her. Colin spread her pussy lips and licked one broad swath across them, making her even wetter. Then he replaced her fingers with his and curled them inside of her. He found her nipple with his tongue and flicked against the sensitive bud. Colin's mouth covered it and he sucked hard, causing a sharp zing to shoot through her. Tiffany threw her head back and lifted her pelvis.

Her body ached with need. Colin removed his hand and positioned himself above Tiffany. He'd gotten hard again already, but he stayed just at the entrance of her slick pussy, teasing her.

"Please," she begged. Her body was on fire.

Colin snatched her up and moved her onto her belly. He rubbed her ass and spread her thighs apart with his knees. His hard cock brush against her drenched center then he gripped her hips and thrust inside of her. *Finally*, the fullness that she craved. He slammed into her. Each stroke was powerful and caused wicked waves of lust to ripple through her. Her breasts swayed below her as he worked her pussy. Colin took a fistful of her hair into his hands. He gently tugged her head back and found her neck. She backed against Colin's hardness and her cunt swallowed more of him, hungry for more and seeking release.

"Tell me how much you need me," he commanded in a low whisper. Colin slid out of her, teasing her aching sex.

"Oh God, please." Tiffany panted hard.

Colin ran his free hand along her ribs then cupped her breast. He grazed her shoulder with his teeth but kept his cock out of her. It drove her crazy as she tried desperately to push him inside again.

"Tell me, Tiffany," Colin said again firmly.

"I need you. All of you," she managed.

"Good girl." With one deep stroke, Colin rewarded Tiffany as he dove into her again.

The flood of heat that swarmed her body was incredible. She just wanted Colin closer. It was as though her body were trying to consume him. Tiffany shuddered as her orgasm rocked her. She fisted the sheets to try to steady herself and ride out the chaotic rush that was crashing over her. Colin continued to steer her into a wild fit of sensations. She cried out when her legs coated with her juices. Light splintered behind her closed eyes as she was racked by another tremor. Colin sent another bolt of electricity through her when he plunged into her as deeply as possible.

"Still need to test drive it?" Colin asked as he tried to catch his breath again.

"Nope, I'm sold," Tiffany replied as they both collapsed on the bed together.

* * * *

Now that they had been home from their amazing trip to Colin's birth home and delightful country, he was all about finding them a more permanent solution when it came their housing. Tiffany actually didn't mind the condo and didn't quite see the need to getting a new home, but Colin was growing more suburban and into a family man as each day passed, and he insisted they had to find something.

House hunting. Tiffany figured it would be super easy. Find a house that had everything—simple enough, right? Not at all.

Colin had created his wish list and she had hers. Luckily, they both wanted a lot of the same things. However, that was proving to be nearly impossible to find in the giant city of Seattle.

"We could always build?" Colin suggested. He was leaning back in his chair, and he thoughtfully rubbed his chin.

Tiffany was in front of him, leaning against the solid wooden desk with her arms folded across her chest. She was beyond frustrated. They'd just returned from looking at several properties and none of them had jumped out at either Colin or Tiffany. It had been a waste of time.

"You have such a great view from here," Tiffany commented as she looked out at the city below. Evening stars were starting to emerge and lights were twinkling from every direction. Traffic stops, headlights, surrounding skyscrapers... It was all gorgeous.

The office was empty. It was quiet—no employees to silently judge her, no old co-workers to throw her nasty looks. It was hard to imagine that months earlier this place had been like a second home. Now it was simply one of her husband's businesses. Her little office was soon going to be home to a new assistant, one that she planned to take out to lunch and hang out with as much as possible — Colin's youngest sister, Penny. Tiffany was thrilled when he'd told her that Penny was interested in working for him. Tiffany had seen how much Penny looked up to her big brother and Tiffany had connected with her instantly when they had visited. Tiffany assured Colin that she would have a friend here. Heck, probably three. Tiffany knew Molly and Mackenzie would love this girl. Colin joked that he was now more scared than ever.

"Did I mention that Owen invited us out on Friday night?" Colin said as he shuffled some papers on his desk, not making eye contact with her. He'd been acting a little strangely the last day or so, but she wrote it off as stress over the house hunting.

"No, it must have slipped your mind. Molly didn't say anything, either."

"Well, I had lunch with him yesterday and he invited us on the boat."

"That will be nice. I need to catch up with Molly. She's been so busy lately," Tiffany commented as she searched Colin's face. He smiled at her, masking any suspicions that Tiffany had.

"I'll just meet you at the dock if that's all right?" Colin asked. "I have several meetings that day and will be getting out a little late."

"Sure, did they invite, Mac?"

"I believe so. You could always come with her," Colin suggested.

He seemed distracted. "Good idea. You ready to head home?" Tiffany asked as she gently kicked him.

"Ouch." Colin rolled his chair closer to her until he was in front of Tiffany. He placed his hands on her hips, keeping her still.

"Oh no, you don't. Not here," Tiffany scolded him. She

knew exactly what Colin was trying to do. She could see the passion light up in his eyes. This man didn't care where they were. When the mood struck, he was willing to answer that call anywhere — be it a plane, hotel room, back of a car or now in his office.

"Yes, here," he answered. Colin moved his hands up and down her bare legs. "These shorts have been driving me wild all day."

They were simple white shorts, nothing special. They weren't overly short. They were cute — she'd give him that — but they were nothing to get all excited about.

He traveled his fingers past the fabric then traced the outline her panties. This man of hers loved to tease. She was discovering that her husband had a very adventurous side. Colin looped his thumb inside the thin material and stayed on her mound, awaiting her approval. His gaze searched hers.

"Colin, what if someone comes in?" Tiffany managed to speak. He'd begun to rub a sensitive spot that was beginning to border on torture rather than pleasure. She was getting wet, even though she was hesitating.

"Then I'll fire them." He lifted her navy-blue shirt and kissed her stomach, dropping her shorts slowly to her ankles and running his tongue along her hips.

Tiffany gave up, threw her head back and laughed. *This man is impossible.*

She tried to move, but his firm grip kept her from getting away. She tangled her fingers in his hair as he began to probe and lap her up. She knew this was bad, but damn, it felt so good. So what if someone walked in? Right now, Tiffany could care less. She was so close to having an orgasm that it didn't matter who came into the office. Her body tensed as he alternately licked and sucked on her clit. Then the dam of need burst and she bucked under his mouth as she found release.

"Oh, Colin," Tiffany breathed when she finally could breathe again. Wave after wave had rocked her.

"Yes, baby? Still want me to stop? Still care about anyone walking in?"

She shook her head. The thrill of being naughty in his office made her want to push it even further. Now it was her turn to show him what tricks she had up her sleeve.

They weren't going to be going home anytime soon.

* * * *

"Mac, you almost ready to go?" Tiffany called out from Mackenzie's living room. Mackenzie was still getting dressed when Tiffany had arrived to pick her up to go to the harbor. "We're going to be late. Traffic was a nightmare just coming here."

"Just a minute. I can't find my other sandal. I have been looking everywhere for it." Mackenzie huffed as she emerged into the living room. She was looking under the table then behind the sofa.

"Why would it be there? It's probably in your closet." Tiffany got up and began to help with the search. It didn't take long. Tiffany had checked in the guest room and right there on the bed was a partially chewed, very expensive mate to the sandal in Mackenzie's hand.

"Um, I think I found it," Tiffany yelled.

"Really?" Excitement filled Mackenzie's voice, then her face dropped when she saw the mangled shoe. "You have *got* to be kidding me."

"This is it, right? Well, *was* it." Tiffany held up the mauled shoe to show Mackenzie.

"That damn bulldog ate my shoe."

"How do you know that Pauly did it?" Tiffany tried to defend him, but they both knew he was the culprit.

Mackenzie glared at her. "You will be buying me another pair."

"These are expensive," Tiffany complained.

Mackenzie laughed. "And you can afford it. So, I'll take two pairs, thank you."

"Fine," Tiffany relented. "We need to go. Molly will kill us with how late we are."

"Are we having dinner on the boat?" Mackenzie asked as she slipped on a different pair of sandals.

They were headed out the door and Tiffany answered, "I think so. Gosh, can you believe summer is nearly over?"

The sun was beginning to set a lot earlier and the tease of the crisp fall air was starting to show up in the evenings.

"Tell me about it. I'm back at school next week to set up my classroom."

They got into Tiffany's small car and sped off toward the waterfront where a line of boats greeted them. Parking in Seattle was one of Tiffany's least favorite things, especially when she was in a hurry or had somewhere to be. Tiffany was looking forward to dinner out on the boat with her friends. Her stomach growled and Mackenzie started to laugh.

"You too, huh?" Mackenzie asked. "I'm starving."

"I hope Owen is making something yummy."

Mackenzie nodded. "I'll eat just about anything."

Tiffany found a spot and parked. The sun was dipping into the sea and the marmalade sky was streaked with lavender. Clouds were stretched across it like pulled-apart cotton candy. The air was pungent and salty. Tiffany inhaled the scent as they power-walked to toward the docks. They spotted Owen's boat and raced toward it.

"Sorry we're late, guys," Tiffany apologized as soon as she saw Owen and Molly out on the portside of the large boat.

"No worries. We weren't going to leave without you." Owen waved then went to help them get on.

Molly stayed back and Tiffany saw it. Her friend's baby bump.

"Oh my God, Moll, you are starting to show," Tiffany cried.

"Ooh, let me see," Mackenzie said as she tried to peek around Tiffany to catch a glimpse.

Molly held her not-so-flat tummy. "Yeah, it just kinda poked out the other day."

Tiffany and Mackenzie both sighed happily. Seeing the bump made it more real, as if seeing the little bean of a baby wiggle at the ultrasound hadn't been enough.

They were all on the boat now and Owen began to lift anchor.

"Wait. Where's Colin?" Tiffany asked.

"Oh, he's around here somewhere. He got here right before you guys did," Molly explained but avoided Tiffany's eyes.

"Everything okay?" Suddenly Tiffany was on high alert.

"All good here," Molly answered.

"You sure?"

Mackenzie looked over the railing. She seemed to suddenly be avoiding Tiffany.

"What the hell, you guys? You're acting weird. What's up?" Tiffany asked.

"Nothing. Want a drink?" Molly tried to redirect the conversation. "I'll go hunt down your hubs for you."

"No, you sit, Mrs. Baby Bump. I will go find him."

Molly smiled and Tiffany couldn't shake the feeling that she'd just been had. *Something is definitely up.*

Leaving her friends to go look for Colin, Tiffany couldn't help but remember the two times she'd been on the boat before—once on that fateful night when too much champagne and a tad of jealousy had put Tiffany in Colin's arms and on his lips then the day where they were forced to be introduced but already knew each other all too well and weren't pleased to learn that they had mutual friends. Now there was tonight. The mist from the sea sprayed Tiffany slightly, causing her face and hair to become damp as the boat cruised out farther into the waters past the harbor. She searched for Colin. This time it was would be different on the boat. He wouldn't be some stranger she was kissing or some guy that she sort of hated. No, this time Tiffany was going to enjoy a lovely dinner with her husband and her friends. Funny how quickly things had changed. Life was full of unexpected twists and turns. Some were downright awful and others were completely wonderful. Sometimes it took riding out those awful ones to finally get to enjoy the wonderful. That's where Tiffany was now, basking in the afterglow of some pretty rotten twists and turns.

Tiffany kept walking, pausing to gather her sea legs a few times, before she spotted him. Colin was standing there, his hands shoved into his pockets and he appeared to be deep in thought. Maybe he was reflecting on everything just as she had only moments ago. She was half tempted to race up behind him and spook him, but Tiffany didn't trust herself to not wind up overboard. That would totally be her luck and she wasn't pressing it.

"Colin," she called out.

He turned and his smile appeared instantly. "Tiffany, I didn't realize you were here yet."

"Um, the boat is moving. That should have been a dead giveaway," Tiffany teased as Colin approached her.

"Sorry. My mind is elsewhere," he admitted.

"Everything okay?" She was really starting to become worried. First her friends were acting strangely, now Colin. Only Owen was acting normally.

"Everything's perfect."

"I'm beginning to wonder. Molly and Mac were acting a bit strange and even you're acting a little odd now," Tiffany countered.

Colin draped one arm around her shoulders. They faced the waves as the boat cut through the water with ease and power. Tiffany became lost in her thoughts again, almost forgetting that they weren't alone on this boat. Sometimes when she was with Colin, the rest of the world disappeared.

"Trust me. Everything is perfect," Colin said after a few moments of quiet, kissing the side of her head.

"It's so beautiful out here," Tiffany commented.

Colin turned toward her and whispered, "Not nearly as beautiful as my wife."

Tiffany flushed with pleasure. He was always

complimenting her, making her feel like some rare and precious treasure, especially the last several weeks. Things had been nonstop bliss since they'd arrived home from Hawaii. She was almost waiting for the other shoe to drop, for something awful to happen to ruin how wonderful everything was going.

"Tiffany, I need to say a few things," Colin began slowly. "We did this the wrong way."

Great, here it is. The other shoe.

"But what counts is that we're here, right? Isn't that what you said in Hawaii?" Tiffany stared at him, searching his eyes for any clue as to what he was going to say next.

"True. But the more I think about it, the more I'm bothered by it all. I can't live the rest of our lives like this."

Wow. Tiffany was gutted. She hadn't expected for him to say anything remotely like this. She felt a pressure, a build-up of emotion threatening to explode — probably from her eyes as they were growing blurry and hot with tears. *Keep it together, Tiff.*

"Oh, baby, don't cry," Colin begged, "Oh dear, let me get on with this. I was trying to find the right words."

"Huh?" Tiffany was confused. She wiped away stray tears from her cheeks. Their salt was rivaling the salt of the sea. Just a moment before, she'd felt as though her heart was being carved out of her chest and dissected. Now she didn't know what to feel.

"Oh, my sweet love, what I mean is that we should do this right way, the way you deserve. I could be happy just as we are, but it's not enough for you."

"But it is. You are enough and that's all that matters," Tiffany replied.

Colin held onto the side of the boat as he got down on one knee. He reached into his pants pocket and fished something out. A small box. He cracked it open and a large emerald and diamond ring peered back at Tiffany, sparkling in the Seattle sunset.

She covered her mouth as the shock throttled through

her. Her ring finger was already heavy with an enormous diamond. Colin grabbed her hand and gently removed the wedding ring from Vegas.

"I was given this ring while we were in Ireland. It was my grandmother's. My mother had kept it hidden until I met the right woman. That woman is you, Tiffany," Colin explained as he slid the new ring onto her finger.

Tiffany began to shake as emotions flooded her. She looked up and saw Owen with his arm around Molly. Mackenzie was wiping tears from her eyes. They stood there quietly and watched as Colin remained solely focused on Tiffany. His gaze never left her.

"I know that you are already my wife and for that, I wouldn't change a thing. But, Tiffany, will you do me the honor of becoming my wife and marry me?" Colin asked as he held her hand.

Tiffany was dazed. *Am I hearing him right? Why is he proposing?*

"But we are already married, Colin."

"I know, but I want us to get married—the right way, with the flowers, all the fuss and your father walking you down the aisle."

"You sure?" Tiffany asked.

"Just tell the poor man yes," Mackenzie yelled.

"God, yes," Tiffany answered.

Colin popped up and scooped her into his arms. He showered her with kisses and spun her around. Claps and a few whistles erupted.

This proposal was exactly what Tiffany had dreamed of. It was sincere and emotional. It involved a man declaring his love for her. It wasn't Elvis or the fake gold of Vegas. This was real. Colin was everything that she had ever wanted in a man and so much more. This was a man she truly loved with every fiber of her being.

"I'm getting married," Tiffany screamed as she admired the magnificent ring. She flashed it to her friends.

Colin released Tiffany and she ran to her girls, her best

friends, her sisters.

"Great. Here comes bridezilla," Molly and Mackenzie said in unison.

Reeling in Love

Excerpt

Chapter One

"I think we got it," Molly said confidently to the almost naked man standing in the corner, wearing nothing but a stark white towel draped across his tan waist.

"You sure?"

Molly nodded as she scrutinized her work. "Yeah, the lighting was brilliant. I don't think we could have done any better."

"If you say so. You're the expert with that thing." The model pointed at the large camera Molly cradled in her hands, the screen displaying the digital shots from the day of working with him.

Molly loved her job as a professional photographer. Her friends were insanely jealous. What woman wouldn't be? She spent her days in her studio behind the lens of her trusty camera, capturing sexy images of some of the most gorgeous men from all over the world. Either she was paid to travel to them or they flew to Seattle to have her work her magic. Authors in the romance industry adored her photos. Her attention to detail had won her awards over the years, but what she loved the most was bringing the characters from books alive. Sure, it didn't hurt to look at well-defined muscles and sculpted abs that begged to be touched and to know what was hidden beneath the scrap of cloth that usually covered these men, but that wasn't how the business worked. Her friends would argue it was just because Molly didn't throw herself at these scantily clad men that she was missing out on these valuable opportunities.

If they only knew how nervous most of these men were, their fragile egos stripped down for her. It took Molly the first half of the shoot to calm them, easing them out of their shells, getting them just to loosen up enough for the right shot. It was more like babysitting rather than staring at a buffet, despite what her best friends thought. Not all the models lacked self-confidence, however. There were some who would stroll in, look directly into the camera and own it. But, for the most part, a lot of the guys were unsure and needed coaxing. Molly often felt more like a counselor than the world-famous photographer that she was.

Today, the Seattle sun was shielded behind soft, white clouds, filtering its rays into her studio that overlooked the Puget Sound. Her tall, glass windows provided the most stunning views of the shimmering water and the bustling city. Molly had worked hard for this view. It hadn't come easy or cheap — or without her busting her ass to make her name known in the photography industry. She had the scars — mostly emotional, but scars, nonetheless — to prove the struggles she'd endured, climbing to the top. Now she was one of the most sought-after photographers. Models from all over the globe wanted her to shoot them. *New York Times* and *USA Today* bestselling authors and publishers almost begged for her to shoot their covers. They wanted the best and…well, Molly was. Her skills proved that she had something special and everyone knew it.

Not bothering to sit down at her desk—bending over, instead—to focus on the images she was uploading to her laptop to edit, she almost forgot to say goodbye to the model she had just worked with. It wasn't until he was standing close to her, now fully dressed, that she realized he was still in her studio. Having him near her like that shifted the atmosphere in the room. His dominating presence was invading her space, creating nervous waves in her stomach. She inhaled his expensive aftershave, looked up from her screen and smiled.

Molly managed to say, "Great shoot today. Thanks again." *Remember to breathe, Molly.*

"Yeah, it was amazing. You're amazing." The man paused, running his fingers along his day-old beard, the perfect blend of refined and unkempt sexy. His voice was silky and oozed well-practiced enticement. Molly watched him stand still, contemplating his next move. She was tempted to grab her camera and snap another shot. The light was hitting him just right and his pose was thoughtful and natural. This man was gorgeous.

He turned his mesmerizing gaze toward her and asked, "Do you want to grab a drink?"

Molly swallowed. It wasn't the first time she had been asked out by a model after a shoot. Sometimes it was the result of having bonded over their frail vulnerabilities. Sometimes they figured she was as good a lay as any while they were in town—another stamp in their romantic passport, so to speak. Molly wasn't so sure about this one. He wasn't overly emotional or guarded about his body, nor did he seem to really desire her. *So, what is he after?* She watched him scan the large studio. There was her answer. This type of square footage didn't come cheap and he knew that.

"You know, maybe another time. I'm really excited to get this edited." Molly pointed at her sleek silver laptop, delivering a fake smile in hopes it would put him off.

He nodded and thanked her again as he saw himself out. *The nerve.* Molly rolled her eyes and released the air she had been holding in her lungs. While she was in mid sigh, her cell phone chirped.

"Hello," she answered, a little more gruffly than she'd intended.

"Wow, so what's with the 'tude, lady? Bad day?"

It was one of her best friends, Tiffany.

"Just got done working with a model."

"Well, then why do you sound all cranky? Was he awful? So good-looking that you couldn't handle it?" Tiffany teased, causing Molly to laugh and her mood to lighten.

"You know the type. He wanted to go out for drinks—"

Tiffany cut her off quickly. "And you said, yes, right? Because if you didn't, you honestly need to have your head examined."

"I'd have to say he was more interested in my real estate than me." Molly frowned.

"Like real estate, as in the prime location between your legs? You know, it's all about location, location, location, baby."

"I wish." Molly huffed in frustration. "No, more like the prime location of my studio."

"That sucks."

"Tell me about it. He was gorgeous and he smelled divine. He was totally your type—tall, dark and devilishly handsome."

She heard Tiffany's disappointment through the phone. "Really? Oh, I just don't know how you do it, Molly. I have to give it to you. I would simply come undone working with those gorgeous men and not taking advantage of them every chance I got."

Tiffany always acted like she was some aggressive sex kitten, but they knew the truth. She was actually quite timid, which was a huge reason why she was single. All three of them were single and not dating anyone special. It didn't usually work that they were unattached all at the same time, but they were now. Their other best friend, Mackenzie, was the mother hen of the group. Well, more like the bossy one—completely overbearing, but with an absolute heart of gold. She, too, teased Molly about her line of work, but Mackenzie loved being a teacher, as it helped fill her maternal void. They had biological clocks that had gone haywire over the last couple of years, but everyone had warned them as they entered the dirty thirties that baby fever would hit soon after, and it had for Tiffany and Mackenzie. Every time they passed a stroller, neither could resist the temptation of peering in to catch a glimpse of some infant swaddled in fuzzy pink or blue blankets. Molly? She had her moments. They were brief and passed quickly when she heard the wail of a newborn or the shrill sound of a tantrum from a toddler. That didn't tempt her to want to rent out her womb for nine months.

She looked at her spotless, chic studio. Her smile went deep into her soul, masking the want for a baby. Her space sparkled and gleamed with the afternoon Seattle sunlight, illuminating sleek lines and utterly contemporary taste.

If she were being completely honest with herself, yes, she did indeed want a child, eventually. But Molly also realized she was missing a very important part of the equation—a man. She didn't want just a sperm donor, though she and her friends had discussed that over far too much wine and Chinese food one night, considering it as a last resort. That had left them laughing for hours. No, Molly wanted the real deal. They all did. They wanted a man—a sexy, successful and simply wonderful man. *Is that really asking for too much?*

Being single, especially in Seattle, came with its challenges. Molly thought the enormous Emerald City should be plentiful with eligible bachelors, but Molly assumed that, as with any place, being single was a mixture of bad luck and an overly detailed list of the personality traits she wanted in a boyfriend. As time passed, her list had grown a lot shorter. She'd crossed off quite a few of her must-haves and was looking to review her available options. Now she figured it was mainly the bad luck that was keeping her single. Molly had been unattached the longest out of her friends, who were more like her sisters. Tiffany had been on a dating spree recently, but Mackenzie and Molly had known that none of the guys were Mr. Right for their friend. Mackenzie also had a pretty extensive list of requirements for her ideal mate, and she was even more stubborn than Molly when it came to sacrificing the qualities she was willing to live with, so she dated very little.

"Well, since you didn't want drinks with that sexy model, how about meeting up with us?" Tiffany asked.

Molly smiled. Yes, a drink with her best pals she could do. "That sounds lovely, actually." She could use some cheering up. The best cure for her bruised ego was some quality time with her besties.

"Great. I'll pick up Mac and we'll swing by the studio and grab ya. Sound good?"

"Perfect. I have some edits I want to go through, so just buzz when you guys get here."

Molly said goodbye and hung up. She stared at the monitor in front of her, the images of the model in various poses looking back her.

* * * *

Lost in her work tweaking the images with an array of filters, Molly was so engrossed that she almost didn't hear the loud buzzing that echoed off the large studio walls. She got up quickly from her desk and jogged to the massive double doors to let her friends in.

"Jeesh, what were you doing? I have been ringing that dang buzzer for, like, *forever*," Tiffany complained as she slipped past Molly into the studio. Mackenzie frowned and hugged Molly.

"We've only been standing outside the door for a minute," Mackenzie assured her.

Tiffany walked over to one of the large windows facing

the Puget Sound. The sun was setting, casting a tangerine hue over the haze of the city. "God, do you ever get tired of this magnificent view?"

Molly shook her head as she joined her, staring out at the glittery lights in the surrounding buildings that seemed to stretch up toward the sky. "Nope."

"Yeah, I didn't think so." Tiffany laughed as she faced Molly. Her dark hair was loose on her thin shoulders. Tiffany's large eyes were a soulful brown and she had the best cheekbones. Tiffany was gorgeous in a unique and completely unexpected way. Molly's brain acted as a camera, capturing shots of her friend's delicate features as the sunset cast a shadowy light on her face. Tiffany sensed what Molly was doing and threw her a pouty look.

Mackenzie stood next them. The willowy blonde towered over Molly, making her feel short and stubby. Mackenzie had the figure of a teenager, slim and athletic. Her sun-kissed hair was cut in a sleek bob, framing the sharp angles of her face. She was another beautiful woman. Molly couldn't help but snap mental pictures of Mackenzie, too. She searched Molly curiously with soft mocha eyes. They all had brown eyes in varied shades of the common color, but resembling their different tastes in coffee. Tiffany had the espresso, dark and bold. Mackenzie was more of an iced mocha with an extra shot. Molly's resembled the instant crap coffee variety that no one really liked. Molly hated her eyes. They were plain. Her friends had tried to convince her otherwise, but they both had spectacular depth and richness in theirs. Molly thought hers looked like a muddy puddle after a typical downpour in Seattle — watery, with a sad, muted tone. Nothing special.

"What's going on with you?" Mackenzie reached for Molly, concern swimming in her eyes and worry creasing her otherwise wrinkle-free face, the result of fabulous genetics.

Molly sighed. *Is there anything going on with me?* They usually accused her of being moody, but she was an artist.

Isn't that sort of the job description? Acting the part of the tortured soul? They sure never let her play that role for very long.

Tiffany stared at her hard and added, "Yeah, you seemed cranky on the phone. So what's up?"

"I don't know. I mean..." Molly really couldn't explain how she felt. She had a blessed life. Granted, she had worked for it, but, regardless, she knew she was lucky. Happy? Well, that was a different ball of wax.

"Drinks. That's what we need." Tiffany perked up, her hand on her hip, taking a sassy stance. She reached for the oversized purse that was slung over her shoulder. A Louis Vuitton knock-off, but it looked as real as they came. It was their little secret. Tiffany dug around and retrieved a bottle of Prosecco, holding it up for them to all gaze at her prize.

"You were carrying that in there? Oh dear. Seriously, Tiffany," Mackenzie scolded.

Tiffany winked and answered with a wicked grin.

"I, for one, am thrilled our friend is lugging around a bottle. You never know when you may need it." Molly grinned happily at Tiffany. "It does make you look a little like a wino, but you're my favorite drunk."

"No, you have me mistaken. I'm fun, not a drunk." Tiffany defended as she moved toward a long table that was against the wall opposite the windows. "Besides, at least I bring the good stuff."

"I have an idea. Let's stay in. Want to order some food?" Mackenzie suggested.

"Yes, let's do that. Molly's got one of the best views in all of Seattle. Let's just hang out here," Tiffany replied while she peeled the label away to get to the cork.

"Chinese?" Mackenzie whipped out her cell phone and started to dial their favorite takeout.

"Hell, yes," Molly and Tiffany answered in unison.

These were her girls. It didn't matter if they stayed in or went out on the town. As long as they were together, they were guaranteed to have fun.

Shortly, they were seated around a large glass table that Molly normally used to lay out prints from shoots. They dined on their fill of chow mein, pork fried rice and more Kung Pao shrimp than any woman should ever eat. White cartons, soy sauce packets and chopsticks were littered around them as they chatted about everything — mostly about the lack of sex or romance in their lives. Biting into a crispy fortune cookie — her favorite — Molly surveyed her beautiful friends. She couldn't understand why any of them were single. Tiffany was gorgeous, sweet and sassy... What was there not to love about her? Mackenzie was stunning, witty and full of love... She had so much to offer. Then there was her. She knew she might not be the sexiest thing on the planet, but she was successful, caring and everyone constantly complimented her on how pleasant she was, even telling her she was sort of hot, especially when she wore her glasses. *So how is it that I haven't landed the perfect guy yet?* Cracking open another cookie, she read the thin slip of white paper. Bold red font stared back at her, reading, *'There is nothing truer than the company of friends.' How right is that fortune?*

More wine flowed and, to keep the mood light, Molly blasted the radio. She and her two best friends danced barefoot in the empty studio, singing their hearts out and putting on a drunken performance that could rival the best pop star's. Tiffany swayed her hips to the song. Mackenzie took a while to loosen up, but then started to bop to the beat. Molly busted out some goofy moves that reminded her of middle school dances, her favorite being the 'running man'. They laughed hard, clutching their sides when Tiffany took a spill on the slippery wood floor. In their feeble attempt at helping her up, they all ended up on the floor somehow, spread-eagled, staring up at the vaulted ceilings. Music continued to play, filling the wide and open space, but the mood had shifted. That was when the laughter died and the deep realness of their friendship was exposed.

"I love you, guys," Tiffany whispered, her dark tresses

fanned out against the honey-colored bamboo floor.

"Me too," Mackenzie added softly.

Molly tried to swallow the lump that was forming in her throat, feeling tears starting to surface. "I love you both. Thank you for tonight."

They all stayed on the floor, listening to several more songs before Tiffany said, "God, this floor is killing my back. I feel old."

Mackenzie and Molly both laughed.

"And for the record, we *are* old," Mackenzie replied.

"I wanted to say the same thing, but figured I would tough it out until one of you cracked." Molly started to get up.

Mackenzie and Tiffany groaned as they eased themselves off the floor. Working quietly as a team, they cleaned up the remnants of their dinner.

"I would totally live here, Molly," Mackenzie commented as she tossed several cartons into a waste basket.

Tiffany was wiping up some sticky Kung Pao sauce. "Seriously. This studio is so fabulous. You need to let me move in here."

"I do love this place." Molly looked around at her kingdom. An enormous clear-glass shelf that held her many awards was against one of the walls. Expensive frames that contained some of her best work were hung precisely in the perfect locations. Various shades, light fixtures and tons of other photography gear were set up in one corner. The room celebrated her. It showcased all of her efforts but, more importantly, it proudly displayed her passion for this form of art.

After every last morsel was cleaned and the work space was back to being immaculate, they made their way back to the window. The sun had long since disappeared, leaving the city lights to twinkle silently as the three of them stared out at the busy traffic below.

"Thank you again, guys. I really needed this tonight."

Mackenzie and Tiffany linked their arms through hers as

she stood in the middle.

She would be lost without them. They knew all her secrets and her fears. They had supported her during her moments of crippling self-doubt. They'd loved her when she was at her worst. They'd dried her tears when critics had given her harsh reviews. They were her cheerleaders. They'd pushed her to continue to pursue her dream so many times when she'd just wanted to give up. They had been the first to celebrate when she finally did become successful and had told her countless times how much she deserved it.

These women were more than just friends. They were her tribe, her sisters. They were Molly's everything.

More books from
Totally Bound Publishing

Book one in the Secrets of Stone series

Once upon a time, there was a girl who dressed up and went to a big party at the palace. When she was there, she met a prince. They danced and fell in love…

Book three in the Beautiful Sinners series

This party girl knows what she wants…but he is everything she needs.

667 WAYS TO F*CK UP MY *Life*

Lucy Woodhull

Sometimes, there's nowhere to go but f*ck up

*Sometimes, there's nowhere to go but f*ck up…*

If you must look back, only look at the best!

About the Author

Gloria Herrmann

Gloria Herrmann is a romance author living in beautiful eastern Washington. All her books have been set in Washington, and she is eager to share with readers how gorgeous her state is.

An avid reader and lover of words, Gloria believes that becoming an author has been a dream come true for her. She still pinches herself all the time and wonders how she got so lucky.

Gloria Herrmann loves to hear from readers. You can find contact information, website details and an author profile page at https://www.totallybound.com/

Home of Erotic Romance